Escapade

Also by Jane Aiken Hodge
in Thorndike Large Print ®

Windover

This Large Print Book carries the
Seal of Approval of N.A.V.H.

Escapade

Jane Aiken Hodge

Thorndike Press • Thorndike, Maine

Published in 1994 by arrangement with St. Martin's Press, Inc.

Thorndike Large Print ® Romance Series.

The tree indicium is a trademark of Thorndike Press.

The text of this Large Print edition is unabridged.
Other aspects of the book may vary from the original edition.

Set in 16 pt. News Plantin by Minnie B. Raven.

Printed in the United States on acid-free, high opacity paper. ∞

Library of Congress Cataloging in Publication Data

Hodge, Jane Aiken.
    Escapade / Jane Aiken Hodge.
        p.   cm.
    ISBN 0-7862-0188-6 (alk. paper : lg. print)
    1. British — Travel — Italy — Sicily — History — 18th
century — Fiction. 2. Young woman — England — Fiction.
3. Sicily (Italy) — Fiction. 4. Large type books. I. Title.
[PS3558.O342E83   1994]
                                                                    94-103

Escapade

1

'But Charlotte.' John Thornton had not expected the refusal. 'We have always been such good friends. Please —' He reached for her hand.

'No, John. No, and no, and no!' She faced him squarely on the solitary cliff path, with only the sound of the sea below, and the cry of gulls around them. He had got her out here, beyond the formal gardens of Windover Hall, on the pretext that an enemy ship was in sight, to the north, off Scarborough. Charlotte Comyn was gazing at it now, without seeing it, the bonnet she had snatched off dangling in her hand, the spring breeze ruffling her cropped curls. Now, at last, her dark eyes focused on his fair, flushed face. 'I doubt I'm the marrying kind,' she went on more gently, seeing how much she had shocked her old friend. 'I'm not fit for it. Not fit for anything.' Her eyes met his levelly. 'Do you remember, you and the boys tied me to that tree once, went off and forgot all about me? Pity anyone came, really. It would have solved everything, saved everyone a lot of trouble.'

'Charlotte!' He looked at the stunted tree with a kind of horror, remembering all the times he and her younger half-brothers had teased and tormented her, a shamefully easy victim. 'It was only our fun,' he said now. 'And we did come back.'

'*You* did. I've always remembered that. You were sorry.'

'Of course I was sorry.' He was remembering how gallantly that younger Charlotte had pretended she had not been frightened, abandoned there, helpless, on the lonely cliff where no one came but scavenging gulls. 'Charlotte —' He reached again for her hand.

'No,' she said again. 'That was then, and this is now. And you should be calling me Miss Comyn. Everything is different, and I don't much like it.'

'Of course you don't like it.' He seized the opening. 'It makes me mad as fire to see the way they neglect you. Everything for the boys, down at Hull, and you sent off to moulder here at Windover, with only servants for company. It will be quite other when you come of age, and the bank and the house in Hull are yours.'

'Four years.' She was looking beyond him, at the wide prospect of sea and sky, as if at an endless, intolerable vista. 'How shall I bear it? What shall I do with myself?'

8

'That's just what I mean. Marry me, Charlotte, and everything will be different. You'll have a place in the world. Father says he will give us a house; he has his eye on one of the new ones in Albion Street. That would do very well until you are twenty-one, he says. And then, trust us to fight your battle for you if there should be any trouble over your taking possession of Comyn's Bank and the house in Hull. But of course there won't be. You know that as well as I do.'

'Do I?' Her long, thin hands were ruthlessly crushing the bonnet. 'You have talked this over with your father?'

'Of course. And with my mother. They say it is what they have always hoped for, Charlotte. A union between our two houses.' If his proposal had been on the formal side, he was becoming eloquent now. 'You know how hard times are, specially for banks like yours and Thornton's. Napoleon's decrees have been death to trade; and then the harvests bad, and this new trouble with those upstarts in what they call the United States of America. When I told my father I meant to ask for your hand, he said it was the first bit of good news for years. Charlotte, you can't disappoint us now. My mother says she quite longs to have the dressing of you.'

'I'm such a dowd?' She looked down at well-

9

washed muslin too large for her thin frame. 'You mustn't blame my mother for that. What pleasure is there in dressing a beanpole like me? Specially when I keep losing weight. But anyway, you know mother, she's too busy with the *Hull Review* to care much about clothes, specially my clothes. And as for old Nurse Jenkins — she just thinks one should be clean, and covered. And what else should I care for, a long thin fright like me?'

'But you're not —'

'I can't do anything right.' She went straight on, ignoring his attempt at protest. 'Not for anyone. And with every chance. Taught alongside the boys; Mark always insisted on that.'

'Should you call your step-father Mark?'

'He likes it. We're all equals, he says. I think he'd like me to call mother Kathryn, but I won't. She was my mother first, after all. I can't help it if I was born less equal than the others. Even little Horatio can reckon faster than I can. I heard mother tell Mr. Jenner she was quite in despair over what would happen to Comyn's Bank when I come of age and take over.'

'My mother always said no good would come of that crazy idea of making you study along with the boys. It stands to reason: girls have different talents, she says. I'm sure you are a dab hand at a syllabub, Charlotte.'

'No, I'm not. And you will kindly call me Miss Comyn, Mr. Thornton. And pray thank your mother from me for the kind interest she has taken in my education, along with everyone else in Hull.' She was angry now, her colour high, dark eyes flashing under heavy brows that contrasted with the fair hair she had worn cropped short since her illness. He found himself thinking this might prove more than the practical marriage he had been brought up to expect.

'Dear Charlotte.' He put a tentative hand on the bony wrist.

'Don't touch me.' She snatched it away as if his hand burned. 'And don't call me "dear Charlotte" either. I'm nobody's dear. And stop taking me for granted.' She fixed smouldering eyes on him, a new thought striking her. 'Tell me, have you discussed this proposal of yours with my mother and step-father too?'

'Well, of course. You surely never thought I would address you without their permission. I most certainly have their blessing.'

'Given with sighs of relief.' Savagely. 'Well, I am sorry to disappoint you all, but the answer is still no. I wouldn't have you if you were the last —' And then, seeing real hurt in his face at last: 'Oh, John, I'm sorry. I think the devil gets into me sometimes. I'm all at

11

odds with myself. Just be grateful I have the good sense to refuse you. You know — all Hull does, thanks to my grandmother — how bad things were between my mother and father.'

'The ravings of a sick old woman.' He did not pretend not to understand her. 'We never for a moment believed that wicked tale of hers about your father killing himself on purpose. It was just what your mother said at the time — and after all she was the only witness — a terrible accident with his gun. My mother says it was a pity old Mrs. Comyn ever recovered from that seizure of hers. A paralysed old lady with nothing to think or talk about but the past, and the son she had lost. Of course she took to imagining things. You mustn't let it trouble you. And those friends of hers, the Misses Harris, as spiteful a couple of cats as you could find in a month of Sundays. Natural enough, my father says, that there was talk when your mother married again so soon, and her childhood sweetheart too. Such a romantic tale; losing and finding each other like that. But you must never think, Charlotte, that your mother was anything but the best of wives to your father. Mother says she quite made a man of him. And she saved Comyn's Bank, you know, after his death. Went off to London, bold as brass, shocking

12

the old tabbies, and persuaded Goldferns the bankers to put up the money that was needed. Of course there was talk . . . You know Hull: there's always talk. That's why — don't you see — Charlotte, I beg you to think again. It would solve everything; settle everything: your position; the talk. Our marriage would end it all. And I do truly love you.' He very nearly believed it himself.

'No.' But she said it more gently now. There had been a moment, while he was speaking of her father's death, when she had nearly told him about that old nightmare of hers. About her grandmother, old Mrs. Comyn, lying among her pillows, in the luxurious bedroom where she was waited on hand and foot by her daughter-in-law, and spitting out her venom about her, day after day. But she would not think about that last scene, the day old Mrs. Comyn died, the things she had said then. Not now, not ever. 'Dear John, we've been such good friends, let's not spoil it now. You've taken my side, time after time, and I've been grateful. But that's not enough, and you know it as well as I do. You'll be grateful to me, in the end, for saying no today.'

'Your parents won't be pleased.'

'No.' She faced it bleakly. 'They really thought they were going to get me off their hands, did they?'

'Don't put it like that.' But he was afraid it was true. Charlotte had always, somehow, seemed the odd one out in the Weatherby family. 'What am I to say to them, Charlotte?' A quick look at the watch on his fob. 'I must be going; I said I would call in on my way home.'

'Oh dear.' She made a face that reminded him of a younger, happier Charlotte. 'So I must expect my scold tomorrow. Unless there is a crisis at the paper and they are too busy. It always comes first.'

'It's a very good paper, the *Hull Review*, and a blessing to Hull.'

'Which is more than anyone could call me.' She chuckled suddenly and again he was reminded of his younger, carefree friend. 'What a miserable, self-pitying wretch I am! No wonder my mother finds her newspaper more interesting. Off with you, John, tell them the bad news and leave me to brush through as best I may . . . With a bit of luck, and some dramatic news from our army in Spain, they may be too busy to scold me at all. And if they do — who cares?'

Standing on the wide steps of Windover Hall's Palladian front to watch him ride away, she was amazed at how confident she had managed to sound. 'Who cares?' Well, who would?

Nobody cares, she thought, and then: why should they? Her very existence was a shame to her mother; no wonder Kathryn preferred the boys.

If I were dead, she thought, the boys could have it all. I ought not to have been born. She thought about the sea, seething and churning below the cliffs, and something practical at the back of her mind whispered to her that the tide was low. Anyway, I don't want to die, she thought, I just want everything to be different, to get away from it all.

But where to go? She was instinctively making her way round the side of the house to her favourite refuge, the stable yard, and the comforting company of horses. Passing the low windows of the servants' quarters, she remembered a story she was not supposed to know, a story of the servants' hall. Her grandmother, the heiress of Windover, had made a disastrous second marriage, to a woman-hunting brute of a clergyman. Failing other game, he had pursued the maidservants at the Hall, and one of them, Beth Prior, had jumped out of one of these very windows to escape him. And, later, that same Beth had been her mother's dear friend, and gone with her on that venturesome journey to London. Beth Prior! Her mother never spoke of her now, but she was a successful actress in London.

15

London. Charlotte patted her horse's nose and hurried into the house.

'She refused you?' Kathryn Weatherby did not want to believe her ears. 'Fool of a girl. Why?'

'She said we did not love each other.' John Thornton had thought of nothing but this interview on the long ride from Windover Hall down to Hull. He had not been sure whether to be glad or sorry when Kathryn Weatherby received him alone, explaining that her husband was still working at the offices of their paper, the *Hull Review*. Now he thought he was glad. 'Mrs. Weatherby —' He took his courage in both hands. 'It's true; and I respect her for it. She's so young; it's too soon.'

'She's almost eighteen.'

'She doesn't look it. What's the matter with her, Mrs. Weatherby?' Might as well be hung for a sheep. 'She's thin as a rail.'

'She won't eat. Says she can't. And if we try to make her, she is sick, poor child. The doctor hoped that country air, and her old haunts up at the Hall would do her good, but it doesn't sound as if it has. And, most of all, I had thought marriage . . . an old friend like you . . . Oh dear, I wish I knew what to do for the best. Thank goodness!' Her face lit up as her husband entered the room. 'There

16

you are at last, Mark. Here's John Thornton to tell us Charlotte has refused him.'

'Pity.' Mark Weatherby poured wine for them all. 'But not a surprise. Forgive me, John; you know we would all have liked the match better than anything, but I did wonder whether our Charlotte was ready for it.'

'But what are we to do with her?' wailed his wife.

'I'll send the carriage for her tomorrow. It's time she saw the doctor again. He had high hopes of the air at Windover; said it was the next best thing to a trip to the south of France. And we all know how impossible that is these days. He will be as disappointed as we are, I know.'

'You won't be cross with her?' said John. 'No scolding? Please?'

'Does she expect one?' A quick look at his wife. 'No, John, no scoldings, I promise you. Not that we aren't disappointed, because of course we are. Do, pray, give our kind regards to your parents.'

It was a dismissal and he was glad to take it as such.

When the Weatherby carriage reached Windover Hall the next day the house was in chaos. 'We've sent a boy riding hell for leather to Hull,' the housekeeper told Kathryn

Weatherby's maid, come to fetch Charlotte. 'He will have taken the bridleways, so you'll have missed him. But she's gone, Miss Prime, the child is gone!'

'Gone?'

'She must have been up at first light this morning. Or maybe never went to bed. I'm sure I don't know what has got into the girl. Mr. Thornton came yesterday; they were talking hours out on the cliff, which is what I cannot approve of, but Mrs. Weatherby said I was to let the child have her head as much as possible. No interference, she said; let her alone; and of course they were children together, those two; I thought no harm at the time. She hardly ate a crumb for her supper, but you know what she is, Miss Prime, it's a waste of good food cooking for her, if you ask me. And when I said something, just in my fun, you know, about the hungry poor at the Hull workhouse, she ups and says good night and off to bed without another word. And this morning she's clean gone. And not a stitch of her clothes missing that her maid can see. She sent Burrows off; said she'd put herself to bed; not one to be waited on, Miss Charlotte, I'll say that for her. Told Burrows to let her sleep in the morning. Come nine o'clock I thought it time she had some breakfast. Mrs. Weatherby was very firm she must be given her meals, even if she wouldn't eat them. And the girl found the room empty. A note for her ma on the pillow; the clothes she wore yesterday neat on her chair — she was always a neat one, Miss Charlotte. Finicking neat, if you ask me.' She paused for breath, both of them aware of the past tense she had used. 'I thought she was over the cliff for certain, but then Tom Barnes comes up from the stable in a right lather to say her horse is gone, saddle and bridle and all.'

'She's run away?'

'Looks like it, Miss Prime, and what a coil that is going to be! There's been talk enough about our family without this. I'm beginning to wonder if I shouldn't find myself another position.'

'You'll go far enough to find one where you are better treated. I'd best be getting back. You sent the letter to her mother, of course.'

'Yes. Well sealed, it was.' An unmistakable note of regret.

'And no clothes missing? No cloak bag?'

'Not that Burrows can see. It's a proper little mystery, Miss Prime, and no mistake. I hate to think what the gossips will say.'

'They'll say nothing if they don't hear about it.' Miss Prime drained her glass of ratafia and rose to her feet. 'And if I were you, Mrs. Piddock, I'd see to it that they don't. This house is lonely enough, lord knows. If you put it about that I came and fetched Miss Charlotte home to Hull no one will know any different, and mind you do, if you value a good position. Mr. Weatherby's a powerful man, with his money and his newspaper and all. I wouldn't want to get on the wrong side of him, nohow. You might find yourself in the workhouse you told Miss Charlotte of. You ought to know by now, Mrs. Piddock, how she hates being fussed about her food. If I were you I'd sit tight and say nothing until you get further orders from the master.'

'Gone to friends, she says.' Kathryn Weatherby handed Charlotte's note to her husband. 'Nothing but a disappointment to us . . . Not to worry — Oh, I could shake her! But, what friends, Mark? Has she any friends?' They faced each other over the bleak question, suddenly aware of a long tale of neglect. 'She had some school friends in Scarborough, I remember, after that year she was in school there, but I thought she had lost touch with them.'

'Do you know their names, their directions?'

'No. She used to get letters for a while; I don't think she answered them . . . We could look in her room.'

'Yes, do that, my dear, while I get ready to ride to Scarborough. Let us hope the school knows the names of her friends. It's the obvious place to start, anyway. She won't have come here to Hull, that's for certain.' But not a pleasant thought. 'Tell me, Kathryn, what does she know of that venture of yours to London? Might she have been copying that? Gone there?'

'Impossible! Oh, she knows she was born in London, of course, but we have never talked about it. How could I, without speaking of Beth, and really, my dear, about her, the least said the soonest mended.'

'I'm still sad you feel that way.' It was an old argument between them, and one he always lost. Beth had been first Kathryn's maid and then her dear friend; now she was well known as a great beauty: one of London's most successful actresses and mistresses of hearts. The stories about her were legion: she had refused her favours to the Prince Regent because he was too fat, and to Beau Brummell because he bored her. Whatever she did, she remained the toast of the clubs and the darling of her audiences. Thinking of her, Mark thought of something else. 'I have it!' he exclaimed. 'Charlotte will have gone to Beverley! The Comyns there are her kin after all, and I don't suppose you have told her any more

21

about George Comyn than you have about poor Beth.'

'Poor Beth indeed! But it's true about George. She knows he is her father's brother, and that we don't speak. But that is all she knows.'

'She must have seen him at her grandmother's funeral. And that wife of his.'

'Yes, but remember the state she was in at the time. I never thought losing her grandmother would upset her so.'

'That old fiend. No, it was odd. But Charlotte had been with the old lady every day, remember, reading to her. They may have been closer than you knew. You did not ask her about it at the time?'

'No.' Regretfully. 'That was a bad time, remember. I lost the baby, and you had to go to America.' She could speak of it at last without tears, but it had been a terrible time.

'I thought it my duty.' They were words all too familiar to Kathryn. 'Mr. Jefferson's embargo on American shipping was a disaster for our trade here in Hull. Someone had to speak up.'

'For what it was worth.' Bitterly. Losing at once the child she was carrying and all hopes of another, it had been the last straw to lose her husband too for almost a year, while he pleaded in vain to the authorities in what

22

he had described as the shanty town of Washington.

'Not much.' He admitted it ruefully. 'And things look worse than ever just now. If it does not come to a war between our two countries it will be a miracle. And how that would delight Napoleon. But we have strayed from the point. You think I should go first to Beverley, and then to Scarborough, if I draw a blank there?'

'I'm sure you will find her in Beverley. And how awkward that is going to be!'

'So long as she is safe and well.'

'Oh, they will look after her all right. She is the heiress to Comyn's, after all.'

'Let me refill your glass.' The Foreign Secretary had invited his younger friend for what he had described as a bachelor glass of wine at Apsley House. 'I have a proposition to put to you, Forde,' he went on now, pouring claret for them both. 'You said something the other night at White's about how you longed for a bolt abroad, now you are out of Parliament, thanks to the idiocy of the voters.'

'What's the use of longing? There's nowhere to go. The French have made travel impossible.' As he spoke, Forde's quick brain was considering possibilities. Was the Foreign Secretary going to suggest some kind

23

of mission to his brother, Arthur Wellesley, now campaigning in Spain? 'You know what an idle, good-for-nothing kind of fellow I am, Wellesley.' He was leaning against the chimney-piece, his splendid head thrown back, and Wellesley, a handsome man himself, thought that his friend had everything: looks, money, intelligence . . . Everything except occupation, and, in his early thirties, a wife. 'I confess I do long for the carefree life of a spa, for Carlsbad or Pau,' Forde went on. 'But I don't fancy seeing the inside of one of Napoleon's prisons, so I suppose it will have to be Buxton or Scarborough.'

'Among the north country misses? I don't quite see you there, Forde. Nor do I believe you when you cry yourself down. You know as well as I do that you are only at a loose end because of your great fortune, and because you have not found anything sufficiently interesting to occupy you.'

'True enough. However much I long to help defeat Napoleon I cannot quite see myself in the army — still less pushing a pen in Whitehall.'

'A lamentable waste of your talents. You are a good friend of Beth Prior's, are you not?'

'A remarkable woman.' Forde concealed surprise at the question.

'So I think too. One of life's enchantresses.

She has not made up her quarrel with the management of Covent Garden, I believe.'

'She can afford to please herself these days.'

'Quite so. Have you ever thought of making a trip to Sicily, Forde?'

'Sicily?' Now he could not conceal his surprise. 'I can't say I have. You're thinking of Brydone's book? Those romantic descriptions of brigands and ruins and volcanoes? Not quite my line, and besides, think of the inconvenience of getting there, just now.'

'Not if I send you in a man-of-war. As a friendly gesture, you understand, nothing official about it. Just suppose Beth Prior could be persuaded to accept a position at the Theatre Royal in Palermo, and suppose, for the sake of argument, that you should be gallant enough to offer to escort her there, what could be more logical than that I, as your old friend and neighbour, should offer you passage on the next ship that's going that way.'

'What a remarkable set of suppositions. And what, I wonder, do they all add up to?' He ran a hand through fashionably short fair hair.

'Some work for you to do, perhaps. And for Miss Prior too, if you can persuade her to go.'

'For Miss Prior?' In amazement, now.

'A great charmer, as well as a remarkable woman . . . Well,' he refilled their glasses,

25

'I don't suppose you know much about the state of things in Sicily, since the King and Queen fled there from Naples, but you most certainly do know that, with Malta, it is our last outpost in the Mediterranean, vital to our operations against the French. And the King is a dolt, led by the nose by his wife, Queen Maria Carolina.'

'Maria Theresa's last daughter; Nelson's patroness.' Forde decided to show that he was not quite ignorant of the state of things in Sicily.

'You have put your finger on it. Nelson's patroness and Lady Hamilton's good friend.'

'So Emma Hamilton tells anyone who will listen to her.'

'But it is true, just the same,' said the older man. 'Queen Maria Carolina is a woman of passionate friendships. With women as well as with men. And her friendship with Emma Hamilton and Nelson was crucial to our fortunes before the Battle of the Nile. She is older now, given to opium and hysteria, I believe, but she is still all-powerful in Sicily. And her granddaughter is married to the Emperor Napoleon.'

'Marie Louise of Austria. Of course. Poor girl.'

'They say he is devoted to her. Specially since the birth of the little King of Rome.

Suppose she were to intercede for her grandmother? There are rumours already in Sicily that Maria Carolina has written to her. But then there are always rumours in Sicily; the place lives on them. That is why I should be so glad to have your intelligent ear on the listen for me there.'

'And Miss Prior's?'

'Well, yes. But better still if she were to make herself agreeable to the Queen.'

'As Emma Hamilton did? Closet councils.' He did not pretend to like the idea.

'I know. It does not sound pretty, put so baldly. But think, Forde, of the alternatives. We have a small army in Sicily, or King Murat would have been over from Naples and taken the island long since. If the Queen were to sell out, either to Napoleon or to Murat in Naples, they would be as good as dead. There is talk that she is in correspondence with Murat, too. The one thing we do know for certain, is that she hates Sicily and the Sicilians and longs to be back on the throne of Naples. Given the offer of that, she would betray us tomorrow. Think about it, Forde, have a word with Miss Prior, in deepest confidence. I am quite sure, are not you, that we can rely on her discretion.'

'Yes.' It was more than either of them would have said of any of the more respectable ladies of their acquaintance. 'I'll call on her tonight.'

'Me! A kind of political emissary?' Beth Prior dissolved into delightful laughter. 'Gareth, my love, I would do a great deal for you, as well you know, but that is going a little too far. To start off with, I should be sick as a dog on the boat, and ugly as sin when we got there, and you would be embarrassed for me, which I would very much dislike. And the Queen would turn up her Hapsburg nose at me, as well she might. And the *lazzaroni* — do they have *lazzaroni* in Sicily, or is that just Naples?'

'Just Naples, I think.' But he was impressed by the local knowledge this suggested.

'They'd throw rotten oranges at me if I appeared on their stage.'

'I very much doubt that. Roses and lilies more likely. And think of the delicious climate.'

'Hot as hell in the summer. I have read Brydone's book, even if you haven't. And talked to poor Emma Hamilton too. She don't speak too highly of Queen Maria Carolina. Never sent her a penny in the way of pension, when she asked for it after Nelson died. Out of sight, out of mind, with that one.'

'Yes, Beth my love, but you will be in sight. You told me just the other day that you were getting tired of doing nothing. Here's your answer. Wellesley promises to organise a profitable engagement for you in Palermo. They rebuilt their opera house the other day, named it for the Queen, are on the lookout for international figures like you. A season there, as successful as it is sure to be, and you can come back and name your terms to that skinflint Kemble at Covent Garden. Wellesley tells me the fashionable world is flocking to Sicily, what with Brydone's book —'

'And the fact that there is nowhere else to go. I confess it is tempting.' She thought about it for a moment. 'But I don't think so, my dear. To gallivant off to Palermo with you, delightful though it would be, would put paid to any rags of character I have managed to hang on to, and I don't fancy that at all. Besides, I may be able to sing in Italian, but I don't speak it too well; how would I ever get next to Queen Maria Carolina?'

'She's Austrian, remember, speaks French as well as German, and as for the Sicilians themselves, they speak some barbarous dialect no one can understand.'

'Not the nobility. Brydone says they are a much more interesting set of people than the Neapolitans.'

'Maybe that is why Maria Carolina is less happy there than at Naples. Think, Beth, how interesting it would be to plunge into a whole new world like that. And to be serving your country at the same time. Who knows what Wellesley might not get Government to do for you if you were able to influence the course of events there.'

'He can hardly give me back my good name.' There was a little silence, while they both recognised that only marriage could go anywhere near doing that for her. And marriage was the one thing they had never discussed.

2

After Forde had gone, Beth Prior prowled restlessly through her luxurious rooms for a while, making herself face the facts of her life. When she had first set up in London, it had been in a house belonging to her friends the Weatherbys, but Kathryn's shocked reaction to her increasing notoriety had made it impossible to stay there, and she had taken pleasure, and run into debt, furnishing a snug little house in Clarges Street to which she invited the select few to whom she granted her favours. The debts had been almost paid off when a ferocious quarrel with John Kemble about the Old Price Riots at Covent Garden had ended with her finding herself out of work for the first time since she had swept to success on the London stage.

It was a pity, she faced it wryly, that this had happened just when Gareth Forde had come into her life and she had begun to find herself increasingly reluctant to entertain anyone else. As a result, the pile of bills in the little writing desk was growing alarmingly. When Forde had asked to see her urgently, her heart had jumped. A proposal of marriage from him would solve everything. No wonder if she had looked askance at his actual proposition.

But now, watching thin rain drizzle down outside, she found it immensely attractive. It would be hot in Sicily, a new world of flowers and sunshine, and, maybe, something worthwhile to do. Even if the Queen were to prove unreachable, she knew her own gift for getting on with people. They talked to her as they did not to blue-blooded Gareth Forde. She could certainly make herself useful as a gatherer of intelligence. The trouble was that she could not give that as a reason for going. But still less could she make the public gesture of accompanying Forde to Sicily as anything but his wife, however much she longed to do so. He was the only man who had ever given her real pleasure. And she liked him too. They could talk. Absurd. She was crying. Beth Prior did not cry; laughter had always been her line.

Her maid Prue was scratching at the door. 'I'm at home to no one, Prue. I'll not go out tonight.'

'Oh, miss, he'll be that cast down. It's ever such a young gentleman. From the north, he says. A Mr. Charles Pennam. I reckon he has run away from school, or maybe it's a wager, miss. Do see him, just for a moment. There's something about him, really there is.'

'Did you say Pennam? A young gentleman?' Pennam had been her lost friend Kathryn's maiden name, but she had only half-brothers called Morewood, and an unmarried aunt down on the Welsh border somewhere. 'I'll see him.' She made up her mind. Never turn a mystery away. And she had always hoped that some day, somehow, she and Kathryn Weatherby would be friends again.

The youth Prue ushered in was even younger than Beth had expected. But that was partly, she thought, because his schoolboy's best suit hung so loose about him. Passed down from an older brother perhaps? 'Mr. Pennam.' She held out a friendly hand. 'How can I serve you? You'll take a glass of wine with me?' She turned to give the order to Prue.

'If I could have milk instead?' His voice had not broken yet. He was looking at her with a speculative glance that she would have found offensive in an older man. But his hand was cold, and quivered a little in hers.

'Milk, Prue, and a glass of wine for me. And some cakes. You've come a long way, Mr. Pennam?'

'Yes. It seemed to take forever. It's good of you to see me.' He moved over to warm his hands at the fire.

'My curiosity, Mr. Pennam. I had a good

friend, once, with your name. Are you kin to her perhaps? Kathryn Pennam she was. Kathryn Weatherby now. She lives in the north.'

'Yes.' He looked up quickly as Prue appeared with a tray. 'That's why I hoped you might see me. I'm so very grateful. And for this.' He accepted the glass of milk Prue poured for him and took a deep draft.

'And a cake, sir?' Prue proffered the dish which was piled high with an assortment as for a schoolboy.

'Thank you.' Choosing a plain bun, he cast an anguished glance at Beth from under the dark brows that reminded her of something. Someone?

'Thank you, Prue, that will do. We'll wait on ourselves.' It got her a grateful look over the half-empty glass. 'And now,' when they were settled facing each other, with the dish of cakes on a table beside him, 'tell me about yourself, Mr. Pennam. I quite long to know.'

'I'm most terribly sorry,' he said. 'I'm going to be sick.' And was, comprehensively.

Beth's hand went out to ring for Prue, hesitated, stopped. She ministered to her guest herself and made a discovery that did not altogether surprise her.

'Charlotte,' she said at last, when she had her settled on her own chaise longue, wrapped in her own negligée. 'It has to be Charlotte Pennam Comyn, but, in the name of goodness, child, why?'

'I'm so *sorry!*' Charlotte had been incoherently apologising between the spasms of sickness. 'It was all so much worse than I imagined. That mail coach . . . the people . . . and the food at the inns . . . I don't know what I'd have done if you hadn't let me in. I do thank you!' In a strange way, the messy scene had made them friends.

'Dear child,' said Beth. 'I was there, holding your mother's hand, when you were born.'

'I didn't know.' The dark eyes were misted with tears. 'Mother never talked about that. Oh, I am glad I came to you.'

'So am I. But you still haven't told me why. I have to know that before we can think what is best to do with you. You can't stay here, child, that's one thing certain. I'm glad you had the sense to come in your brother's clothes.'

'I can't stay?' The desolation in the girl's voice went straight to Beth's heart.

'Well, for tonight perhaps. Prue can keep a secret, and she knows I'm not at home to anyone. We'll fudge something up in the morning.'

'But, why? Oh —' Charlotte looked down at the little pile of boys clothes on the floor.

35

'Your reputation?'

'No, yours. That's the whole point, child. I have none. That's why your mother cut the connection all those years ago.'

'Oh,' said Charlotte. And then, 'Oh, I see.' There was a little silence. 'I'm still glad I came.'

'Then so am I. But tell me the whole story. I suppose there is a man in it. There usually is.'

'Yes. My oldest friend. John Thornton.'

'The banking family? I remember them. A starchy lot, but reliable.'

'That's it. John used to visit us at Windover when we were all children. He's a bit older than me, but it didn't seem to matter then. We had good times, the five of us.' She looked back at them wistfully. 'Then he went away to Cambridge. When he came back it was all different. And I've not been well. They sent me up to Windover, said the air would do me good. He came up the other day; asked me to marry him. Just like that. As if it had all been settled in advance; we merely had to go through the motions. And it had been settled too!' She was angry now, her eyes sparkling as she remembered the scene. 'He'd talked to his parents first. And to mine! Everything was fixed; we were to have a house in Albion Street until I came of age. It's the bank, of course,' she explained. 'Nothing to do with me. Just the two banks getting together.'

'John Thornton can hardly have said that.'

'He didn't need to. I understood.'

'So you refused him.'

'Yes. And he rode back to Hull, to tell them all, and I thought and thought, and in the end I couldn't face it. Mother doesn't much like me, you see. I'm a disappointment to her. Oh, they try to be fair. You can see them trying. But how can they be, when any fool can see it would be better if my brother Mark could inherit Comyn's rather than me. I can't even add,' she wailed.

'What's that to the purpose? Just because your mother had to manage things at the bank, and did it so well, it doesn't mean that you will need to. And as for this talk of her disliking you, that's the greatest nonsense I ever heard. She adored you, Charlotte, when you were little.'

'That may be, but she has had a new husband and three sons since. How could she go on liking me? I know all about my father, you see. My grandmother told me, when she was dying. How could my mother help but hate me after what she did to him?'

'Dear child, what can you mean?' The candles were burning low and it was getting dark in the room, but Beth would not stir to trim

37

them. This was important. This was the heart of the matter.

'Didn't you know? Surely you must have. You were there, weren't you? That my mother killed my father. Grandmother thought it her duty to tell me; a sacred confidence, she called it. The voice of God speaking through her. What did you say?'

'Nothing. Go on. What else did old Mrs. Comyn tell you?'

'About my mother and Sir Henry Etherington. About how I am probably not a Comyn at all. And then you talk about my reputation! The reputation of a bastard! Of course I couldn't marry John Thornton. Not even if I wanted to. Which I don't.' Defiantly.

'Oh, the wicked woman,' said Beth.

'Mother? No, not wicked. I've thought about it so much. She must have been terribly unhappy, poor mother, to do such things. Pushed too far. Not wicked. Just unlucky. Like me. Grandmother said my doom was written in my face. I don't look like anyone in the family. I don't look like Sir Henry either,' she admitted. 'I've studied him over and over in church, and there's not a trace. But I don't know about his parents.'

'Fool of a child.' Beth was sitting close to the chaise longue now, holding the thin hand in hers. 'Did you never look at your great-grandfather's portrait at Windover? Lord Eskdale? He used to hang in the study. Over the chimney-piece. A Kitcat; his wife facing him. He's got your eyebrows. I knew you reminded me of someone, the minute you came into the room. And as for the rest of this nonsense; that's all it is: nonsense. Your grandmother was a truly wicked woman, I think, and I don't often think that of anyone. You're quite right. I was there, when it all happened. And I saw how she worked at poisoning your father's mind against your mother. I truly think they might have had a kind of practical happiness together, those two, if it had not been for her and that devil, Mr. Jones.'

'Mr. Jones?'

'I'd forgotten; you wouldn't know about him. He was run out of town after your grandmother had her stroke. He'd been extorting money from her; telling her all kinds of tales about your mother. Well, of course, there was talk. Kathryn stood out among the married ladies of Hull like a swan among sparrows. Watching what happened to her, I vowed I'd never marry. She saved the bank, by that dash to London of hers, and all the thanks she got was gossip and enmity. Your Uncle George Comyn meant to have her put in a madhouse if you had been a boy. Lord knows what would have happened to you. That's why we ran for it to London the second time. She knew she had no chance of facing him out, in the teeth of all the talk. And then, after you were born, it turned out that the will didn't specify male heirs. One in the eye for George Comyn. But he's the heir now!' She realised it. 'After you. It don't matter a tinker's damn whether your mother and step-father would like one of their sons to take over Comyn's. He has no more right to it than I have. If you don't marry, George Comyn and his brood — I suppose he has a new wife and children by now — will get the bank, and that is not a day I wish to see. No wonder they are so eager to get you married, up there in Hull. Comyn's is vital to Hull trade, and we all know how bad things are in business. George Comyn in charge would be a disaster. But I'm tiring you out.' A quick glance showed her visitor drooping on the chaise longue. 'We'll get you to bed. Things will look better in the morning.'

'They look better now.' Charlotte pulled herself upright. 'I'm not a bastard, I'm a fool. And I'm going to be sick again.'

In the morning, the sun shone. Charlotte, waking in the tiny sliver of a spare room found her hostess standing over her with an armful of clothes. 'These won't fit,' Beth said. 'Nothing I have will. But they'll do for the moment.

You are my friend Miss Pennam, up from the wilds of the Welsh border. I expect I met your family when I was on tour in those parts, don't you? We'll think of a story when we've more time. For the moment, I want you to eat what you feel like of your breakfast and get ready to see my doctor. You'll like him; he's a sensible fellow and doesn't think all women hysterical fools. Whatever we decide to do, we can't have you being sick all the time. It's too tedious. And besides I can't afford the washing bills.'

It made Charlotte laugh, which was what Beth had intended, and she was glad to see her dispatch the toast and tea she had ordered for her. 'You don't get any more,' she said, noticing a wistful gleam in her guest's eyes. 'Not till the doctor's been.'

'Quite right.' Alone with Beth after examining Charlotte, Dr. Soames had listened with interest to what she had told him of her young visitor's story. 'Less to eat than she wants, but regularly. I hope you aren't thinking of launching her in society, Miss Prior; she's not fit for it. I can't think what her people have been thinking of, to let her get into this state. And any talk of marriage is absurd. She's a child still, in every way. Distraction, she needs, exercise, rest, fresh air. A change of scene but not into the London season.'

'That's just what I thought.' Beth looked at him with friendly approval. 'It should be the south of France, shouldn't it, or Italy, perhaps.'

'All quite out of the question, of course, with that madman loose in Europe, but, yes, that is precisely what I meant. So — Buxton, perhaps, or Scarborough? One thing,' more cheerfully, 'she tells me she has not been sick today. Perhaps the change of scene and your bracing company are doing her good already. I'll send round a tonic draft for her and call again in a week or so to see how she goes on in your wise hands.'

Beth had cancelled all her engagements for the day, congratulating herself on having established it that no one, be he however exalted, might call at her house uninvited. This went for her women friends too, such as they were. She had never fraternised with professionals like Harriet Wilson, though they met amiably enough in the haunts of the demi-monde. Mrs. Siddons had become a good friend, and so had Mrs. Inchbald, when both these ladies realised that she would never push herself in when she was not wanted. Those two had managed to retain their position in the eyes of the world, despite being visibly independent and self-supporting females. Mrs. Inchbald's husband had died; Mrs. Siddons' hung around her like a bad debt, but husbands they had, or had had, so they were socially acceptable.

'I'd rather die,' Beth told herself, and went back to wondering, as she had been all morning, what she was going to say to Mark Weatherby when he came. She had written a note to Kathryn the night before, and seen to it that it caught the night mail to Hull. They must be distracted with worry up there, and she was a little surprised not to have heard from them already. They would surely be exploring every avenue in search for their lost child. But then, she remembered, Kathryn thought her daughter ignorant of her own adventures in London. How extraordinary to think of such a gap developing between the mother she remembered as entirely devoted to her baby, and her only daughter. But then, childless herself, and grateful for it, how was she to understand the feelings of parents?

She might not know what she was going to say to Mark Weatherby, but she was very sure she was not going to let him take Charlotte back to Hull. Their meeting was going to be awkward enough, though. He had thought himself in love with her once, asked her to marry him, just when Kemble had offered her a start in the theatre. She had laughed at him, and he had not liked it much, but, later, she thought he had taken her side when Kathryn had come out suddenly and surprisingly so strait-laced. Not that one could really blame Kathryn, she had been too close to the abyss herself. Of course she was afraid of being pulled down again.

Prue brought her a note from Gareth Forde. 'Lord Amherst is here, back from Sicily,' he wrote. 'Government think he has been too easy on them there. They talk of sending Lord William Bentinck, a man of iron if ever there was one. I know him a little; it would be easy to arrange to go out with him. Dear Beth, think again. When did you ever refuse a challenge?' There followed two closely written pages of persuasion; not one word of marriage.

Well, why should he? He had had her without. But there was no word about money either, and this was something else again. Another handful of bills had arrived that morning; something drastic would have to be done soon. And she began to think she saw what it would be. She sat down and wrote a temporising answer to Forde and sent a footman to deliver it and buy her a copy of Mr. Brydone's useful book on Sicily.

Mark Weatherby arrived two days later, just

as Charlotte was getting impatient at being confined to the house. She was looking much better, Beth thought, but she still meant to see Mark alone first.

'It's been a long time.' She held out a friendly hand to him and thought how much older he looked, his nabob brown faded to yellow.

'Too long, dear Beth. It's good to see you at last. And best of all that you have Charlotte safe. We have been sick with worry about her, as you can imagine.'

'A little late in the day.' Dryly.

'I know. It's been a mismanaged business, one way and another. There's been no way to get through to the child since her grandmother died. We'd never have thought, Kathryn and I, that she would take it so hard.'

'No.' Beth had promised to say nothing about that last scene. 'When it was such a relief to you.'

'Quite so. We had high hopes of John Thornton's proposal. They were the best of friends as children.' How very odd to find himself justifying their actions to Beth, who had once been Kathryn's maid. 'We truly thought it would be the answer for her.'

'As well as for the Comyns. Tell me, has George Comyn children?'

'Oh yes, he remarried soon after we did. A raft of boys.'

'I'm surprised you hadn't thought of marrying Charlotte to one of them.'

'Cousins? And with that father?' And then because it was somehow difficult not to tell the truth to Beth. 'We did think of it, of course, but they are a set of good-for-nothings. George wanted us to take the eldest into the bank, but there was no way we could, not on his record.'

'And what is not good enough for Comyn's is not good enough for Charlotte. I'm glad you see that at least, you and Kathryn.'

He flushed, unused to criticism. 'We have acted always for the child's best, as we saw it. The question is, what is best for her now? Kathryn thinks she should come back to Hull, face out the talk.'

'Kathryn would. And I might even agree with her if the child were stronger. I have had my doctor to her. He prescribes rest, fresh air, exercise, a change of scene — a trip to the sunshine, in fact.'

'And where do we find that?'

'In Sicily.' Beth surprised him. 'I have been considering an offer to appear at the Theatre Royal in Palermo. The snag is: the money's not right. I did not think I could afford to indulge myself in the trip. But if you and

Kathryn were prepared to put up something towards it, I think I might really be tempted to go, and take Charlotte with me. I like her very much, Mark.' She had been meaning to call him by his Christian name, as he had her, and was amused to see how this surprised him. And she was even more amused as she watched him consider her proposal, both as he reacted to it, and as his wife would. An ideal solution: the difficult child taken off their hands. If only her own circumstances were otherwise. She took pity on him. 'She wouldn't come as herself, naturally. I don't suppose you know, but she arrived in your son's clothes, sensible child, calling herself Charles Pennam. And a very nice boy she made too. I have given it out that she is the daughter of friends I made when I was on tour in the west. And I have kept her strictly at home, which is beginning to bore her very much, now she is feeling better. But she could come with me as Charlotte Pennam, and nobody the wiser.' She could see how it tempted him.

'But what would we say in Hull? We've managed to cover the wretched business so far. They think at Windover that she has come home to Hull and in Hull that she is still at Windover. But we can't keep that up for ever. There's young Thornton, to start off with. It's a funny thing, but her refusal seems to have made him more eager.'

'Well, of course,' said Beth. 'Tell me. Are the two ladies still going strong down at Ross?'

'They were at Christmas.'

'Well, there's your answer. Tell the gossips that Charlotte has gone to them on an extended visit. I suppose everyone in Hull will know she turned young Thornton down. What more logical than that you should send the child away for a change of scene? Specially granted her state of health, which you all seem to have taken so lightly.' But she must not make him angry. 'I know how busy you must be, you and Kathryn, with that splendid newspaper of yours. I have watched its success with the greatest pleasure. It's no wonder if domestic affairs have had to take something of a second place. Specially now, with all the turmoil of the poor King's madness, and the Regency. Tell me, do you think, you and Kathryn, that the Prince of Wales is going to continue the present government in power?'

'It begins to look like it. Certainly for the year that the restraints on his actions continue.'

'And what a fuss that was! I went to hear his royal brothers speak up for him in the House of Lords; such a field day for the press!'

'Are you acquainted with them?' He felt himself blushing as he asked the question. For himself? Or for her?

'Oh, a little. Mrs. Jordan is a friend of mine, so naturally I see something of Billy Clarence.'

'And Mrs. Clarke?'

'That shabby woman has never darkened my doors. Selling commissions and involving the Duke of York!'

'So you were glad when he was reinstated as Commander in Chief?'

'So should everyone be who has the good of our army at heart. Arthur Wellesley says York's done more for the poor bloody man in the line than a thousand royal commissions.'

'You know Wellesley?'

'Oh, yes.' Smiling to herself. 'We all know Arthur Wellesley.' But if she must not make him angry, still less must she shock him, though she was glad to have impressed him with her knowledge of the Royal Dukes. 'This has happened at a good moment for me,' she told him. 'You see before you a reformed character, Mark. I know Kathryn will be pleased to hear it. I have decided it is time to turn over a new leaf and concentrate my talents on the stage. But it's not an easy thing to do, not here in London. Old habits die hard. Specially other people's. That's why, when this Sicilian offer came along, I found myself thinking about it seriously, even though the money was so miserable. It would be a break, do you see; a chance to make the change.

When I came back, everything would be different.' And the surprising thing is, she thought, that this is all perfectly true. Or almost. 'And having young Charlotte with me would be a kind of guarantee, do you see? I promise you, and you can promise Kathryn, that if you let her come, we will live the blameless lives of two lady tourists.'

'But you would be appearing in the theatre?' The fact that he was even discussing it was surely encouraging.

'Oh, yes. But that is not in itself an impropriety, except with the most rigid of Evangelicals. Look at Sarah Siddons.'

'Yes.' He thought about it for a few minutes, and she could see him working out the pros and cons of her proposition and Kathryn's reaction to it. 'Beth.' He surprised her at last. 'Are you by any chance thinking of marriage?'

'Oh, my dear creature! We all think about it all the time. But it doesn't happen to many of us, and, frankly, if it does, not much good seems to come of it. Look at poor Dorothy Jordan, working as hard as ever, at her time of life, to support all Clarence's children. If she were not so devoted to them, I'd say she would be better on her own. No, what I am thinking of is an independent future. And the snag about this easy come, easy go life of mine, is there always seems in the end to be more go than come about it. Look there.' She opened her little writing table. 'All bills, Mark, that would have to be paid before I could leave town. It will cost you and Kathryn a pretty penny if I take Charlotte abroad with me, but I promise you, I will see to it that you get value for your money. I like the child: I wouldn't offer if I didn't. I think I could maybe give her life the new turn it needs. And I'll tell you something else, very much to the purpose. I don't think she dislikes that young Thornton at all. If you ask me, a lot of the trouble was that she did like him, but felt his proposal was a mere matter of business. Something like her mother's first marriage.'

'Oh, I see. And if being refused has made young Thornton more eager, not less —'

'The best thing we can do is separate them for a while. I can see that the match would be an admirable one from all kinds of points of view, if they should find they like each other enough. And you know about absence —'

'I should rather think I do. What do you think we should tell young Thornton?'

'I'd be inclined to tell him the truth, if you feel you can trust him with it. And if you don't, can you trust him with Charlotte?' She was delighted to notice that they were now discussing her proposal in practical terms.

'And with the bank,' he reminded her. 'And the answer is yes. But, Beth, what will Kathryn think?'

She smiled at him and he understood why men were her slaves. 'That's your problem. The case is, I have a chance of a ship, any day now. You have to make up your mind to it fast; no time to consult Kathryn.' She rang the bell. 'But I think we should put it to Charlotte, do not you? And — no scoldings, Mark, please.'

3

After that, it was all cheerful confusion. Having agreed terms with Mark Weatherby, Beth was able to surprise Forde with a new proposition. 'The child's been ill,' she explained. 'Her parents are mad to get her abroad, and where better than to Sicily? They will pay the half of my expenses, and all of Charlotte's. It is only for you and Wellesley to match their half, and the thing is done. But before you agree, I have to tell you that I have undertaken to be Caesar's wife on this expedition — above suspicion.' She put a hand on his lips. 'Think a minute, dear friend. It would have been necessary anyway. If I am to get next or nigh to Queen Maria Carolina I must appear in society. And if I am to appear in society, you, my dear, will have to keep the line. After all, there is a Lady Bentinck, is there not? With Evangelical leanings and no children? She must receive me in Palermo, if I go, or my going is useless. Can you achieve that small miracle for me, do you think?'

'Oh, I imagine so. She is devoted to her husband, I know, and to his career.'

'He's the brilliant one of the Bentincks, isn't he, but something went wrong in India?'

'That's the one; recalled after a mutiny. This is his chance to make a new start, and nothing is going to stop him. But you are right, dear Beth, as you so often are. You must be the prima donna, and I your devoted slave — at a distance. Intolerable! And I warn you, if you have no obvious male protector, you are likely to find yourself open to the advances of King Ferdinand the Stupid.'

'Which certainly would not endear me to his wife. But let me alone to deal with that. Making men keep the line, when I don't want them, has never been a problem to me, as you should know, my dear.'

'That's just why I shall find this new regime so hard to bear.' He took her hand. 'But it hasn't started yet.' He began to pull her towards her bedroom door. 'Come, love, let's have one more gaudy night.'

'No, sir.' She withdrew her hand. 'Quoting Shakespeare will get you nowhere. We are going to have a business meeting, you and I, and then, if the dibs are in tune, you are going to meet my protégée.'

'Tell me more about her, Beth.' Resigning himself. 'It's a new come-out for you, acting preceptress to the young.'

'You are to start calling me Miss Prior, if

54

you please. And, as to Miss Pennam, you shall see for yourself, and draw your own conclusions.' After some thought, she had decided to resist the temptation to tell him Charlotte's story. A secret shared with a man is one shared with all his friends. This one, she would keep to herself. 'But first, we must talk finance,' she reminded him.

She had expected to have trouble pinning him down, and did, but he had brought the news that the Bentincks were to sail for Sicily at once, and this inevitably strengthened her hand. Forde really wanted to go on this odd expedition, and really wanted her to come too; it was but to show up his wrigglings, civilly, for what they were, and in the end she was satisfied, and sent for Charlotte.

'You drive a hard bargain.' She could see that he respected her for it.

'I need to. I have my future to consider, as well as the child's.' She had let him think, without actually saying so, that Charlotte was a nobody whose parents were hard put to it to pay her expenses. Nobody must know that she was an heiress until she was very much better able to look after herself.

Forde's manner with Charlotte, when she joined them, was perfect, something between the gallant and the avuncular, and Beth was amused to see the child blossom under his tact-

55

ful handling. With a bit of luck, and a touch of good management, this should prove part of her cure. She also noticed that Charlotte had her own resources. When Forde turned the conversation to the Welsh border country from which she was supposed to come, she put on a good show of confusion, covering her ignorance by a pretence that thoughts of home made her worse.

In fact, Charlotte was enjoying herself. She was breathing new air in this surprising household, run by a woman for her own ends. Looking back, as she watched her hostess spar with her handsome guest, she thought that all her life, so far, had been based on the assumption that somewhere there was a man whose convenience came first. It had been a revelation to her to see how Beth treated Mark Weatherby. At home in Hull, her step-father's word was law. Here, in Beth Prior's house, she saw him on his best behaviour, submitting even to being teased a little by his hostess. And now, here was this outrageously handsome Gareth Forde, also deferring to Beth as if her opinion were of value. When he had left, she turned to her hostess with sparkling eyes. 'Oh, I am going to enjoy this, Beth! May I call you Beth? How lucky I am!'

But she begged in vain to be shown something of the sights of London before they left. Beth knew too well how small the world of society was, and how swift the voice of gossip. It only needed one north country neighbour to recognise her guest, and the story was blown. Which reminded her of something. She sat down and wrote a note to Lavinia Pennam, the old aunt in the west country, telling her enough of what was going on so that the old lady, whom she remembered as nobody's fool, would be equipped to fend off any enquiries that might come her way. That done, she applied herself, heart and soul, to spending the money she had wrung out of her two sponsors on preparations for the trip. She and Charlotte were going to cut a dash in Palermo society or she would change her dressmaker.

Charlotte loved the clothes, though a disparaging remark by Madame Gros the dressmaker about her skinniness made her sick again, and she ate nothing on the last day in London. But Beth just laughed, and ate her own devilled kidneys, and sent her to bed early with Miss Burney's *Evelina*. 'I'm going to put you on a diet of entertaining novels,' she explained. 'But don't read late. Gareth Forde is calling for us betimes in the morning.'

Tucked snugly up in the comfortable bed, Charlotte gazed across the room at the new dress hanging ready for the morning, and told herself it was not all a dream. She had got away; she was free; and she was Charlotte Pennam Comyn, nobody's bastard. *I'm so lucky,* she thought, *to be me,* and slept.

And in the morning, she was hungry, ate all the tea and toast Beth allowed her, and put on the new dress, forgiving Madame Gros everything. She looked — what was the word?

'Willowy.' Beth had caught her gazing into the glass. 'Not thin, but willowy. I look forward to seeing Gareth Forde's face when he calls for us.'

'He thought me such a fright?' Charlotte could ask it now.

'He thought you a schoolgirl, hardly out of the nursery.'

'But a mile high,' said Charlotte, putting her finger on it. 'I'm glad he's so tall, Beth. I don't have to stoop.'

'Don't ever stoop,' said Beth.

Gareth Forde's carriage was luxurious, like everything else about him, and it was a happy drive down to join the brig that awaited them at Spithead. Arriving there, the parties separated, to spend the night at different inns.

'This is where the game begins,' said Beth.

'At last.' Charlotte had been on tenterhooks lest a last minute message from Hull should catch them and summon her home. Would she have gone? She was not sure. But it was a relief not to have been summoned.

When they went on board, early next morning, they found that the Bentincks were already established, and Lady Bentinck had taken to her bed. 'My wife is a sad invalid, I am afraid.' Lord Bentinck had greeted Beth with stiff civility that did not auger well, she thought, but had unbent a little to Charlotte.

'I'm a poor sailor too,' Beth told him. 'I think I shall follow Lady William's wise example.' She was glad to retreat from this cold, formal man, but reminded herself that Gareth Forde had warned he had a name for shy reserve, which his wife's voluble friendliness did something to mitigate.

A storm in the Bay of Biscay laid both the older ladies low, but Charlotte throve in the sea air, regained her appetite and adapted naturally to the rhythms of the ship. Beth's maid Prue was also groaning helplessly in a corner of their tiny cabin, and it was Charlotte who looked after her new friend. When she learned that Lady William's maid was prostrate too, she nerved herself to approach her husband as he paced the deck and volunteer her own services.

'You wouldn't mind, Miss Pennam?' He looked suddenly human. 'She's in a wretched way, I am afraid.'

'So is Miss Prior,' said Charlotte. 'But a little nursing does make things pleasanter.'

'Then come along, child, if you really mean it, and thank you.' He led the way to the cabin, where his wife was indeed in a wretched state of unmade cot and unemptied slops. 'Here is an angel of mercy for you, my dear. I hope she will help you to feel more the thing.' He took a horrified look at the sordid cabin, and fled.

Half an hour later, propped up on pillows in a cabin that looked and smelled quite different, Lady William managed a small smile as Charlotte bathed her head with lavender water. 'Angel of mercy is the word, Miss Pennam; I can't begin to thank you. But tell me about yourself. You have been ill they tell me.'

'I'm better now,' said Charlotte. 'And you should get some sleep, Lady William, now the movement of the ship has eased.' She found she very much did not want to tell lies to this kind, friendly Irish lady.

'There has been some trouble in your life, hasn't there, and you don't want to talk about it.' Lady William might be a great talker, but she was no fool. 'So we will not do so, but you will remember that if you should ever need my help, or my husband's, it is there for you.'

'Oh, thank you,' said Charlotte, and fled.

★ ★ ★

When the bland air of the Mediterranean, and news that Sicily was in sight drew both the older ladies up to the deck at last, their meeting proved surprisingly easy. Both had dreaded it, but they had heard enough about each other from Charlotte, as she moved between their cabins, so that they met almost like friends.

'I don't know what I would have done without your Miss Pennam,' said Lady William.

And, 'No more do I,' said Beth.

'Miss Prior,' Lord William joined them, 'I have to thank you for all your young friend's goodness to my wife. Lady Bentinck has quite lost her heart to the child. We look forward to seeing something of her when we are all settled in Palermo.'

And that was a piece of good news, thought Beth as he turned away for a keen glance at the preparations for their reception on the crowded quay. She moved across the deck to join Charlotte who was gazing eagerly at the widening view of bay and mountains, all bathed in the amazing Mediterranean light.

'I do hope there will be someone to meet us from the opera house,' she spoke her anxiety to Charlotte. The trouble was that she must not be seen to rely on Forde for more help than any gentleman would give to a lady in distress. 'It looks a proper muddle to me.'

'Yes, doesn't it?' Charlotte agreed cheerfully. 'They look like a tremendous set of brigands, and Brydone says the only hotel in Palermo is quite unfit for human habitation. I've been reading him aloud to Lady William. Beth,' with a quick look, 'do you feel all right? You've eaten so little.'

'I've felt stronger.' Beth was touched at finding their roles reversed. 'I confess I can think of nothing but toast and tea.'

'Let's hope we can find them for you. Oh dear, this looks like trouble.'

Beth turned to see Prue approaching with a look at once shame-faced and smug. 'Where's your portmanteau, Prue?' she asked. 'We will be going ashore any moment now.'

'Not me, I won't.' She looked both apologetic and defiant. 'Lot of murdering ruffians there in Sicily by what I've heard, and I've had an offer, miss, from a gentleman on the lower deck. He'll make it all right and tight with the captain, he says, and I've said I'll go back with him. I'm sorry, miss.'

'After all these years —' It had hit Beth hard.

'It's my life, miss, my chance in life. And I've took it.' She turned and flounced away across the deck.

'Never mind, Beth,' Charlotte took her hand. 'I'll look after you. We'll be better off without that girl, if you ask me. I thought she was shamming it about being so sick.'

'I thought we were friends,' said Beth sadly. 'And how I wish I knew where in those handsome streets we are going to find a lodging. Don't, I beg of you, let yourself get separated from me when we go ashore. They look a sad enough set of ruffians.'

'Yes, but do you see, Beth, further back on the quay there are carriages drawn up. One of the officers told me that it is a pastime among the gentry to come down and watch ships come in. May you not find a friend among them? He says the place is full of the English since our troops are here. Oh, look, the Bentincks are going ashore.'

And Gareth Forde with them, Beth saw, catching a guilty backward glance from him. 'We had best follow,' she said.

They found themselves, at last, standing on the quay, their baggage piled around them, being importuned by a gang of ruffians, whose language neither of them could understand. Beth kept saying, *Il teatro,* and thought she was understood, but nothing came of it. The bandits merely went on snatching bits of their luggage from each other and jabbering away in their incomprehensible argot.

'You stay here.' Charlotte saw Beth sway where she stood. 'I'll fight my way through to the carriages, ask for help. Someone must speak an Italian I can understand. Oh, thank goodness —' She had seen a ripple in the crowd that surrounded them and now a tall, swarthy young man pushed his way through, speaking savagely to right and left. Their luggage was dropped and the threatening crowd stood back as he addressed it with one last sibilant, incomprehensible phrase, took off his hat and bowed to them. 'Can I perhaps be of assistance ladies?'

'Oh, thank goodness, you're English,' said Beth.

'No, ma'am, American, but at your service just the same. Our countries are not at war yet, to the best of my knowledge, and even if they were, I would still feel in honour bound to serve two such charming damsels in distress. You came with Lord Bentinck, I take it, and your friends have failed to meet you? Or perhaps they have missed you in the confusion of the ceremonial welcome Bentinck is getting. Organisation is not a strong point of the delightful Sicilians, as you will have noticed. They need it all done for them, and, if I may, I will do it for you. But, first, let me introduce myself. Nathan Peabody, from New Bedford, entirely at your service.' His admiring glance, moving from one to the other, suggested that this was nothing but their natural due.

'What a relief!' Beth smiled at him warmly. 'I am Beth Prior, sir, come to appear at the theatre here. And this is my young friend, Miss Charlotte Pennam.'

'Miss Prior! The prima donna!' He made it an accolade. 'I should have known. And how disastrously characteristic of the management, if you can call it that, of the Theatre Royal that no one is here to meet you. But they will have arranged lodgings for you, I do trust. The place is as full as it can hold, with you British in occupation.'

'Occupation?' Beth took him up on it, as they began to move slowly through the noisy crowd towards the row of carriages. 'A strange word to pick, surely?'

'You'd not think so if you were to go to Messina, Miss Prior, where your army has its headquarters. You English do tend a little to behave like the lords of creation, don't you think? After all —' His smile took the sting out of his words. 'Look what happened to you in my country.'

'And may again,' agreed Beth. 'I agree that our behaviour at sea has been, simply, outrageous, but —'

'This is no time to be talking about it.' He turned to Charlotte, who had followed the exchange with interest, while admiring his dark good looks. 'I don't suppose you know anything about our war of independence, Miss Pennam.'

'On the contrary.' Almost as tall as him, she looked him straight in the eyes. 'My grandfather was killed on the Heights of Haarlem.'

'There's one in the eye for me. Miss Pennam, what can I say? On behalf of my country, I grovel. But here,' with relief, 'is my carriage. I have told these rascals to take your luggage to my place.' He helped Beth into the open carriage, then turned to offer his hand to Charlotte.

'Thank you.' Beth was glad to sit down. 'What a miracle that you speak their language, Mr. Peabody. Miss Pennam and I both flattered ourselves on having some Italian, but we could not understand a word.'

'It's the Sicilian dialect, shaped by their history. Their island has been a central point in the Mediterranean, for trade, for conquest, for everything, down through the ages. Naturally they have picked up words, phrases, intonations from their various conquerors. And as to my speaking their language, that is easily explained. My grandmother came from here. The island is full of my cousins; it is a great advantage.'

'That's why you are here?' Beth had been

wondering a little about this.

'Yes.' He had given an order to the coachman and the carriage was moving slowly to extricate itself from the now fluid crowd of vehicles on the quay. 'I thought I would come over here on a voyage of exploration, before I put my nose to the family grindstone as my father wished. I'm interested in antiquities,' he explained, 'and we don't have that many of them in our United States. I started in Naples, of course, for a sight of those extraordinary temples they have found near there, at Paestum. And I am hoping, in the end, to go on to Greece, but that seems to take a good deal of arranging. The Turks don't much love strangers. Besides, I have found such a warm welcome here, from my mother's family, that it is going to be hard to tear myself away. But I am failing in my duties as cicerone.' He saw that Charlotte's attention had wandered. 'We are going through the Porta Felice now, leaving the Marino for the Corso, the main street of the town. I am taking you to the theatre,' to Beth. 'There we will be able to find out what arrangements have been made for you. Is it not a handsome city, Miss Pennam? I, myself, like it very much better than Naples, and as to the inhabitants, there is no comparison. But then, I am prejudiced, of course.'

'How very interesting to have been to Naples.' Beth was thinking they were lucky to have met this knowledgeable young man. 'What did you think of King Murat's regime?'

'We don't talk of that much, here in Sicily.' He had given, she noticed, a sharp look forward to the coachman, and back to the liveried footman behind. 'Freedom of speech is a good English and American habit that should be practised here only with circumspection. What we think in Sicily, of course,' raising his voice, 'is that it is high time King Murat and his upstart Queen Caroline gave way to the true monarchs of Naples: King Ferdinand and Queen Maria Carolina.'

'I see.' She took the warning, and was grateful.

'This is the Ottangolo.' He turned again to Charlotte, who was admiring the big square with its handsome symmetrical buildings at the corners. 'Where Palermo's two main streets cross. The theatre is higher up. Not long now, Miss Prior. You won't mind sitting in the carriage and watching the world go by while I knock their heads together for you?'

'We shall enjoy it,' Beth told him. 'It is a most animated scene.'

'And the air is delicious,' agreed Charlotte.

'For the moment.' The carriage had

stopped. 'Just you wait till the sirocco starts to blow, Miss Pennam. It's an alibi for murder, you know.' And on this disconcerting note he left them.

'Well, what a godsend,' said Beth.

'I should say. I like him, don't you?'

'Very much. So far. And he certainly turned up in the absolute nick of time.' It might have been politic of Gareth Forde to abandon them like that, but she could not much like him for it.

Nathan Peabody returned quite soon with the manager of the Theatre Royal and bad news. Wringing his hands, Signor Bartolucci explained that superstition had prevented him from believing that the famous signora would really arrive to grace his humble theatre. If he had made arrangements for her, she would most certainly not have come. So, he had made none. 'And now what is to become of the beautiful signora and the exquisite signorina? Even the hotel is full, as I know to my cost, and, besides, it is no place for beautiful ladies.'

'If I might make a suggestion,' said Peabody. 'I had been rather expecting this, to tell you the truth, Miss Prior. Thought for the morrow is not our strong suit, here in Sicily. Now, I have a modest little palazzo not far from here, lent me by one of my cousins. I spend most of my time with him and his delightful family anyway. Do, please, let me go and stay with them, while you make use of my house until you can find something that suits you better. It is a charming situation, open to the sea breezes, and set in its own garden. Please, let me lend it to you?' He had said all this in English, now turned to translate the proposal for Bartolucci, who greeted it with obvious relief. 'He undertakes to pay me a reasonable rent,' turning back to Beth, 'so you need have no scruples on that score. I shall be making a handsome profit out of the arrangement.'

'You are sure your cousin will not mind?'

'Mind! He will be delighted and honoured. And Signor Bartolucci will give us a box for the season. What could be more satisfactory for everyone? You will find the little house ideal for entertaining, Miss Prior. It has been sadly wasted on me, and the servants have been getting restive. I merely insist on being invited to all your parties.'

'It seems too good to be true,' said Beth, an hour or so later, as the two of them stood on their balcony and listened to the soft hush of the sea, several terraces below. 'There must be a catch in it somewhere.'

'Or the age of chivalry is really not dead, here in Sicily.'

'Or in America. We have yet to meet the cousins, remember. They may be dreadful people with whom I should not let you associate.'

'It doesn't seem likely, when he is so charming.'

'I wish we would hear from Gareth Forde.' Beth had sent him a note, care of the Bentincks, as soon as they were settled in the charming little house. 'He will find out about them for me, I am sure.'

'The least he can do.' It was the nearest either of them had got to criticism of Forde's behaviour. 'But, surely Bartolucci would not have been so enthusiastic if there had been anything doubtful about the cousins — I wish I could remember their name.'

'I am afraid Signor Bartolucci is going to prove a thoroughly broken reed,' said Beth. 'I have the most uncomfortable feeling that it is going to turn out that he cannot easily fit me into his company; that it was one of those splendid ideas, you know, that no one expects actually to come to pass. He is probably being torn to pieces by his present leading ladies at this very moment.'

'Oh dear,' said Charlotte. 'Will that be very bad?' She put out an impulsive hand. 'Beth, you do know, don't you, that the very minute I come into my money, I am going to pay you back every penny of what you are spending on me.'

'You are a dear child, and you are not to be worrying about a thing. Your parents have funded me lavishly for your expenses. We could probably manage on that, if we had to, specially as Signor Bartolucci is at least paying our rent here. But we are not going to have to.' She did not mean Charlotte to know about the funds Forde was providing, and was glad when a servant appeared to announce a visitor. 'The Countess Falconi? Mr. Peabody's cousin, of course. How very civil. I just wish we had heard from Gareth Forde.'

'Another broken reed?' suggested Charlotte wickedly as they moved to their salon to greet their guest.

The Countess Falconi looked about fifteen, but had the manner of a great lady. She held out both hands to Beth. 'You must forgive this early intrusion.' She spoke excellent English. 'My husband said I must come at once to welcome you and tell you how absolutely delighted we are with what our cousin has done. Is he not a charming young man? We want to keep him here in Sicily for ever, and I am sure having you two ladies here will be the greatest help. You are to come to us for anything you need, whether it is advice or something more practical. And my husband asked me to say to you, Miss

Prior, that he proposes to take the liberty of saying a word to Bartolucci about you. You probably are not aware — how should you be? — that his squawking wife has been our prima donna here for longer than we care to remember. There may be a little difficulty about her standing down, but Carlo told me to tell you that it was just to wait, for a little, in patience, and leave all to him. And now, I must not keep you any longer from your unpacking. If you have any trouble, of any kind, with the servants, you must let me know, but I do not think you will.'

'No, I am sure not.' Beth had seen the obsequious respect with which the Countess was ushered in. 'We can only thank you a thousand times.'

'And join us for the promenade tonight, I hope. My husband said to tell you we would drive past on our way, if you wouldn't mind being ready in the carriage to follow us? That way, we will be able to make you known to all our friends.'

'You overwhelm us,' said Beth, and meant it. 'That's a great lady.' She turned to Charlotte when the Countess had left. 'No need for Gareth Forde to tell me that.'

'Not much need for Gareth Forde, it seems to me,' said Charlotte. 'But what is this promenade, Beth?'

'It's the evening meeting, down on the Marino. I read about it in Mr. Brydone's book. They turn night into day here, because of the climate. After the theatre and the evening's entertainment, everyone gets into their carriage and drives down to the Marino for an hour or so of friendly talk.'

'But isn't that the Marino, down there?' They had moved back on to the balcony after the Countess left. 'Why take the carriage? It would take only a few minutes to walk.'

'Nobody walks in Palermo. According to Brydone, it is a worse social error than —' She paused, suddenly remembering how young her guest was.

But Charlotte was laughing. 'I read that bit in Brydone's book,' she said. 'I remember now. You have to put out your flambeaux as you go out at the Porta Felice; this happy conversation takes place in the dark. I take it there is a good deal of movement between carriages.'

'I think there must be,' said Beth, laughing too, partly with relief. 'But you and I are going to stay very strictly together.'

'I should just about think we are. Anyway, there is a full moon tonight, or almost, which must have rather an inhibiting effect on the goings on, wouldn't you think? I noticed last night that it was almost as bright as day.'

'And what were you doing out on deck last

night, if I may ask?'

'Of course you may. Saying a fond farewell to the second officer. Oh, Beth, doesn't
England seem a million miles away, and aren't
you just glad to be here!' And then, on a practical note. 'What shall we wear?'

4

They were both comfortably aware of looking their best, as they waited in the luxurious little open carriage that belonged to the house. 'Everything handsome about us,' said Charlotte happily, and then, 'And here they come, prompt to the minute.'

'Admirable ladies!' Nathan Peabody jumped down from the other carriage. 'I said you would be ready. My cousin presents his compliments and looks forward to meeting you when we reach the Marino. In the meantime, will you allow me to join you? It is not just the usual thing for ladies to drive down unaccompanied.'

'We shall be delighted.' Beth had not been best pleased to receive a scrawled, apologetic note from Forde, promising to call 'tomorrow'. 'You will be able to tell us who everybody is, since we know no one.'

'But everyone will know you,' said Peabody. 'I should warn you ladies that news travels like lightning here in Palermo. Never forget that. What you say in the Toledo tomorrow morning will be subject for conversation on the Marino tomorrow night.'

'As fast as that?' Once again, Beth felt she was being given a warning, and once again she was grateful. 'We must mind what we say, must we not, Charlotte?'

'Oh, look,' exclaimed Charlotte. 'They are putting out the lights just the way Mr. Brydone said.' They had emerged from the Porta Felice and could see the moon path across the still sea, and feel the soft touch of the sea breeze. Further off, was the sound of music, but all around them was talk, and soft laughter, the creak of harness and the small friendly sounds of horses.

'There's a concert in the Flora Reale tonight.' Peabody explained the music. 'It's a garden belonging to the King; he often gives us a concert these summer nights.'

'Is he here?' asked Beth.

'No. He spends most of his time at La Ficuzza, his hunting lodge in the country. But the Queen is in residence. I am sure she will wish to have you presented to her, Miss Prior, though I should warn you that she is not too delighted with you British these days. But here is my cousin Carlo, longing to meet you both.'

Bowing over their hands, Carlo Falconi looked surprisingly fair in the moonlight. 'I would have thought you were the American,' said Beth after she had thanked him prettily

77

for all his kindness.

'Ah, it's the Norman in me, Miss Prior. Always remember that we Sicilians share something of your viking, freedom-loving heritage.'

'I will.' She recognised another warning. The night seemed full of them and she wished more than ever that Forde had made time to call. He would have only himself to blame if she were to put a foot wrong among all these pitfalls.

And here was what looked to be another one. A tall, solidly built man had loomed up behind Falconi. 'You are not to monopolise our new prima donna, Falconi. I am charged with welcomes from my wife, who quite longs to hear Miss Prior sing.'

Beth was beginning to find these moonlight exchanges maddening. She thought something had changed in Peabody's face, but how could one be sure in this romantic, deceptive light.

'As do we all,' said Falconi. 'May I make Monsieur le Duc d'Orléans known to you, Miss Prior. And to you, Miss Pennam.'

Saying the proper things, Beth was aware of Charlotte also taking this introduction very much in her stride, and was proud of her. The Duke of Orleans was married to Maria Carolina's daughter, she knew, but he was also the son of Philippe Egalité, the Duke of Orleans who had voted for the death of his cousin, King Louis of France. And here he was, offering to guide their carriage through the crowds to where his wife waited in hers. It was as good as a royal command, and she noticed that neither Peabody nor his cousin the Count accompanied them as they made their way through the murmuring crowd, which gave way at sight of the Duke, now sitting in the carriage saying agreeable things in good English to the two of them. She was amused to catch a glimpse of Forde, with the Bentincks, and wished she could see his expresson. This moonlight was really very frustrating.

The Orleans carriage was tucked away among sweet-scented shrubs in the Flora Reale and Beth saw that a space had been conveniently left beside it. She had been wondering about the etiquette of such a meeting, began to hope that it would prove less formal than she feared. As their coachman pulled his horses to a halt, the Duke leaned towards her. 'My wife very much hopes for a word with you alone, in this quiet corner, Miss Prior. Will you trust your charming young companion to me for a few minutes?'

What could she say but yes, which got her a wry, understanding look from Charlotte.

Entering it, she noticed that the Orleans carriage was a good deal plainer than the one she had left. The Duchess was plain, too, the moonlight unkind to her high colour and unmistakable Hapsburg nose. 'Miss Prior, this is truly good of you.' She held out a firm hand to clasp Beth's. 'I so much wanted a word with you, before you plunge into the vortices of our society. You understand French, of course?'

'Yes, your highness.'

'No formality please. My husband and I like to be treated as the plain citizens we truly are. But it is about my mother I wished to speak to you, Miss Prior. She is a sick woman, though she conceals it gallantly. Our present discontents are putting a terrible strain on her. Tell me about this Lord Bentinck. You must have seen something of him on the voyage out.'

'He's a soldier,' said Beth. 'He likes things just so. He says things like "my word is my bond". You know the kind of man?' She found herself liking this plain, plain-spoken Princess.

'I certainly do, and it is just what I feared. And Mr. Forde?'

'He's a friend of mine,' said Beth.

'And you do not feel you can discuss him? Quite right, Miss Prior. But you would feel able to give him a message.'

'Oh, yes.'

'Tell him, please, that I am truly worried about my mother's health. We all are. She carries a great burden, here in Sicily. Do, please, beg him, Miss Prior, to urge his friend Bentinck to go easily with her.'

'I'll gladly do so,' said Beth. 'But I don't think it's just Bentinck's line. He's very much the man of action, I think, and he has past failures to make up for by a resounding success here in Sicily.'

'And is going to find nothing but trouble here,' sighed the Princess. 'But I am keeping you too long from your young friend, Miss Prior. I hope that our bland Sicilian air will soon restore her to full health.'

It was at once a courteous dismissal and an indication of how well informed the Princess was. This was indeed a place where one should walk warily. Beth did not see Forde again that night, and thought he must have been learning this lesson too.

He called early next morning, full of apologies.

'And so you should be.' She had taken him out to admire their perfumed terrace garden where they were sure of being alone. 'I hope I've not made too much of a mull of things, for lack of your advice.'

'You seem to have managed admirably. I knew I could trust you to do so. Tell me about this young American, Nathan Peabody? Nobody seems to know anything about him, except that he is cousin to the Falconis, who move in the very first society, here in Palermo. You were lucky to meet them.'

'We most certainly were.' She did not mean to make heavy weather of his neglect on the quay. 'They are charming, and have been kindness itself. As to Peabody, he's one of those antiquarian gentlemen who think nothing of interest unless it is hundreds of years old. He's been in Naples, you know, talks a great deal about Pompeii and a place I have never heard of called Paestum. And he has invited Charlotte and me to go and look at some of the antiquities here — somewhere with another odd name. Segesta, perhaps?'

'So that is why he was at Naples?'

'Yes. He talks of going on to Greece presently, if he can get passports from the Turks. Only he says his cousins are being so good to him he thinks he may stay a while longer here in Sicily. I have a message for you, by the way.'

'Oh?'

'From the Duchess of Orleans. She says her mother is a sick woman, and begs you to remember this. She wanted to know what

82

Bentinck is like. I had to tell her he is a martinet and she begged me to suggest that he temper the wind to her mother.'

'It's not in the man's character. And there is so much to infuriate him! That sick Queen you speak of seems to have spent the money they were supposed to use to raise a real Sicilian army on everything else you can think of. It has been nothing but bad news since we came ashore. She has bullied the Parliament — if you can dignify it with the name — into new taxes that have outraged her own nobility. Has anyone told you that she had five senior barons arrested the other day, for protesting against these taxes, had them sent off to island fortresses? It seems to have been touch and go whether your friend Orleans was among them. No wonder his wife is anxious. One of them — Prince Belmonte — is kin to your hosts, by the way, but not much seems to be known about the Falconis' politics.'

'I should think they are too young to have any,' said Beth.

'No one in Sicily is too young for politics. Don't ever forget that, my dear. I confess I am beginning to wonder whether I should have brought you and Miss Pennam into this hornets' nest.'

'You didn't bring us,' she told him. 'We came.'

'One good thing though,' he went on. 'Bentinck was so angry at not being received at once by the King and Queen, and by the interview he did have with Circello, the Foreign Minister, that he has got on his high horse and is going straight off to Messina to review the British troops there. He has left it to me to make the first contact with their majesties. Or rather with the Queen, since everyone knows that she is the one who matters. The King is off at La Ficuzza, as usual, with his mistress and his hunting, but the Queen is receiving tomorrow night at the palace, and I mean to go and pay my respects. Mr. Fagan, our Consul will present me. He is a painter and has painted her portrait: they are on good terms, I am told.'

'Not so good as they were.' She surprised him. 'Countess Falconi says he is under the same cloud as the rest of us English. The Falconis very much want to meet you, by the way. They hope for Lord Bentinck's intercession for their cousin and the other barons who are under arrest. They are true friends to England, I think, the Falconis.' She looked about her, but the jasmine-hung terrace was deserted. 'They say nothing has gone right, here in Sicily, since the King and Queen had to flee here from Naples. The King likes it well enough here, since the hunting and fish-

84

ing are so good, but the Queen thinks of nothing but how to get back to Naples. And all the high offices go to the Neapolitans who fled with her; no wonder the Sicilian barons are dissatisfied. And as for the new taxes, they think the Prince de Tabbia is out of his mind, but he is all-powerful with the Queen, they say, having lent her money. What are you smiling at?'

'I was congratulating myself on asking you to come, and wishing that you could be at the palace tomorrow night.'

'Oh, but I shall be.' Smiling in her turn. 'The Queen has graciously asked me to sing for her guests.'

Beth was not sure whether to be glad or sorry that Forde must attend the Queen's reception under the aegis of Mr. Fagan. Nathan Peabody had already volunteered to escort her and Charlotte, but she was beginning to wonder whether she should not try to put a brake on his attentions to her young friend. He was politeness itself to both of them, but his looks, his true attention were all for Charlotte. It was too quick; she did not like it; the child might so easily lose her heart, and then what would the Weatherbys say?

In the end, she decided on a word of warning. 'Mr. Peabody is delightful, is he not?'

She was adjusting the set of Charlotte's sash. 'Such charming manners, but I do wonder a little how much of it he really means.'

'Oh, none at all,' said Charlotte cheerfully. 'Sometimes I'm hard put to it not to laugh when he ogles me so. He smirks at me, but he listens to you, Beth. If those are American manners, they can keep them. Your Mr. Forde is ten times the gentleman. Now I wouldn't mind if he were to pay me a little attention, instead of treating me like a miss from the schoolroom. Will he be there tonight, Beth?' Eagerly.

'Yes; he's coming with Fagan, the British Consul.' Now Beth had a new source of anxiety.

Beth and Charlotte had been asked to come to the palace early, to arrange about the singing, but they found the gardens and salons already crowded when they arrived with Nathan Peabody. The Queen's friends were there because they were her friends, and everyone else was there because they were afraid not to be. Besides, everyone wanted to see how Lord Bentinck's stand-in was received.

A liveried page approached Beth as they climbed the grand staircase. 'If you would come this way, signora? It is about the singing.'

'Thank you.' Following the page, she did not much like leaving Charlotte alone with Peabody, but was reassured by memory of their talk. Charlotte was no fool, and she seemed to be growing up at lightning speed. It had done her immense good, Beth thought, to find herself so useful on the voyage, and to be treated like a grown-up by Lord William and the officers. She could surely cope with the American.

Beth had expected to be taken to some kind of master-of-ceremonies, was amazed to find herself in the royal apartments, handed over to a lady-in-waiting.

'This way,' the lady said. 'No need to be alarmed, Miss Prior, it is quite informal, just curtsy, and listen.'

'Welcome to Sicily, Miss Prior.' Queen Maria Carolina was splendidly gowned, ready to receive her guests, but looked haggard, Beth thought. The white hair was dressed high, to hold the little crown, and infinite pains had been spent on a complexion that had once been fairest pink and white. Despite her diamonds, her low-cut gown was hard on the tired body that had borne so many children.

It's a hard world for women, thought Beth, rising from her curtsy. 'Your majesty is too kind,' she said. 'To be received like this —'

'We are planning your programme,' said Maria Carolina. 'What are you going to sing for us, Miss Prior?'

'I thought a little Mozart and some Cherubini? Nothing too serious, and not too much?' Diffidently.

'Quite right. I have sent a message to that fool Bartolucci, by the way. You will hear from him in the morning. But that is not why I sent for you. I want to speak to you, Miss Prior, as one woman to another. Will you listen to me?'

'Of course.'

'You are come here at a bad time, Miss Prior. Everything is at sixes and sevens, here in Sicily.' She reached out to drink from a glass that stood on the ormolu table beside her. 'Forgive me: my medicine. These new demands of Lord Bentinck's have quite overset me. Her colour was rising already behind the rouge: it must be strong medicine. 'We are to raise an army, forsooth, to help drive the tyrant Napoleon out of Spain. Nobody could want that creature's downfall more than I do! Think what the French have done to me. My sister killed! My husband and I driven from our kingdom of Naples! If I could raise my hand and have him dead at my feet, I would do it, Miss Prior, without a qualm.' She was heavily flushed now, and the hand she raised trembled a little. 'But one must be realistic.' Lowering her voice. 'You have only been here a day or so, but you must already have seen what the Sicilians are like. An idle set of good-for-nothings who won't work themselves, and grumble when someone else does. Tax them: they won't pay. Enlist them: they won't fight. They don't much like having us here, my husband and I, but they'll never exert themselves to help us back to our throne in Naples.' She took another pull at the glass of 'medicine'. 'You are a woman, with a woman's heart, Miss Prior, and I am told that you are a friend of this Mr. Forde, who is to be presented to me tonight. Will you try to make him understand how things really are, here in Sicily?'

'I wish I understood it myself,' said Beth. 'But I do beg your majesty to believe that Mr. Forde has only the most sympathetic feelings towards you. And of course we all share your detestation of Napoleon.'

'And those Murats,' said the Queen darkly. 'What does that Mr. Peabody say about them, Miss Prior?'

'That they are nothing but Napoleon's puppets.' The question had taken Beth aback, and she was thinking fast, because in fact Peabody had spoken with surprising warmth of the new King and Queen of Naples. She was charming, he had said, and he was the kind of flamboyant figure the Neapolitans liked. But Napoleon called the tune. 'And the taxes they have raised have made them unpopular,' she quoted something else Peabody had said.

'I sometimes think taxes are the root of all evil,' said the Queen. And then, 'I shall look forward to your singing, Miss Prior, and you will count on me for any help you need.' She looked exhausted now, and Beth wondered how she would get through the evening. Her daughter was right, she was obviously a sick woman, keeping herself going on stimulants, and Beth felt both sorry for her and, somehow, frightened.

Her singing went as well as could be expected, with an audience that had so much else on its mind. When it was over, she looked about for Charlotte. 'You are looking for your young charge?' Forde joined her. 'I saw her a while ago, centre of a happy group of young aristocrats. They let their young into society sooner than we do, Mr. Fagan tells me. May I present Mr. Fagan, Miss Prior?'

'Delighted.' The British Consul bowed over her hand. 'I have an earnest request to make to you, Miss Prior. Will you let me paint a joint portrait of you and your charming protégée, to whom Forde here has just made me known?'

'Well,' doubtfully. Then, catching an appealing glance from Forde, 'Why, it would be a pleasure, Mr. Fagan, if you would really like to.'

'I most certainly would. May I call on you tomorrow to discuss arrangements?'

'Very well, but late, if you please. I am expecting to hear from the Theatre Royal, and their arrangements must naturally come first.'

'I am more than grateful.' He bowed and left them.

'So Bartolucci has come to heel.' Forde took her arm to lead her out into the illuminated gardens.

'The Queen said she had sent word to him; that I might expect to hear from him in the morning.'

'That is something at least. But tell me about the Queen. You saw her alone?' He was both surprised and, she thought, disconcerted by this.

'Yes. Was it not gracious? To discuss my music. I hope you enjoyed what we agreed on. Mr. Peabody,' turning to greet the American. 'Have you abandoned Miss Pennam?'

'I can't get near her, Miss Prior. She is quite surrounded by young Sicilians who want to hear about fashions in England. And not just in clothes either, in case you were thinking so.' With a bright, challenging glance from one to the other. 'When I crept unnoticed away she was being asked about books and making rather heavy weather of her answers, I thought.'

'And you abandoned her to her fate?' Beth smiled at him. 'How very ungallant, Mr. Peabody.'

'Oh, she can look after herself, can Miss Pennam. A most unusual young lady.'

5

Calling early the next day; Bartolucci congratulated Beth on her choice of music. 'Nothing by Paisiello, I hear, how wise. The Queen didn't much like his staying on in Naples, toadying to the Murats. And we must all be ruled by her taste.'

Agreeing with him, Beth was relieved when he proposed that she make just a few starred appearances at the theatre, as honoured guest artist. She had never had any great illusions about her voice, which John Kemble had described as a good working instrument, while her gift for comedy would be largely thrown away as she struggled in an imperfectly known language. The pay Bartolucci offered seemed to her lavish for what he was proposing, and she wondered if it was perhaps being supplemented by the Queen. This was undoubtedly the kind of thing Maria Carolina spent the British subsidy on, rather than the enlistment of troops.

Returning from the theatre, where Bartolucci had taken her to meet the other actors, Beth found Forde with Charlotte, and was glad she had not stayed out longer. Something Charlotte had said about Forde had made her a little anxious. She very much wished that she had not had to lie helpless in her cabin during the voyage from England. It was really a little disconcerting to see what easy friends Charlotte and he had become. He had been full of justified praise, all along, for her care of Lady William, but from time to time some small remark of Charlotte's gave a disturbing hint of the friendly, casual terms on to which the child had got with both the two older men.

Of course, that was it, they looked on her as a child. And there was no question but that the voyage had done her immense good. She had not, so far as Beth knew, been sick once since they landed, and though she still ate only tiny amounts and was thin as a rake, she was almost disturbingly bubbling with spirits. 'I have been entertaining Mr. Forde as best I might,' she said now. 'But it's you he wants. And I am late for my first German lesson.' She rose, smiled impartially at them both, and left them.

'She is learning German, industrious child?' asked Forde.

'Yes, she has a real gift for languages. Her French and Italian are both better than mine, and she has seized on the chance of German lessons from one of the refugees stranded here

94

in Sicily.' Charlotte had explained that Comyn's Bank was increasingly dealing with such German courts as had survived the French onslaught. 'We can't let the Rothschilds have things all their own way,' she had said, surprising Beth. But this was not a subject for Forde, who knew nothing about Charlotte's fortune, unless, disconcerting thought, the child had told him about it herself?

'I was grateful to you for taking my cue with Fagan,' Forde came down to business. 'He has not called yet?'

'No. You would really like Charlotte and me to sit for him?'

'Very much. You see, he is what one could call the permanent British thread, here in Palermo. People like Amherst and Bentinck come and go, Consuls go on more or less for ever. And he is in charge of commercial relations. I am beginning to think that a great deal of the trouble here is because of their lunatic arrangements about exports, specially of corn. The result is that huge fortunes are made, corn piles up and rots in warehouses, and the peasants are so poorly paid that they leave the land and turn to the more profitable trade of banditry. Sicily used to be the bread basket of the Mediterranean, and yet we have had to import food for our soldiers here. What do you think of that?'

'It sounds a characteristic Sicilian muddle. Lisa Falconi was telling me about their legal system last night, and that doesn't sound as if it made much sense either. And again, immense fortunes being made by all the wrong people. It's no wonder there is disaffection. Lisa is terribly anxious about their cousin Belmonte, by the way. They truly seem to fear that he might die on the island to which he has been exiled.'

'But he's a man in the prime of life. The incarceration will not surely be so bad?'

'The King's confessor died not long ago,' Beth told him. 'He had been influencing the King to stand up against his wife's intrigues. Everyone thinks he was poisoned.'

'Beth!'

'I am only telling you what I have learned. And they are not fools, the Falconis. Just two very anxious young people. I like them so much; I'm really glad that Charlotte will have them for company when I am working. She will be safe with them, I think. And, Gareth,' she was trying not to use his first name, but it came out in this moment of tension, 'I am truly sorry for the Queen. She is an old, sick woman; she is taking some powerful stimulant; I do not think she can be considered as entirely responsible for her own actions.'

'You truly think she might have been behind the confessor's murder — if murder it really was?' They had drawn close together, in the centre of the room, to talk in low voices.

'I don't know. She might have said something, in a moment of passion — Like King Henry and Becket? And the palace is full of ears. Didn't you feel that?'

'All of Palermo is full of ears. I'll speak to Bentinck about Belmonte and the four other barons the moment he gets back. He said he would not stay away for long, but had to know what the state of things really is at Messina. We might find we need troops here.' And on that disturbing note, he left her.

Charlotte found her new German teacher awaiting her in the little salon Beth had set aside for her use. Herr von Achen came highly recommended by friends of Lisa Falconi's. 'He's some kind of connection of the Villermosas,' Lisa had explained. 'Blown here by the winds of war, and having a hard enough time making ends meet, by what they say. I fear they are beginning to think they have funded him about long enough, poor fellow, and he should be looking about for himself.'

Something she had said had given Charlotte a picture of a frail elderly scholar, struggling for survival in a Palermitan garret. So Gustav von Achen came as a surprise as he bowed impeccably over her hand.

'But you are a young man.' She spoke in German.

'That is a surprise?' he answered in English. 'So it is to me that you speak German already. But —' He looked about him. 'You are thinking you should have a chaperone, fräulein? I apologise for my youth,' with a wry smile. 'It is a fault that starvation will soon amend.'

'Starvation?' Appalled. But it was true, the elegant, old-fashioned clothes hung loose on his gaunt frame; there were dark circles under the clear blue eyes, and hollows under the high cheekbones. Her hand went out to the bell. 'I will ring for refreshments.'

'No, please. First we must understand each other. After the lesson — if there is to be a lesson — I will eat your food and be grateful. I must earn it first. I may be poor, fräulein, but I am not a pauper, yet, nor quite without pride. If these lessons are merely a charitable sham, to put bread in the poor refugee's mouth, you will be so good as to say so now and end the affair.' He had drawn himself up to be taller than she had thought and looked suddenly formidable.

'No, no, you don't understand.' She put out a pleading hand. 'My German is quite good enough, I know, for taking a journey or ordering a dinner, but suppose I really wanted to talk to someone — to discuss politics, or business, or what is going on here in Sicily . . .'

'I should think you a very unusual young lady, fräulein. But if that is what you really wish, to learn German conversation rather than German grammar, I will be more than happy to oblige you. It will be a pleasure, for which I will be paid.'

'Yes,' she said. 'How much, Herr von Achen?'

When they had settled that, he smiled for the first time. 'Now the pleasure begins.' In German: 'Shall we discuss life, fräulein, or literature, or the pursuit of happiness? I do not entirely recommend talking about the state of affairs here in Sicily.'

'No, that was a — How do you say rash suggestion?'

After a stimulating hour of general talk, Charlotte rang for the promised refreshments. 'Now,' smiling at him, 'I wish you will tell me how you come to be starving here in Palermo, Herr von Achen.'

'Oh, it is easy for a younger son to find himself starving.' For a moment she thought he was going to put her off with this, but then he smiled again, looking younger still. 'Shall I tell you the story of my life, and will you stop me when you do not understand? Good.' He accepted the glass of wine she had poured for him, and the cake she offered, nibbled and slowly sipped. 'My family's estates were in Poland, fräulein, Eastern Poland. We owned miles and miles of open steppes, thousands of serfs. It was then, when we were something in the world, that one of my aunts married into the Villermosa family. No wonder if they are not so happy to have her impoverished nephew on their hands now. Though, mind you, I can only be grateful to them.' With a warm look. 'Anyway, we lost everything — almost everything — at the iniquitous Polish partition of 1793. Oh, if my father had been prepared to crawl before the Empress Catherine, he might have saved something. He preferred to go into exile; move into a small estate in the Rhineland that had come into the family by marriage. Do I need to tell you the end of the story?'

'I am afraid you do.'

'I shall teach you history, as well as German.' She had in fact had to stop him several times, to make him slow down, or to ask him the meaning of a word. 'Perhaps you should pay me double.' It was a joke. They exchanged a friendly smile. 'When Napoleon's armies swept through the Rhineland, my father bowed his head to the storm. Two of my older brothers were conscripted and killed in the Austrian army. That leaves four of us, and two sisters. All to be supported from our small property. I was meant for the Church, the fate of youngest sons, but our occupying masters thought otherwise. I was to be drafted, fräulein, into the French army. The army that had killed my brothers. Intolerable. My mother smuggled me out by the back way while my father kept the recruiting officer in talk over his wine. I went to Vienna; we have cousins there too.'

'It seems to me that you are all cousins, here in Europe.'

'It is something that needs always to be borne in mind. I joined the Austrian army, of course.' He had quietly eaten several of the little cakes as he talked, and Charlotte wished she had felt able to order something more substantial. 'But a devil of a wound I got at Austerlitz put paid to that, and I have been scraping for expedients ever since. My father paid for my escape by losing his estates under the reorganisation at the Treaty of Paris. No help there. Vienna is full of useless men scraping for a living. I fought at the barricades in the year nine, and that did me no good either when the French took over the city. In fact, it is why I am here now.'

'Oh?' She poured him more wine.

101

'I speak good French,' he explained, 'having grown up in the Rhineland. They all speak it in Vienna, of course, but you should hear their accents. When Napoleon proposed for the hand of the Archduchess Marie Louise, and her father made her take him, they wanted someone to polish her French a bit. I was the lucky man. I thought my fortune was made. A nice girl: kind, frightened. I was sorry for her; she was sorry for me; we got on. When it came time to go, she was scared, do you wonder? Asked her father if she could take me along in case she ever needed an interpreter. The Emperor Francis would have said yes to anything, just then. So — a whole new outfit to make me fit to appear in Napoleon's overdressed parvenu court, and off we all went.' He stopped; ate another cake.

'What happened?'

'A splendid journey, at first.' He paused, looking back on it. 'Fêted like the saviours of the civilised world at Melk. And next day, when we got to the frontier, there was Napoleon's sister Caroline, I'll never forgive her, all smiles and embraces for her new sister-in-law. And explaining that everything and every person Austrian was to be put away now. They re-dressed the Archduchess in French clothes, straight from Paris, they sent away her ladies-in-waiting. And they sent me away with a flea in my ear. They knew about the barricades, do you see? They know everything, those French devils. Don't ever forget that, fräulein. Fouché has the best secret police in Europe.'

Signor Bartolucci had made a box at the theatre available to them, and they went to see Haydn's *Fedelta Premiata* that night so that Beth could get the feel of things. 'I imagine it will be just the same as London,' she told Charlotte. 'More conversation than listening, and the gentlemen moving about all the time, from box to box. Mr. Forde comes with us, and I was wondering whether to ask Mr. Peabody.'

'I don't see why not,' said Charlotte. 'Safety in numbers, you know. But he will probably be with the Falconis; I know they are to be there.'

But Peabody expressed himself as delighted to accompany them, and they were a cheerful little party as they drove through the warm sweet-scented night to the opera house. The streets were full of people, aristocrats in their carriages, the rest of the world on foot, buying oranges and ices from movable stalls.

'They seem a cheerful enough lot,' said Forde, as the carriage moved slowly through the chattering crowds.

'Not exactly a hotbed of revolution, it seems to me,' agreed Peabody, watching a man buying oranges for his children.

It got him a sharp look from Forde. 'What in the world makes you say that, Mr. Peabody?'

'Oh, just something someone said to me. They were talking about Paris in '89, how you felt the tension in the streets. I certainly don't feel anything here.'

'I should rather think not.' They were talking English, of course, but Forde had an anxious glance for the driver in front and the footman up behind. 'Not just the subject for public conversation, Peabody, if I may say so. And particularly not with ladies present.'

'For fear it offends our sensitive ears?' asked Beth.

'No, Miss Prior, for fear it puts you in danger.' But the carriage was drawing up outside the brilliantly illuminated opera house and they were able to let the subject drop.

It had taken them longer than they expected to get through the crowded streets and the house was already full, and the orchestra tuning up, when they entered their red plush box. 'Signor Bartolucci has done well by you,' Forde held a gilt chair for Beth.

'Yes, a good view of both stage and audience. Hard to tell which is the more important.' She was looking along the row of crowded boxes. 'There is Lady William. So she didn't go to Messina with her husband. Ah.' With concealed relief, as Lady William saw their party, smiled and bowed. 'The Queen's not here.' She recognised the Duke and Duchess of Orleans in the Royal Box, where they must have arrived early to avoid ceremony. 'Odd to think we shall soon know most of these people.' She hushed as the overture began.

'I'm sorry if I spoke out of turn back there,' Peabody said quietly to Forde under cover of the outburst of applause at the end of the short overture. 'But things I have been hearing have made me a little anxious about our two delightful companions. This place seems a tinderbox to me. And you British perhaps not quite so popular as you were? It's always hard for an occupying army to be loved, and your men do seem to behave as if they owned the place.'

'Hush,' said Beth as the curtain rose.

When it fell again, to resounding applause, Forde excused himself and made his way to the Bentincks' box, where he had been glad to see the Consul, Fagan. He found Lady William doing her best not to be shocked by the low-cut dresses and light flirtations all around her. She was known as something of an Evangelical, he remembered.

'You have not left your two young ladies alone, I hope, Mr. Forde?' was her first question. 'Things seem to go on with a good deal of ease here in Palermo, and I would not wish that delightful young Miss Pennam to have any kind of awkward experience.'

'No, I left Nathan Peabody with them.' He was grateful to her for asking.

'That young American.' Fagan took him up on it. 'What do you know about him, Forde?'

'Not much, except that he came gallantly to the ladies' rescue on the quay the other day. And he is a relative of the Falconis.'

'A very right-minded young couple.' Fagan approved of the Falconis. 'And cousins to Belmonte, another of our friends. As Peabody is to them. But did you know that he came here by way of Naples?'

'Yes, to look at the antiquities. The advantage of being a neutral American.'

'While they stay that way,' said Fagan darkly. 'But that's another story. The thing is, I had a report from Naples today.' It was an open secret that spies plied constantly to and fro across the narrow strait between Sicily and Italy. 'Peabody did indeed visit the ruins — Pompeii and Paestum and all that. But he was fêted by the Murats too. And cut quite a swathe in Neapolitan society.'

106

'Which he is now doing here.' Forde could see the young man prominent among the little crowd around Beth and Charlotte. 'As I say, the advantage of being neutral. And the son of a rich father.'

'That, too,' agreed Fagan. 'I had enquiries made. He's the only son, and his father in a very thriving way indeed, what with whaling and the eastern trade. I'm surprised his father let him off the leash to come gallivanting here to Europe.'

When he returned to Beth's box, Forde found Falconi there, joining with Peabody in urging the two ladies to consider a party of pleasure to look at the ruins at Segesta. 'My wife longs to go.' He turned to appeal to Forde. 'We have often discussed it, but she has never been able to find a female friend intrepid enough to go with her. Or if she has,' with a smile, 'her parents have forbidden it. But if we all went,' his glance included Peabody and Forde, 'there could be no possible objection. And it would give the ladies a chance to see something of our Sicilian countryside. It would be a pity to come here and see nothing but the streets of Palermo. You go by way of Monreale,' he explained. 'The road is good to there. We could start in the cool of the evening; I have a friend in Monreale who will lend us his house. A look at the magnificent Norman cathedral either evening or morning, and an easy day will take us to Alcamo, where a tenant of mine will put us up. From there, it is merely a morning ride to Segesta. Do say you will all come.'

'Do let us!' Charlotte was eager, but Forde thought Beth looked doubtful, as well she might.

'We must talk more about it.' He was relieved that the signal for the next act sent Falconi back to his own box.

'It's not just the proprieties.' He was escorting Beth to the carriage after the opera. 'It's the danger. I noticed young Falconi said nothing about the bandits who are supposed to lurk everywhere in the hills.'

'Oh, I think he feels himself safe from them,' said Beth. 'It's his own country, you know. The Sicilians' sense of honour would protect us. Charlotte longs to go, and I confess I should rather like to. It would be an adventure! One has so few of those, as a woman.'

'We must think more about it.' They had reached the carriage.

It was nearly midnight, but the streets were as thronged as ever as they drove down for the evening concourse on the Marino.

'Does nobody ever go to bed here?' asked Charlotte.

'I'm not sure how many of them have beds to go to.' Peabody threw some small coins to a beggar who had put up appealing hands as the carriage paused in a traffic jam in front of the Porta Felice. 'There is terrible poverty here in Palermo, Miss Pennam. Falconi warned me never to leave the main streets after dark. The narrow byways are full of perils, and I hope you and Miss Prior will never think of venturing out, even in daylight, by yourselves. I know Palermo presents a smiling face to the world, but it is not one I would trust for a moment. Now in New Bedford, one could carry a bag of gold safe through the streets at midnight.'

'If it was not too cold to be out,' suggested Forde. 'No wonder if the Sicilians live out of doors, with their delightful climate.'

'We've not had a taste of the sirocco yet,' warned Peabody. 'My cousins say everything stops when it blows. And it is likely to hit us any time now, they say. That's why I would like to get our plans made for Segesta as fast as possible.'

'We must talk more about it in the morning,' said Forde.

He visited Fagan early next morning to tell him about the plan. 'It seems a hare-brained enough scheme to me,' he said. 'But Peabody

109

has talked the two ladies into great enthusiasm for it.'

'I do find myself wondering why.'

'Just so.'

'Then perhaps you should go, in the hope of finding out. Leave it to me to make sure no harm comes to the young ladies.'

6

Beth was surprised by a summons to the palace next day. She and Charlotte were giving Robert Fagan a preliminary sitting for their joint portrait when the message came.

'Goodness.' She read the note, looked at Fagan. 'A royal summons. A carriage is coming for me at six; I'm to go alone.'

'Alone?' He did not like it any more than she did.

'The Queen sends a lady-in-waiting,' Beth told him. 'I suppose that makes it all right?'

'I think so.' Looking at the watch on his fob. 'I shall be much interested to hear what her majesty has to say, Miss Prior, and so, I am sure, will Mr. Forde. We will see you at the theatre tonight, I hope?'

'Yes, indeed. We are looking forward to *Lodoiska*. When does Lord Bentinck return?'

'I don't rightly know, but he said he would be gone for as short a time as possible. We shall all feel safer when he gets back.'

'That's the way I feel.' Like him or not, and she was not quite sure about this, she felt Bentinck could be counted on for firm action in a crisis. But what was there critical or threatening about a summons to the palace? It was just surprising, that was all.

Flora Cottone, the lady-in-waiting, was fading into her thirties, and fluent in English. 'My uncle, the Prince Castelnuovo insists it is the language of the future,' she told Beth. 'We are all to forget our French and learn English. Will you please to tell me if I say anything that is not quite right?'

'I shall be glad to.' Beth was beginning to feel that she had been absurd to be alarmed.

'And, please, you will try and reassure our poor Queen, signora? Nobody understands what she suffers! An old woman; seventeen times a mother; and now she must fight for her life, and for the future of our country. All alone. No one to turn to. No one to trust. I am trusting you, signora, when I tell you this. But I want you to understand, when you see the state she is in. It is these cruel men who have brought her to it. Your Lord Bentinck with his insulting messages! It is not the first time she has been threatened by you British, signora, as you must know as well as I do. If she talks somewhat wildly, remember, she has cause. She hopes great things of you: I do beg you, for all our sakes, try not to disappoint her; leave her some hope? Or she might be pushed to do something des-

112

perate. But here we are.' The carriage had drawn up at an inconspicuous side entrance to the palace. 'Her majesty will see you alone, quite informally. I will be waiting to take you home. I do beg you, give her some comfort.' She put a hand on Beth's. 'The doctors fear for her reason,' she whispered.

Ushered to the same room as before, Beth found Maria Carolina at her desk, frantically scribbling at a letter.

'Miss Prior!' The grey-white hair was dishevelled today as if she had been running her hand through it as she wrote; the contrast between the red and white of her face was more extreme than ever. Beth could see why her doctors were anxious. 'Sit down,' she said. 'No ceremony. I am beyond ceremony. They have taken ceremony away from me, turned me into an old woman, fighting for her life, for her future, her children's. Are you going to help me? Say you will help me.'

'I will most certainly do my best, your majesty. But what can I do?'

'A great deal, if you will. You and your young companion are friends of this churlish Lord Bentinck and the toady, Forde, he has brought with him. Make them see reason, Miss Prior! They blame me for everything that is wrong, here in Sicily. Make them listen to me when I tell them about these brutes of

Sicilians, who can do no wrong in their eyes, because they talk about parliaments and democracy! Let them just try it! Sometimes I am tempted to give up, to go home to my nephew Francis in Vienna, to let them try and make some sense of this benighted island. Let them try and raise a Sicilian army! Collect Sicilian taxes! Grow Sicilian corn! Sweet talk, they'll get: sweet, enlightened talk. My Sicilians are good at that. But action! Pah!' She reached for the glass that stood on her writing table. 'I have to explain this to them, Miss Prior.' The drink seemed to steady her. 'But they refuse to listen, even to come to me. Imagine that! To refuse to attend a Queen who asks to see you. What would my mother, what would Maria Theresa have said, if she had been so affronted? But they do not think of her; they think of my poor sister, of Marie Antoinette who was killed by those French barbarians. What has been done before, they think, can be done again. No wonder if they feel free to insult me. But how can I explain to them if they will not come to me?'

'But how can I help, your majesty?' Beth was still standing.

'Oh, sit down, do, and listen to me. They won't come to talk business, so they must come for pleasure. They think pleasure is all I understand. All I spend my money on. Well, let them think what they will, so long as it brings them to me, gives me a chance to put my case. So you are going to tell me what kind of entertainment would please Lord Bentinck and that starchy wife of his, and you are going, pray God, to help me put it on for them, and get them to come to it.' Another pull at the glass. 'How can I explain to them, if they will not listen?' Her mind was going round and round on the same desperate track.

'How could they not come, your majesty, to an entertainment specially arranged for them?'

'Oh, he will find a way, that hard Lord Bentinck. I know his English kind. Polite as be damned, and do just what they want. So let us think of his wife. Persuade her, surely he would come?'

'I'm not so sure,' said Beth. 'But I agree it would be better if it were to be something that seemed specially arranged to please her. It would certainly make it harder for him to say no.'

'I knew you would be a good friend, Miss Prior. A good ally. I felt it in my heart, when we met. So, what is it to be?'

Beth had been thinking hard. 'An entertainment Lady William could not resist? I wonder if there is such a thing. She is a very religious lady.' She thought what a gulf there was between Lady William's stern Evangelical beliefs and the emotional saints' worship of the Sicilians. 'A concert, perhaps, of religious music? Nothing too long or heavy? I don't believe music is Lord William's passion, or his wife's. But if it were to be Handel perhaps? Something they were used to hearing, or hearing of, in England? Or Herr Haydn? Some of the music he wrote while he was visiting England? His *Creation* perhaps? Or some of it?'

'Impossible!' exclaimed the Queen angrily. 'Have you forgotten? Or are you too young to know that an attempt was made on Napoleon's life on his way to *The Creation*'s first performance in Paris. If it had only succeeded! And anyway there is something very free-thinking about the text of that oratorio. It would not do at all. But you are on the right track, just the same, I am sure of it.' She was sounding calmer, Beth was relieved to hear, the rational talk of music soothing her.

It suggested something. 'I know,' Beth exclaimed. 'Handel's *Ode to St. Cecilia*. Nothing controversial about that; it's not too long and should not be too hard for Signor Bartolucci to get up.'

'You will sing in it?'

'Your majesty, my voice is not suited to

116

oratorio. I must beg to be excused.'

'Maybe that is for the best,' said the Queen. 'If you are to be in the audience, we can be sure of Mr. Forde, and let us hope he will persuade Bentinck to condescend to come too. Thank you, Miss Prior, I will have it put in hand at once, to be ready the instant Lord William returns, satisfied, no doubt, that his English troops are ready and willing to march on us here in Palermo if he so wishes.'

'Your majesty!' Beth was equally horrified at the possibility, and at the Queen's awareness of it.

'It surprises you that I know of his plans?' The Queen's voice was rising again. 'Give your friend Forde a message from me, Miss Prior. Tell him I may be an old sick woman who loses her temper, and is sometimes afraid, but thank the good Lord, and my good servants, I am well informed. Yes?' Angrily, to a nervous servant. 'I said I was not to be disturbed.'

'Signor Castroni is here, majesty. He said it was most urgent.'

'So soon? Very well.' She thought for a moment, then. 'Show him in. I think I would like you to meet him, Miss Prior, or rather I would like him to meet you.'

Beth did not much like the look of Castroni. His clothes were too rich, his manner at once obsequious and, somehow, over-confident. Told by the Queen that Miss Prior was her good friend and to be respected as such, he bowed low over her hand and said it would be his pleasure, with an appreciative look she did not like at all. She was glad when Flora Cottone appeared to take her away.

'Who is Signor Castroni?' she asked in the carriage.

A warning hand descended on hers. 'He is our Chief of Police,' said Flora Cottone, 'whom we all revere.'

'And fear,' said Forde at the Marino that night. 'And so should you. He came with the King and Queen from Naples, where he had made himself so much hated as a police informer that he can never go back. But he is indispensable to the Queen, I understand. Not only as informer but as spymaster, if the reports are to be believed. Well, I suppose we should be grateful that the Queen has introduced you to him as someone to be protected. But tell me about the rest of your interview. The Queen did not just get you there to meet Castroni?'

'Oh, no. She was angry, at first, when we were interrupted. But Castroni's name seemed an open sesame. He's her spymaster, is he? She's alarmingly well informed, you know. I

have a message for you, to tell you just that.'
She explained the circumstances.

'Frighteningly well informed,' Forde agreed
when she had finished. 'Spies in England as
well as here. What a blessing she has taken
a fancy to you, Beth.'

'I doubt you can call it that,' said Beth. 'She
means to use me, just as you do.'

'Beth!'

But Peabody and Charlotte had returned
from the Falconis' carriage, and the conversation inevitably turned to the proposed trip
to Segesta. It seemed to be more and more
of a settled thing, but must be postponed until
after Bentinck's return and the entertainment
at the palace. They would none of them wish
to miss that.

'And that postponement is a great relief,'
Forde told Fagan next day. 'I don't much like
that project.'

'I know. But if the Falconis are going,
there really can be no danger. I should think
it must be an opportunity for Peabody to meet
someone who dares not show his face here
in Palermo, and I would dearly like to know
who that is.'

'Yes,' said Forde. 'There is something very
much too good to be true about that young
man.'

'There was a ship in from America this

morning,' Fagan told him. 'They have voted in a very belligerent Congress there, by what I hear. War Hawk Republicans to a man. I don't much like it, Forde. We could do without a war with them.'

'We most certainly could. But what has that to do with Peabody, who must have left home some time ago? Do you know how long he was in Naples? He is purposely vague, I think, when one asks about it.'

'No, and I don't know how he got there either. I have been trying to find out, but the men who risk their lives crossing to the mainland usually have more serious errands to do.'

'Yes. Interesting that the Queen banned *The Creation* on the grounds that Napoleon was nearly assassinated on his way to it. You would think that was to his credit, in her eyes.'

'You're not thinking, Forde. No monarch can afford even to seem to countenance the assassination of another monarch. It opens too many doors. And Maria Carolina never for a moment forgets the death of her sister, Marie Antoinette.'

'Will we be able to persuade Bentinck to go to her entertainment?'

'God knows. I imagine it depends a good deal on what he has found at Messina!'

'Will the King come to it?'

'I doubt it. He is much too comfortable at

La Ficuzza with his mistress and his sport. He doesn't mean to be bullied, whether it's by his wife or by Bentinck.'

'And can you blame him?' They exchanged a masculine, sympathetic glance.

Beth and Charlotte were also discussing the events of the previous day over the late breakfast they made a point of having together. 'You met one chief of spies,' Charlotte summed it up. 'And I was warned against another. It does make life seem exciting, does it not?'

Beth laughed and reached out to pat her hand. 'Oh, I am so glad I brought you, Charlotte. And yet, I'm not sure I should not send you swiftly home.'

'No need to think of it.' Charlotte smiled sweetly at her. 'I wouldn't go. I am having far too entertaining a time here.' She reached out for another roll. 'And I am getting fat, too! Tell that to my mother and step-father. I must take more exercise. Which reminds me,' too casually, 'Nathan Peabody would like to take me riding. With the Falconis, of course. You wouldn't mind, Beth? I can't sit at home all the time you are working at the theatre.'

'No, of course not. But would it not be hideously hot?'

'That's what Lisa says, but I would so much

rather ride to Segesta than go in one of those curious chairs they use, and you have to admit it would be sensible to get into practice first.'

'I suppose so.' Doubtfully. 'I wish I felt quite happy about that Segesta trip, Charlotte.'

'Oh,' smiling brilliantly, 'I think you and I can go without a care in the world now you have been officially introduced to the Chief of Police. I shall cling to your skirt tails, Beth, I warn you of that. Something very havey-cavey is going to happen on that trip, is it not?'

'Well, I certainly think so.' Relieved. 'But Forde thinks we should go. Just so long as —' She paused, wondering how to word the warning.

'I'm not letting myself be fooled by Nathan Peabody's sweet looks? I'm not the fool from the nursery he thinks me, Beth. Having so many brothers does teach one a thing or two about men. I know a lie when it's acted out to me. Do you know, I actually find myself missing those boys.'

'I'm delighted to hear it. We should both of us write to your mother, Charlotte.'

'Careful letters.' Charlotte grinned at her. Charlotte was enjoying herself. Amazing to look back at those sad days in Hull, all that unnecessary misery. It had truly surprised her to hear herself telling Beth she missed her half-brothers, but it was still perfectly true. She had been so much fonder of them, and they of her, than she had realised in what she now looked back on as her wallow of despair. And her mother? She did not think she was quite ready to write to her mother yet, though she had told Beth she would do so. That was going to be so difficult. Should she tell her about old Mrs. Comyn's lies? She could not decide, and, until she did, she could not write.

'Bentinck is back.' Forde had arrived to escort them to the theatre, where Beth was not performing that night. 'In no better temper than he left.'

'No worse, I hope,' said Beth. 'Will he come to the Queen's entertainment?'

'I left Lady William doing her best to persuade him. If she cannot, no one can.'

'There are to be illuminations in the palace gardens after the performance, I understand.'

'Which doesn't much please Bentinck. Money spent on fireworks that should be equipping a Sicilian army.'

'All the more reason for seeing the Queen and telling her so.'

'He says she won't listen.'

'That's just what she says of him!' She looked at the clock on the chimney-piece. 'It's getting late; we should be going. I do not like to be late for the theatre, as a member of the troupe.' She rang the bell. 'Tell Miss Pennam we're ready to go, please,' she told the servant.

Charlotte arrived a few minutes later, her colour high from hurrying into her clothes. 'I am so sorry, Beth. We got arguing and forgot the time.'

'Arguing?' Forde had a special tone for Charlotte. 'About the set of a sleeve or the colour of a ribbon?'

'About neither.' Her colour higher than ever. 'About the way to run a country. It's my German lesson,' she explained. 'Herr von Achen believes in firm government by a benevolent despot. He says we British will never get anywhere with our democratic notions, and as for any idea of trying them out here in Sicily — balderdash, he says.'

'In German?' Forde asked, teasing. 'Naturally. It's a very expressive language.'

'And we are going to be late for the theatre.' Beth interrupted before the argument could develop any further.

'This von Achen.' Forde seized a moment alone with her, down on the Marino after the performance. 'What do you know about him?'

'Just what Charlotte does. That he is a refugee, like so many others, from the French. You are anxious too?' It was at once a relief to find their minds were working on the same lines, and disconcerting that the subject of their joint anxiety should be Charlotte. She was feeling more and more, disturbingly, out of touch with Forde, in these circumstances where they never seemed to have more than a few minutes alone together. It had all seemed such a good idea, when they planned this trip. Enforced separation would bring the passion back into their relationship. He would recognise that he could not do without her. Having to behave like mere friends would add a new strength to the bond between them.

And what was happening? Having to behave like mere friends, they showed signs of becoming just this. She could no longer see into Forde's mind, feel his feelings. They were beginning to drift, slowly, inexorably apart. She would not believe it. It was this sinister court, full of intrigue and strange overtones that made her imagine these horrors. She and Forde had been one; they would be again when this charade was over.

'I think I would like to meet this von Achen.' Forde had paused for a moment in thought. 'I feel in some sort responsible for young Charlotte. She is looking much better, by the way. At least the cure seems to be working.'

'Better than I had hoped. Her parents

should be pleased.'

'Just so long as we get her safe home to them.' And with that mildly reassuring 'we' Beth had to satisfy herself.

There was no performance at the theatre next day and they were all invited to an evening's entertainment at the Falconis' palace. Beth had learned to enjoy the friendly, informal way the Sicilians entertained, with a little music, a great deal of conversation and unlimited ices to make the heat bearable. And she had also learned that she did not need to worry about Charlotte on these occasions, since there was always a cheerful group of young people somewhere, playing games like Cross Purposes. Charlotte fitted easily into these groups, though she pointed out wryly that in Sicilian terms she was almost an old maid, since Sicilian girls married as early as thirteen or fourteen, and could easily be grandmothers by thirty. They were used to growing up along with their brothers and cousins and had none of the British miss's bashfulness when it came to relations with the male sex. But then, it struck Beth, neither had Charlotte, older sister of three half-brothers. Was that, perhaps, the secret of her charm for Forde? Because, slowly, reluctantly, wretchedly, she was beginning to admit to herself that Charlotte had charm for Forde. Could this be the reason for the increasing estrangement she herself felt from him? It would make unbelievably painful sense. He had come to her in the first place, because he could buy her, which made the relationship easy for him, as for so many other Englishmen. Had he, bitter thought, learned the way of it from her, so that he was ready, now, to fall in love and marry someone else? She had hoped so much that it had all changed between them: that they had become friends as well as lovers; that it would go with them as it had with Charles James Fox and his mistress, Mrs. Armistead, whom he had shocked society by marrying, and with whom he had lived happily ever after. Had she been the world's fool to think this might happen between her and Forde? She was beginning to fear so.

But here was Bentinck approaching her, and she pulled herself together to be glad that he and Lady William had come to the Falconis'. It boded well, she thought, for their coming to the Queen's entertainment next day.

'Miss Prior. I had been hoping for a word with you!' Bentinck took her arm to lead her into the discreetly illuminated gardens.

'And I with you, Lord William.' She was not going to let the initiative rest entirely with him, and felt this surprise him.

'You have been to the palace, I understand. Helped to arrange this entertainment for tomorrow?'

'You are well informed.'

'I need to be. Come, Miss Prior, don't fence with me. Tell me what it is all about.'

'Simply that the Queen very much wishes to talk to you and feels that an informal occasion like tomorrow's might be the best way. All she wanted to know from me was what form of entertainment was most likely to please you and Lady William.'

'I suppose we should be grateful to you for your choice.' He did not sound it. 'But there was more to it than that, surely?'

'Yes. That is precisely why I am glad to have this chance of speaking to you. She's a sick woman, an old, sick, sad, frightened woman.'

'Drugs and drink,' he said.

'That's not fair!' But anger would get them nowhere. 'Think of her position, Lord William. So far from home; a dolt of a husband —'

'Whom she has bullied so unmercifully that he keeps away from her.'

'Yes. Publicly, with his mistress. She has borne him seventeen children, endured defeat and exile at his side, worked like a Trojan to hold things together here in Sicily —'

'A Trojan woman,' he interrupted again. 'It would be very much more suitable if she were to let her son, the Crown Prince support his father.'

'Have you met the Crown Prince?'

'No.' Surprised.

'He's a cipher; a nothing. Bends to every wind that blows.'

'No doubt because he has a harridan for a mother.'

'That may well be true, but it does not alter the facts of the case. The King thinks of nothing but his own pleasure, his son is useless, only the Queen worries about the state of affairs here in Sicily.'

'And plenty to worry about.' His face closed. 'But we'll not talk of that. What you are saying, Miss Prior, is that it will add to the Queen's set of grievances against us British if I do not see her and give her a chance to rant at me as she has done at all our other representatives.'

'I want you to listen to her, my lord. Give her a chance to explain herself. Think if she were our own poor Queen Charlotte, bearing her load of grief, or your own mother.'

'My mother is a lady. And knows better than to embroil herself in men's affairs.'

Beth very nearly lost her temper. But what use would that be? She made herself smile at him. 'That's one in the eye for me, but do, pray, remember that I was asked to come here in the hope that I might have some kind of influence over the Queen. She thought he muttered something about 'idiotic notion' but pretended not to hear. 'And in fact the Queen did talk to me quite freely. She wants you to understand what a useless lot the Sicilians are, says they won't co-operate, won't join the army.'

'Exactly.' He pounced on it. 'Because they know that all she wants is to get back to Naples. She'd let Sicily sink to the bottom of the Mediterranean if it would win her Naples back. Never forget that, Miss Prior, when you are thinking your wise political thoughts. But you have convinced me, just the same. It would be the act of a coward not to go and let her loose off her batteries at me, and no Bentinck has ever been accused of cowardice. I shall look forward to seeing you at the palace tomorrow night, Miss Prior.'

She very nearly said, 'Don't go.' In this frame of mind, he would do more harm than good. But opposing him would not improve his temper either. She accepted his brusque dismissal with deceptive meekness, but went home with the gloomiest expectations about next day's meeting.

While Bentinck was talking to Beth, Gareth Forde found Charlotte among a laughing group of young people. 'Miss Pennam, it is stifling in here. Can I persuade you to take a turn in the garden with me? I have a favour to ask you.'

'Why, of course.' Surprised and flattered, she accepted his arm and they moved out through wide open doors to the terrace. 'A favour?' She turned him a smiling, friendly face. 'Something for Beth?'

'No, Miss Pennam, something for me. Miss Prior can take very good care of herself, I think.'

'Well, of course she can.' Surprised. 'It is what I so much admire about her.'

'Admirable.' He had got her off into a secluded alley by now. 'But not womanly. Miss Pennam. I think it was only when I saw you ministering, like an angel of mercy, to those two poor ladies on board ship that I realised what a woman should be. Loving and cherishing; kind and tender; not always standing up to a man and discussing things with him.'

'But that's not really my line at all, Mr. Forde; the loving and cherishing thing, that was just an accident —' She did not at all like the turn the conversation was taking.

'You're young, of course. Naturally you enjoy the success you are having among the young people here in Sicily, but I have seen enough of you to know that you want more out of life than that kind of social success. You want to do something in the world, Miss Pennam.'

'Yes, that's true.' Now he had surprised her again.

'Then I have a suggestion to make — an offer to make. I beg of you to think of it in all seriousness, Miss Pennam. I am older than you, I know, but Shakespeare says somewhere that that is how it should be. You would make an admirable wife for a diplomat, Miss Pennam — may I call you Charlotte —' He had her hands now, as if he were sure of her answer.

'You don't — you can't mean — But, Beth!' It was the first, and paramount, of all the objections that leaped into her mind.

'I am asking you to marry me, Miss Pennam — Charlotte. Miss Prior has nothing to do with that.'

'Then she ought to,' said Charlotte roundly. 'And you may not call me Charlotte, Mr. Forde, and I would not dream of marrying you, whatever Shakespeare says. And now I will go back to my friends, if you please, and we will try to forget that this conversation ever happened.'

'How can I forget, when my heart is yours?'

He felt, too late, that he had set about it wrong and turned on her the loving, languishing look that had made so many women his slaves.

'Oh, stuff,' said Charlotte, and left him.

7

'I have a favour to ask of you, fräulein.' Gustav von Achen took the volume of Goethe's poems from Charlotte, his hand lingering for an instant on hers. 'A great favour.'

'Yes?' Her hand tingled and she was afraid of a blush. 'How can I serve you?'

'This entertainment tonight. I long to see the palace, hear Herr Handel's fine music. But I am an outcast, here in Palermo. Having no lands, I am nobody. You have shown me such kindness, gracious lady, that it emboldens me to ask if you might not be able to smuggle me into the palace tonight, in your train.'

'Hardly a train.' Doubtfully. 'I would have to ask Beth — Miss Prior.' It weighed on her mind that she had not told Beth about Forde's outrageous proposal, but how could she?

'Who would feel she had to say no. Forgive me for asking, and please forget I did so. I will remember my place better in future.'

'No!' Horrified. 'It's not like that at all. It's monstrous you are treated like this. I only wish I could help. I am so sorry —' What could she say?

'If you are sorry for me, it makes it bearable, fräulein. It was a happy day for me, when you decided to improve your already admirable German.'

'And for me.' Now she really was blushing.

Considering how short a time the singers had had to learn their parts, Beth thought, the performance of a shortened version of Handel's famous *Ode to St. Cecilia* went well enough. Dryden's words were quite impossible to understand, but that was just as well, considering the Queen's objections to the text of *The Creation.* Dryden's idea of music as the life force, 'the diapason closing full in man', would hardly be approved by the Queens's confessor, who had already objected to the performance on the grounds that St. Cecilia's day was not in fact until November.

From the modest seats allotted to her and Charlotte at the back of the concert hall it had not been possible to see whether the Bentincks had come, but when the civil applause ended and the audience rose for the royal party to leave, Beth was pleased, she thought, to see them in the little group behind the royal family. The Queen looked surprisingly magnificent tonight, in crimson with a little tiara perched in an elegantly restrained coiffure. Beth could only hope that the knowledge of appearing as a Queen would make her behave like one, and that Bentinck was in a better temper than he looked.

'Do let us go out into the garden,' urged Charlotte. 'It's stifling in here. Oh!'

The crowd was thinning, and Beth turned to see Nathan Peabody approaching them accompanied by another man it took her a moment to recognise. Both of them were impeccable in the dark coats and black satin knee-breeches that were still de rigueur for court appearances, and she had never seen von Achen in anything but the most shabby and casual dress before. But everyone knew that King Ferdinand had once almost hanged a man for appearing before him in what he considered revolutionary garb. Everyone knew, and everyone was careful.

'I know I don't need to present my friend von Achen,' said Nathan Peabody, while Beth wondered just where they had met. 'We are hoping for the pleasure of finding you ladies some ices, and a quiet place in the gardens to watch the fireworks, which I believe are to be superb.'

'Thank you.' Beth had been looking about for Forde, but he must be on duty with the Bentincks. It was unhappily significant of the new, remoter relationship between them that she had not heard from him all day.

It was good to get out into the heavily perfumed air of the terraced gardens, and to find the Falconis already established in a little yew-bordered enclave, with views both to the main terrace and to the sea. Falconi joined her at once, to congratulate her on the singers' performance, and she was glad of it. Used to being the centre of attention, she had found it mildly disconcerting to see the two young men quietly competing for Charlotte's notice. The child was in remarkable looks tonight. Was she actually a little glad that Forde was not with them?

If so, it served her right that he joined them a few moments later. 'I have found you at last.' Bending over her hand. 'May I congratulate you on the performance? I thought Lady William actually enjoyed it.'

'I am glad. And her husband did not mind it too much?'

'Of that, I am not so sure. He is with the Queen now. We must just hope that good comes of it.'

'But you doubt it as much as I do?'

'I am afraid so. Flint and tinder, those two, and neither of them just in the listening vein. But I think it had to be done.'

'So do I.' She was glad to feel their minds in tune again. 'If only they will try to understand each other. After all, they want the same

137

thing, as do we all — Napoleon's downfall.'

'Yes, but do we all want it by the same means?' He was looking past her now at the rest of the group. 'Who is it absorbing young Charlotte's attention?'

Did he usually call her Charlotte? Beth looked around. 'Oh, that is Herr von Achen, her German tutor. He came with Peabody; I hope he was invited.'

'The one she argues with?' Forde surprised her. 'If I were you, I would keep an eye on her dealings with that young man. I heard a rumour this morning I think you should know about. The talk in the town is that your Charlotte is an heiress. Is there truth in it, by any chance?'

'Oh dear!'

'So there is. I rather thought so. It's interesting how the possession of money, or the expectation, gives a girl confidence. And no one could say your Charlotte lacks that.' His tone was cool, and she was ashamed to be pleased.

'No,' she agreed thoughtfully. 'But, do you know, I don't think it's just the money. You are right, there is money. I am sorry the gossips have got hold of it.'

'And you chose not to tell me, for fear I turn fortune hunter?'

'Gareth!' Appalled. She was still trying to

think what to say, how to explain, when the first firework went up and the little group moved forward to the edge of the clearing to watch. There was no more chance of private conversation, and she was not sure whether to be relieved or desolate.

She turned from watching a pyrotechnic display of the royal arms over the sea to find a page trying to catch her attention. 'The Princess sent me for you, signora. You are wanted in the palace. Urgently.'

Princess? Which princess? They were all princes and princesses in Sicily; it meant nothing. She looked for Forde, but he had moved a little way to bend over Charlotte, explaining the royal arms of Naples and Sicily as they appeared emblazoned in the sky.

'Urgently, signora,' the page repeated.

'I am summoned to the palace.' She turned to Falconi. 'Would you explain to Miss Pennam? Tell her I will look for her here?'

'Should I come?'

'The message said alone.' She caught an exchange of glances between the page and Falconi.

'We will await you here,' Falconi decided, as a new burst of rockets distracted everyone else.

'This way.' The page led her swiftly through a maze of steps, yew walks and terraces, in at a side entrance and up a privy stair to a door concealed in the panelling of a small receiving room.

'At last!' It was the Duchess of Orleans who awaited her there, tension in every line of her. She was standing by a small table on which lay a little pile of the flowers she had been unconsciously shredding from her bouquet as she waited. 'Miss Prior, you must help us; I cannot think of anyone else who can. My husband says it is the only chance of saving something out of this ruin.'

'Ruin?'

'My husband thinks so. He has lived in England, you know, truly believes you British are our only hope here in Sicily. And Lord Bentinck has thought fit to quarrel with my mother. They have said things to each other; unforgivable things. Ones that must be forgotten. I won't tell you. If she should do so, you must promise not to listen. She wants to see you, Miss Prior; she has taken a great fancy to you. If you wouldn't mind? To let her talk about it; to listen; try to convey to her that all you English are not bigots like that Bentinck. Oh,' impatiently, 'my husband insists it is her fault too, but think of it, Miss Prior, try to understand. After all these years a queen, to be given the lie to her face, accused of God knows what. We are afraid for her health, for her reason . . . The doctor is with her now, but when he goes . . . You won't mind? And to say nothing of it afterwards? You see how we are trusting you, Miss Prior.'

'You can. I am overwhelmed.' It was true. 'Anything I can do . . .'

'Just let her talk. The doctor says she must speak out her rage or it will destroy her. He means it. Let her talk, Miss Prior, and try and steer her thoughts into more pleasant channels. Ah, here is the summons.'

A lady-in-waiting had appeared through the concealed door. She looked distraught and seemed quite unaware of a great stain, presumably of some dark medicine, down the front of her dress. 'This way.' She led Beth back through the door and up one flight of the privy stair to emerge in the royal apartments.

It must be one of the smaller reception rooms, Beth thought, more formal than the one in which the Queen had last received her, with a state chair that was almost a throne. The Queen was sitting huddled in it, her hands running convulsively through the streaked grey-white hair; the tiara she had worn earlier hung at a rakish angle on the chair arm. Another lady-in-waiting, kneeling beside her, was trying to persuade her to drink from a silver goblet that steamed a little and smelled of wine and spices.

'Let me.' Beth took it gently from her. This was no time for ceremony.

'The doctor urges it,' the woman whispered. 'She is tearing herself to pieces, our poor lady.'

They love her, Beth thought. Her servants love her. It had to mean something. She did not think Bentinck's much liked him. 'Your majesty.' She put down the goblet and bent to take a writhing hand and kiss it. 'I am come to apologise for my countryman, and for my own mistake in urging the meeting.'

'Apologise!' The word had caught the Queen's attention. 'Too late for that! I would not speak to a serving maid so. Treachery! Who dares speak to me of treachery? I'll tell the King! I'll tell my son!' Beth was appalled to see tears show in the red-rimmed eyes. And yet, might this not be a good thing, a way to relief? 'What's the use,' said the old lady who was also a queen. 'They wouldn't listen. I'll tell —' She looked about her, suddenly surreptitious. 'Why should a woman not write to her own granddaughter? Poor child. Who else will help her? Who else can help me?' She was muttering now, and Beth was glad to see that the lady-in-waiting had moved away, probably out of earshot. The Queen's granddaughter was Marie Louise, wife to her enemy Napoleon. 'And those Murats,' Maria Carolina went on. 'Sitting on my throne. To say I was in correspondence with them! I am the Queen.' She sat up suddenly, straight in the ornate chair. 'I write to whom I please. I'll not be insulted, do you hear?'

'Nobody would dare, your majesty.' Beth proffered the cup. 'Try a little of this?'

'He dared! Oh, God! What would my mother have done to him? No one insulted her. She was a truly great queen — an empress. And she fought for her throne, as I have had to fight for mine. But it was hers! Born to it! I married mine. Do you know,' she seized Beth's hand and fixed her with a fierce, mad eye, 'my sister should have married Naples, poor Josepha. Sometimes I wish I'd died of the smallpox as she did. All those years of marriage, of wooing him. Putting on my white gloves — he could never resist me in white gloves. And now — I'm a bad influence. Did you know that? The great Lord Bentinck thinks me a bad influence. He'd have me out of here if he could, but I'll surprise him yet. I am Maria Theresa's daughter, and I am still not without friends.' She was tiring now. Her hand reached out half-consciously for the silver goblet. She sipped. 'At least I showed him his place.' A note of satisfaction now. 'To speak to a queen like that. Unendurable.' She sipped again, the draught visibly taking effect, and Beth caught the goblet as it was about to fall from her hand.

'We do thank you, signora.' The lady-in-waiting came quietly forward. 'We can see to her now. She will sleep the clock round, and wake, please God, feeling better.'

And how would Bentinck feel? Who would be listening to him? Trying to make him see reason.

Returning to the gardens, Beth found the firework display over and Forde missing from the little party.

'Lord Bentinck sent for him,' said Falconi. 'Time to go home, I think.'

'So soon?' Charlotte had heard him. 'The air is so delicious now, can we not stay a little longer?' She was sparkling with happiness, Beth saw. Why? For whose benefit?

'I'm on stage tomorrow,' Beth reminded her. 'I don't like to be too late.'

'Of course not.' Charlotte was contrite at once. 'I clean forgot. It's the Piccini, isn't it, and you said you needed a run through.' She rose from the seat she had shared with Peabody and von Achen. 'You do look tired, Beth. What's going on at the palace?'

'I'll tell you in the morning.' It came out a little more quelling than she had intended. And, in fact, she had already decided that she was not going to tell even Forde what she had heard. Every instinct told her that her first duty was to the Queen, as one woman to another. To tell Forde that the Queen had as good as confessed to corresponding with Napoleon's wife could only cause infinite trouble. Had she confessed to writing to the Murats too? Of this, Beth was less sure. The ravings of a drugged, angry woman should not be used in evidence against her. Besides, she told herself, the Queen must surely have said very much the same things to Bentinck himself. She would hear about it in the morning. Normally, she saw no one on the days when she was appearing at the theatre, but tonight she left orders that if Forde should call, he must be admitted.

But she woke, undisturbed, at her usual hour. Breakfasting in bed, she thought she was actually beginning to get used to the scandalous hours the Sicilians kept. But where was Charlotte? She usually came tapping on the door when breakfast was brought up, and ate hers sociably on the chaise longue. 'Where is Miss Pennam?' she asked the maid.

It got her a voluble reply. The signorina had been up for hours, it appeared, and had gone riding, 'with two gentlemen'.

'No lady?' Surely Lisa Falconi had meant to go too.

'No, signora.' The woman was shocked, and so in fact was Beth. But at least two escorts were better than one. She found herself hoping that Forde was not one of them. He was bound to visit her today. But the long day dragged on with no sign of either him or Charlotte and she left at last, in a bad temper, for the rehearsal of Piccini's time-worn comedy, *La Ceccina.*

The theatre was alive with rumours. Everyone knew that something had happened at the palace the night before, nobody knew what. Questioned eagerly by fellow members of the cast, Beth described the fireworks with enthusiasm and managed to talk about nothing else. But she was relieved when it was time for the performance to start.

The house, too, was restless, with even more than usual of the movement between boxes that was so maddening for performers whose reputation might depend on the reception of one solo.

When the curtain fell at last Beth changed quickly and hurried round to the usual meeting point at the front of the house, hoping for a word alone with Charlotte. But of course she found her surrounded by cavaliers. Lisa Falconi was there too, and had a pretty apology for Beth. 'I am afraid we made Miss Pennam late,' she said. 'I am so sorry. I was unable to ride with them today so I persuaded the gentlemen to bring her to me for a luncheon afterwards, and you know how time drifts away, these hot days. I promise you, she was not late for the theatre.'

'Unlike everyone else,' said Beth ruefully. 'One might as well have sung in the fish market when the boats were in. What is going on today?' She made the question general, but Falconi answered it.

'We were hoping you could tell us that, signora. You were the one who was summoned to the Queen last night. There is nothing but talk today, and where is Mr. Forde?'

'I don't know.' Beth's eye had been quick to find him missing from the little group. 'I have not heard from him all day.'

'And the Bentincks were not in their box,' said Falconi.

'Were they not?' This was indeed surprising. She had never thought the Bentincks enjoyed the opera, but they came, as a matter of social punctilio.

'Nobody has stirred from the Bentinck house all day,' said Peabody. 'Except messengers who have come and gone like bees from the hive. We had been counting on you for information, Miss Prior.'

'Then I am afraid you have counted in vain. I know no more than you do.' She did not enjoy admitting it.

'But the palace,' persisted Peabody. 'Last night's summons must have meant something, Miss Prior?'

'Oh, that.' She had had time to think about this. 'I got a great scold for agreeing to perform in Cimarosa's *Matrimonio Segreto*. Nobody told me he had been imprisoned and threatened with death for his liberal principles after the first occupation of Naples. We have cancelled the performance, of course.' A little silence fell, as she had known it would. Nobody liked to remember the bloody reprisals Ferdinand and his wife had wreaked when they got back to Naples in ninety-nine. And still less did anyone like to think of what this might mean for any future return. And in the silence, nobody asked just who it was who had scolded her.

She had rather hoped to find Forde waiting for them down at the Marino, but there was no sign of him. The Duke and Duchess of Orleans were missing too, and so was Circello, the Foreign Minister. Rumours ran from carriage to carriage. The Queen was ill. Bentinck was ill. No, it was Lady William. The Queen's own doctor had been sent to her from the palace. No, he had been sent for to the palace, but it was the Duchess of Orleans' baby son who was ill. Constantly appealed to, Beth continued to plead ignorance on every count, but it was a relief when everyone began to drift home, rather earlier than usual.

'Lord, what a long day.' Charlotte paused at Beth's door, as if hoping to be asked in.

'Yes. Bed at once, I think. And, Charlotte —'

'Yes?'

'I'll see you at breakfast? You're not riding again?' She tried to make it question rather than command.

'Not if you don't want me to. Are you cross with me, Beth?'

'I'm tired. And, yes, I think I am a little cross. But, in the morning, Charlotte, please.'

She was roused long before her usual hour by her maid to say that Signor Forde wanted to see her urgently. 'Oh, very well. My swansdown negligée, and breakfast for two.' Another Sicilian custom which had surprised her very much at first was that ladies thought nothing of receiving gentlemen in their bedrooms. She and Charlotte had already paid a duty call on a new mother and found her entertaining royally from her bed.

'Quite like old times, is it not?' she greeted Forde, happily conscious of looking her best after a good, if short, night's sleep.

But he had no time to spare for courtesies.

'He's gone,' he told her. 'Bentinck sailed for England this morning.'

'What?' She actually did not believe her ears. 'Gone? And Lady William —'

'Left here. As a hostage to fortune, I suppose. At least as a sign that he means to return. With the fullest possible powers. That's what he has gone back for. He says there is no dealing with the Queen. We made a fatal mistake, you and I, in contriving for them to meet. Fatal.'

And he blamed her for it, of course. 'The Queen is furious too, if that is any comfort to you,' she told him. 'He made her ill; she's an old woman, Gareth.'

'A witless old hag. If only she would admit it, and stop meddling with affairs of state. There's no getting anywhere so long as she goes on doing so, Bentinck says, so he has gone home to get absolute power. To be able to send her into exile if necessary.'

'Exile? He wouldn't?' But she remembered something the Queen had said about going to Vienna. If she had said this to Bentinck, it could have given him the idea. 'Does she know, Gareth?'

'I expect so. She knows most things, it seems to me. What did she say to you, Beth?'

'She was beyond reason. Outraged. Said her mother would never have endured such insults. Do you think it was people like Bentinck who drove George III mad, Gareth?'

'More likely his wife's nagging.' But she had successfully distracted him from her talk with the Queen.

'But it's madness,' she said. 'Bentinck has insulted the Queen. Let her know he wants to be rid of her, and now he sails for home, calm as you please, leaving the rest of us to cope with the consequences. Who is in charge here, now he has gone?'

'General Maitland, of course.'

'He is going to run things from Messina? Has Bentinck actually left, Gareth?'

'Yes, I told you. This morning. I spent all yesterday, all night trying to dissuade him. No use. He's gone.'

'I wish you had let me know. I would have sent Charlotte with him.'

'He'd not have taken her.'

'No, I don't suppose he would. A very dictatorial gentleman, is Lord William.'

'He says there is not the slightest cause for alarm. He will be back before he is missed, he says.'

'Having instantly caught the undivided ear of a government that is embroiled in a death struggle with Napoleon? Believe that, Gareth, you will believe anything!'

It was true enough to make him angry and

she was sorry, and did her best to soothe him, but without much success. She would have to wait for a more propitious moment to try to explain to him just how outraged the Queen was, and how dangerous she thought that might be. The problem was how to do this without betraying the Queen's confidence, and this was certainly not the moment to try.

He left soon, still ruffled, and she faced the next interview, with Charlotte, with less than her usual equanimity. Inevitably, they quarrelled. Used to freedom at home, Charlotte did not see why she should trouble herself about what she described as 'small town Sicilian nonsense'.

'You're always too busy to ride with me,' she burst out with it at last. 'Or waiting around for one of your confabs with Forde, or some excuse or other! Even I can see that it won't do to go out alone. So what is wrong with two cavaliers? Safety in numbers, after all! I never heard such a fuss. Or is it that you would rather they stayed around here turning the pages of your music for you?'

'Charlotte!' She must not lose her temper. 'The trouble is —'

It was a confession she had not wanted to make. 'I don't like riding. I'm not good at it. I didn't learn until a few years ago, don't you see, and have never taken to it naturally.

I hate it!' She burst out at last. 'Horses frighten me.'

'I'm sorry!' Charlotte surprised her with a quick, loving hug. 'Truly sorry. I won't do it again, if you really don't want me to. I did honestly think Lisa meant to come too. But don't you think you should try and get to like it better, Beth? We could go out quietly together, just you and I. I taught all my brothers to ride; I am sure I could get you used to horses, if you would just give me the chance. I'd dearly love to do it, so good as you have been to me.'

'Why, thank you!' Beth was amazed to find herself near to tears. 'I'd like to try; it's a handicap, no doubt about it.' Unspoken between them was the knowledge that Forde never walked when he could ride.

8

The sirocco struck the day after William Bentinck left, and Beth, prostrate on her bed in a darkened room, was almost grateful. Life stood still in Palermo while the devilish, hot wind blew. The servants hung damp blankets over the shutters and sprinkled cold water through the rooms, and she lay on her bed and thought bitter three o'clock in the morning thoughts. She had been mad to come, madder still to think that this shared venture with Forde would bring them closer together; maddest of all to bring Charlotte.

This was the worst of it. Because, under all the other anxieties, there now ran a sharp, new sense of danger. Bentinck had insulted the Queen and sailed away, leaving nothing but threats behind. Threats to an already maddened woman. No good could come of it.

The vile wind blew for two days, and when it was over, all of Palermo seemed to sigh with relief and get back to the business of living, under its new layer of white dust. It was the day for the weekly *conversazione*, subscribed to by the nobility of Palermo, and

Beth and Charlotte found the rooms fuller than usual. They always enjoyed these informal occasions given up mainly to talk and the consumption of ices and iced drinks, though some rooms were set aside for cards. But tonight these were empty. Everyone had a tale to tell, whether of the unendurable discomfort of the sirocco or, more often, of the events that had preceded it.

Forde had told Beth he had promised Lord William to support his wife in his absence. When she and Charlotte arrived, escorted by Nathan Peabody, she saw that Lady William was already there, Forde in attendance, fending off questions as best she might. Easy enough to plead ignorance of her husband's intentions since everyone knew him for a silent law unto himself.

Beth soon found herself surrounded by a similar group of eager questioners. It seemed to be generally known that she had been sent for by the Queen on the night of the entertainment at the palace, but she stuck to her story that it had just been to talk about music.

She was grateful for the good manners of the Palermitans, which made it impossible for them to press her, so that she was able to leave it in doubt whether she had seen the Queen before or after the scene with Lord William. And the sirocco provided a useful channel of escape if any question did need dodging. She found Peabody helpful here. He stayed close beside her this evening; it had been his first experience of the baleful wind as well as hers and he was happy to expatiate on it. He and von Achen had had themselves rowed out into the bay for a swim in the warm sea and had seen the sun set over the water. He waxed lyrical in describing the experience, and Beth was grateful. She noticed, with interest, that von Achen was also present tonight. Having appeared at the palace function had obviously given him the entrée elsewhere, and she wondered how she felt about this as she saw him dancing attendance on Charlotte.

But here was a stranger being led up to her by Fagan. She thought she would have known him for an Englishman even if he had been on his own. He was tall and fair, with a fresh outdoor complexion and the confident manner of one who knows his world. Her instant and informed assessment placed him as a junior member of the aristocracy, so it was a surprise when Fagan introduced him as John Thornton, a new Vice Consul, just out from England. She had noticed that Sicily was beginning to be a place where younger sons came hoping for rich pickings from the island's muddled trade arrangements.

John Thornton. The name echoed in her

mind as she said polite nothings in exchange for his. And then she had it, and her glance flickered past him to Charlotte on the other side of the room, who had just seen him and dropped her fan.

'And I very much hope you will make me known to your young friend Miss Pennam,' John Thornton was saying, 'who is some kind of cousin of a friend of mine at home, Miss Comyn.'

'You are from Hull then, Mr. Thornton?' Her mind was in a whirl.

'Yes, my father is a banker there. I have worked for him since I grew up, decided it was time to see the world, what there is to be seen these days, with Napoleon's shadow so long over it. My father is a young man still, doesn't want me throwing new-fangled notions into the works for a while yet. I think he was glad to let me go. And Palermo strikes me as a delightful place. Do you not find it so?'

'Even with the sirocco blowing?'

'Oh, that! A little weather never did anyone any harm.' He was looking thoughtfully across the room to where von Achen had picked up Charlotte's fan and returned it to her with just a shade too much grace. 'Will you present me, Miss Prior?'

'If you wish it.' With a questioning look.

He must know Charlotte very well, if he was so sure she would carry off this surprise meeting without betraying herself.

'Oh, I do, Miss Prior.' His face was a civil blank as he handed Beth across the room to where Charlotte still stood, gazing at him. But his confidence had been well grounded. She read the message of non-recognition in his face, and went through the introduction with almost complete aplomb. Only the fan, twisting in the fingers of her left hand, betrayed her.

When Charlotte looked across the crowded salon and saw John Thornton talking to Beth, she felt dizzy for a moment, then furious. If he thought he had come to take her home, he must think again. The two of them were looking at her now, the moment of confrontation was at hand, von Achen was saying something to her, she dropped her fan, to distract herself, or him, and then, at last, got the message of non-recognition on John Thornton's face. So what in the world was he playing at? She went through the farce of the introduction like a civil automaton, was aware of von Achen watching her curiously, and was furious all over again with John Thornton for landing her in this imbroglio.

'You must be sorry,' he was saying now

as Beth turned away, 'not to be at home when your cousin is visiting your family in the west country.'

'Oh, is she?' carelessly. 'I did not know. We may be cousins, Mr. Thornton, but we are not particularly close friends.'

'You surprise me.' He was teasing her, she thought angrily, and there was not a thing in the world she could do about it. 'Such a charming creature as Miss Comyn is. I am quite devoted to her, you know, have been ever since we were children together. Hull seemed such a sad place without her that I decided it was time I came abroad to see something of the world.'

'Such of it as you British are able to visit,' put in von Achen. 'No Grand Tour these days, Mr. Thornton.'

'No Grand Tour ever for the likes of me,' said John Thornton. 'I'm a businessman, not an idle sprig of the aristocracy. I am here to earn my living, not to see the sights. Though,' smiling for the first time at Charlotte, 'I rather hope that I may contrive to do a little of both. May I hope to see you and your delightful friend Miss Prior at the Marino later on, Miss Pennam? I know I should not detain you longer now, but I am very much hoping that you will be kind enough to give me some advice as to how I should go on, here in Palermo.

I do not expect to stay very long, and mean to make the most of every minute. I can hope to see you later?'

'We shall most certainly be there.'

'Surrounded by cavaliers,' said von Achen. 'You must not expect to monopolise Palermo's two leading ladies, Mr. Thornton.'

'No, why should I?' Thornton smiled at him blandly, refusing to take offence. 'I shall look forward to seeing you later, Miss Pennam.' There was something about the way he used the assumed name that was at once tease, challenge and reassurance. He turned away and Charlotte saw him return, as to a magnet, to Beth.

'A very self-confident young man, like all your English merchants,' said von Achen. 'Because they have no blood themselves, they refuse to acknowledge it in others. For a moment, there, I was tempted to call him out, Miss Pennam, for the familiar way he addressed you, but I resisted the temptation because I was sure you would not like it.'

'You were quite right,' she told him. 'I hope you will go on resisting it.'

'You have my humble promise. But I hope you will recognise how I suffer when I see another man treat you so cavalierly. You, who should be throned above the crowd, cynosure of all eyes, respected by every tongue.'

'It sounds a dead bore to me,' said Charlotte, suddenly at odds with the man she thought she adored.

'If you only knew how I suffer, seeing the free-and-easy way you are treated, Fräulein Pennam. But I am afraid it is the inevitable result of the company you keep. How could your esteemed parents let you come gallivanting to Europe with no better chaperone than —'

'Be careful what you say,' she interrupted angrily. 'You are speaking of my friend.'

'The woman who has pulled the wool over your eyes so successfully. But I am dumb.' He had caught her look of pure rage. 'Oh, fräulein, if only I were the man I ought to be. But I promise you, the day will come when I can lay lands and honours at your feet, when I can match my dignity with your beauty —' He stopped in mid-sentence, and she was half sorry, half relieved as Nathan Peabody joined them.

'I am sent by Miss Prior,' he told her, 'to tell you the carriage is waiting. May I —' He held out his hand, to lead her through the crowded rooms.

'On the contrary, the privilege must be mine —' Von Achen too held out a hand.

'Absurd!' Charlotte was aware of tension in the air. 'You will both take me, since I am

161

so frail and need such protection.' But she was glad to join Beth, who was deep in talk with John Thornton.

'Mr. Thornton has been telling me about the hard times poor Mr. Wilkinson has been having on his visits to the Theatre Royal at Hull, now the Evangelicals are so deeply entrenched there,' Beth explained. 'You'll let us give you a lift in our carriage, will you not, Mr. Thornton? The other gentlemen know their way well enough.'

Charlotte did not think the other gentlemen liked it much, particularly von Achen, but there was nothing they could do about it, except walk very close to the carriage, which they did, making any *éclaircissement* impossible. Charlotte thought she was glad, but John Thornton was still talking theatre with Beth, and she could not help feeling a little out of things.

The Marino was unusually crowded that night, since everyone was out to compare notes about their sufferings during the sirocco. If John Thornton had hoped for a word alone with her, it was soon obvious that it would not be possible, and once again she thought she was glad. But it was altogether one of the most unsatisfactory evenings she had spent since they arrived.

John Thornton on the other hand, was thoroughly pleased with his evening, though he had managed a swift exchange with Beth about his one anxiety. 'I wonder whether knowledge of German is really such an important element in a young lady's education,' he said quietly as he handed her out of the carriage, while von Achen was doing the same for Charlotte.

'Do you know,' Beth's voice was friendly in the darkness. 'I have been wondering that too, Mr. Thornton.'

Beth could only assume that the duties of a Vice Consul were light because Thornton was soon a regular caller at their house. If she had not known better, she would have thought that it was herself, rather than Charlotte, whom he was coming to see. He soon contrived to insinuate himself into the riding lessons Charlotte was giving her, and proved an admirable teacher, so that she began to find herself actually enjoying them.

But when he learned the purpose of them, the plan to ride to Segesta, he made an instant objection. 'But, Miss Prior, you have not been thinking enough about the Sicilians, and their prejudices.'

'Prejudices? I would have said they had none; it seems to me a most tolerant and delightful society.'

'Oh, society, yes indeed. But it is not society

you will be meeting on the road to Segesta. Frankly, I am a little surprised that the Falconis have even suggested the plan, but they must know what they are doing. But I cannot believe you have told them of your idea of riding?'

'No, I don't believe it has come up,' she admitted.

'I thought not. You have forgotten your Brydone, Miss Prior. He says somewhere that one young member of their touring party looked rather like a lady, and they got stoned by peasant women as a result. I would not at all like that to happen to you and Miss Pennam. I am sure, if you do decide to go, that you will be much better in those curious mule-borne sedan chairs that Sicilian ladies use. I don't think it is just laziness, do you see? They may act as they please, here in Palermo, but in the country I think you will find they conform to the prejudices of the peasants.'

'Oh dear, I am afraid you are almost certainly right,' she admitted. 'Poor Charlotte will be disappointed.'

'Better disappointed than mobbed. I wish I could persuade you to have second thoughts about this expedition. Frankly, I am amazed that Forde has not advised against it.'

'On the contrary, he is proposing to come.' She was not going to discuss Forde with this surprising young man, but she was beginning to think Charlotte might have been foolish in refusing him. And more and more she wished she knew just why he had come to Sicily.

Charlotte was discussing the Segesta trip too. While Thornton had hung back with Beth on the pretext of adjusting her stirrup, she and von Achen had ridden ahead for a favourite view of Monte Pellegrino. They turned to watch a felucca put out to sea, and von Achen put a delaying hand on her bridle. 'One moment, Miss Pennam. I have been longing for this, a word alone with you. You are so surrounded, these days, by admirers, how is a poor devil of a German tutor to get a word in?'

'You get enough when we are at work.'

'That's not alone! Why does your dragon of a guardian distrust me so? Oh, she does not actually sit in on our lessons, but you know as well as I do that she is in and out like an old wife at a peep-show. I can only be grateful to this plebeian Mr. Thornton for attaching himself to her, though it is hard to understand his motives. How anyone could, when here is metal so much more attractive — but that is not what I wished to say.' He knew he had gone too far. 'Miss Pennam, what I have longed for the chance to say to you is that

I am deeply anxious about this proposed jaunt to Segesta. This is neither the time nor the place for parties of pleasure. You British ladies are beyond a man's comprehension. You behave, abroad, as if you were at home, or even more freely! Look at you here, riding alone with a man, or as good as alone. What my mother would say! And what in the world is Miss Prior thinking of. But of course we all know about Miss Prior —'

Now she was angry. 'I suppose she trusts me, Herr von Achen, if she does not necessarily trust you. But let us by all means remember your mother's strictures and ride back to join them.'

'I've done it all wrong.' His hand was hard on her bridle now. 'What I am asking, what I am begging, Miss Pennam, is that you find a way of making it possible for me to come too on this mad venture to Segesta. If there is danger, as I truly believe there may be, then I wish to be there to protect you.'

'Danger?' she said thoughtfully. 'You really mean that?'

'Indeed I do. This island is full of danger, of plotting and distrust. It is only on the surface that it smiles, Miss Pennam. Never forget that.'

John Thornton was saying very much the

same thing to Beth. 'If you do decide to go, Miss Prior, I hope and trust that you will allow me to come too. I think I have some kind of a right to ask that.'

'Do you know, I believe you have.' They had never discussed the curious charade in which they were involved, and she was grateful, increasingly aware that even Sicilian gardens had ears. Your secluded terrace, with its screen of well-watered, heavily perfumed shrubs, lay just below your neighbour's. You talked secrets on it at your peril. But out here they were alone, except for Charlotte and von Achen, ahead of them, down by the sea. She and Thornton watched as von Achen leaned forward on his horse to say something eagerly to Charlotte. 'I'm sorry I've done nothing about the German lessons,' Beth said now. 'But I thought it might do more harm than good.'

'I am absolutely sure you were right,' he told her. 'I have the greatest respect for your judgment, Miss Prior. Tell me, does Mr. Forde mean to accompany you on this trip to Segesta?'

'I wish I knew,' she told him. 'He most certainly did in the first place, but now Bentinck has gone so unexpectedly back to England, he feels he has a duty to his wife.'

'Understandable,' he said. 'But there are

duties and duties, Miss Prior. I am more than delighted that you will let me join you on this venturesome trip. Shall we join the others?' They had both seen von Achen put his hand on Charlotte's where it held the reins.

Forde called on Beth that evening just before it was time for her to leave for the theatre, where she was to sing Violante in a rare production of Mozart's *La Finta Giardiniera*. It was a part that suited her, she was looking forward to it and wished he had picked any other time. Back in London, she would have refused to see him, but back in London everything had been different.

'I am come to apologise for neglecting you so shamefully.' His first words failed to please her. 'But I am sure you understand the duty I feel to Lady William.'

'Of course I do, Mr. Forde.' She found it suddenly easy to use his surname. 'She is not used to facing the world alone.'

'And it is not something you ever have to do, dear Beth. You and Miss Pennam are quite thronged with cavaliers these days. Who is this new young Englishman?'

'Mr. Thornton? A charming young man. And a friend of Miss Pennam's cousins in Hull. He is from the banking family, you know.'

'The only son, Fagan tells me. I am surprised his father can spare him, but he makes a most creditable addition to your society. I wish I could say the same for that young German. It's a great pity, if you ask me, that that egalitarian young Peabody contrived to get him the entrée into Palermitan society. We got on very well without him, and if I were you, Beth, I would be inclined to consider making an end to those farcical German lessons he is giving your young companion. His constant company can do her nothing but harm.'

'And you think forbidding him the house would improve matters? It's a pity you have no sisters, Mr. Forde.' This time she saw him notice her use of his surname. 'But, forgive me, if that is all you had to say to me, it is more than time I left for the theatre.'

'One more moment, please . . . This trip to Segesta . . . Do you and Miss Pennam still mean to go?'

'We are to discuss it with the Falconis this evening. I know Lisa is eager to go, and so is Charlotte. Why? Do you advise against it?'

He hesitated, taken aback by the direct question. He and Fagan had agreed that there was something odd about the trip, that something might be learned from it. But was he justified in not warning Beth? 'Oh, I don't

169

believe so,' he said at last. 'Not so long as the Falconis arrange for adequate guards, as I have no doubt they will — and so long as I am permitted to come too.'

'Oh, everyone is coming.' With her sweetest smile. 'As you say, Charlotte and I certainly do not lack for cavaliers. And now I really must leave you or I shall be in blackest disgrace with Bartolucci. Do you intend to hear my Violante, Mr. Forde?'

'You keep calling me that,' he protested at last.

'And I would be pleased to hear you calling me Miss Prior,' she told him. 'Indeed, I must insist on it if you do propose to accompany us on this excursion. Something Charlotte has said has made me a little anxious. No, there is no time to discuss it, if I wished to, which I do not. Good day, Mr. Forde.' She was not sure afterwards whether she was glad or sorry that she had been so firm with him.

But she was happily aware that she gave the performance of a lifetime as Violante that night. The strange part of the woman whose lover had tried to kill her exactly suited her mood, and she enjoyed every moment of the scenes, some comic, some near tragedy, in which, disguised as the gardener's girl, she teased and tormented the man who thought he had killed her. When it was over at last, she was amazed at the wave upon wave of applause that filled the usually lethargic house.

'You made us all listen, Miss Prior. I did not think it could be done.' Nathan Peabody contrived to be the first to greet her when she came round to the front of the house at last. 'It's an absurd tale, and, forgive me, I have always thought opera an absurd enough business, but there was a moment, back there, when I felt a mist in front of my eyes.'

'Why, thank you.' Her eyes met his for a moment, then she had to turn to receive a barrage of compliments. She had reminded von Achen of all the great opera singers he had ever heard; she thought she had surprised Forde very much indeed; Falconi simply kissed her hand and thanked her.

'Oh, Beth!' In the carriage at last Charlotte turned to her with starry eyes. 'I didn't know; I didn't understand —'

'I don't believe we any of us did.' Peabody had managed somehow to ride with them tonight. 'Did you know the Queen was there, Miss Prior? She came at the last minute, technically incognita, to the Orleans' box.'

'No, did she?' Beth was not much interested. All she wanted was to get home to bed; the performance, catching her up in its own momentum, had left her exhausted, drained.

'You are tired out.' Peabody surprised her by recognising this. 'You two ladies should make an early night of it.' He directed the suggestion to Charlotte.

'Oh, but we have to plan for Segesta,' she protested. 'And, besides, everyone will want to congratulate Beth.'

Everyone did, and Beth was so worn out by being kissed by ladies and thanked by gentlemen that when she found the Falconis in a quiet corner at last and they told her that all arrangements were made for their departure in three days' time, she simply agreed.

'Bartolucci would let you go to the moon, just now, if you were to ask it,' Falconi summed up the situation, and that was that.

9

Too tired to think about it that night, Beth woke in the morning to face what had been disconcerting about how Forde had taken her triumph. He had not much liked it. She knew him well enough to know this, and it both puzzled and disturbed her. She had made a great stride forward in her career, and Forde had not much liked it. What kind of a friend was this?

She was imagining things. He had simply not wanted to rejoice with her in public; he would come this morning. Perhaps she would share another sociable breakfast with him. It was more than time that they got back in touch with each other. When a maid came scratching at the door with an early message, she greeted her eagerly.

But it was a summons to the palace.

'You made me cry, Miss Prior.' It was hot again, and Queen Maria Carolina received Beth on a shady terrace at the back of the palace. She looked herself again today, composed and regal; only a slight tremor in her hands betrayed tension. 'You may leave us,' to her lady-in-waiting. 'Miss Prior and I will take a turn in the gardens, while I tell her how much I admired her performance last night. You surprised yourself, did you not?' She had taken Beth's arm, and leaned on it heavily, guiding her down the steps from the enclosed terrace.

'Yes, I did.' Surprised herself at the Queen's perception.

'I have seen it before,' Maria Carolina told her. 'The moment when an artist outperforms himself. Or,' smiling, 'herself. I remember once at Schönbrunn, oh such a long time ago, a child prodigy — he was famous later . . .' They had reached the bottom of the steps and she moved forward to a low wall with a far view of the sea. 'My favourite view. And my favourite place for confidential talk. There are no hidden ears here.' The terrace below them was empty and the one above too far off. 'They sent you here to spy on me, did they not?'

'Your majesty!' But it was true.

'I told you I am well informed.' The Queen was smiling now. 'I had meant to use you, as I used that poor, stupid Emma Hamilton. But that was a long time ago, and everything is different now. I held my husband by love then; now I do it by fear. It does not work

174

so well. And you, how do you hold Mr. Forde?'

'I don't.' Beth surprised herself.

'Ah. So that is why you did not tell him.'

'Tell him?' Now she was entirely at sea.

'What I said to you the other night. I'm an old, passionate fool, Miss Prior, and I cannot always control what I say, but I do not forget it. And, as I have said, I am well informed. So I scolded you about wanting to perform *Matrimonio Segreto*, did I? It was well thought of; I congratulate you. And I do not want to lose you. We can deal together, you and I; two women. So, let me give you a piece of advice, in return for your discretion. This plan to go to Segesta, Miss Prior. Give it up. It's not safe.'

'That's what I have felt, but how can I? It's all fixed.'

'So is the kidnapping.'

'Kidnapping?'

'Too many people know that your young friend is an heiress. Imagine the scene. She is snatched from you, expensively ransomed — and compromised. Some gallant young man offers to marry her, save her from shame. What can you do but consent? The kidnappers get the ransom; their accomplice gets the heiress. And meanwhile —' Seeing Beth speechless, she carried smoothly on. 'Meanwhile who knows what treasonable meetings have taken place. I have this from Castroni, the Chief of Police. He cares nothing for Miss Pennam, if that is her name, which I doubt. He is merely intent on catching the plotters, or, better still, learning their plans. He'll not lift a finger to save Miss Pennam, when the moment comes. In his eyes, she is expendable, and so are you; never forget that. And remember something else; I cannot be seen in this. You must think of some way of withdrawing from this mad expedition without involving me. You came here this morning simply to be congratulated on your performance last night, and to be asked to take part in the festival I plan in honour of St. Rosalia.'

'St. Rosalia? But I thought her day was past?'

'So it has, with the usual pomp and circumstance, back in July, and a small fortune it cost us all, as usual. But it keeps the people happy, making the elaborate preparations. That's the whole point of bread and circuses; they give employment to the vulgar. And we need that badly just now. I am planning just one day of festivities this time. That will be enough, I think, to give the public mind a new direction, away from all this revolutionary talk about democracy and constitutions. I only wish St. Rosalia was as obliging as our friend St. Januarius back in Naples. The Holy Fathers there could mostly be counted on for a miraculous liquefaction of his precious blood, when it was needed to calm the mob. But St. Rosalia's bones keep the plague at bay, if they are carried through the town. Why should they not keep off the French threat? And the English one, too, if need be. I am sure it is worth giving it a try, and you, my good friend, are going to have another of your brilliant ideas about a suitable entertainment for me to give. Perhaps down on the Marino, granted the hot weather. Some more Handel, and you singing this time, perhaps? And no Lord Bentinck to cast a gloom over the occasion.'

'May I not plead your majesty's request as a reason for crying off from Segesta?'

'No,' said the Queen. 'I want no part in that. But one thing I can tell you; your party will be safe enough until past Monreale. It is at Alcamo that the danger lies. You could do worse than go as far as Monreale — a place that is very well worth seeing. After that it should be easy enough for an actress like you to find a reason for abandoning the project.'

'Yes.' Doubtfully. 'But when is St. Rosalia's festival to be?'

'Early in September; it takes time to prepare for these occasions and in fact it is the preparation that does people good. Now, we have talked quite long enough, Miss Prior. I count on your discretion. Trust no one. No one is to be trusted.' She turned to lead the way back up the terrace steps. At the top, she paused, turned, smiled at Beth, and took a diamond bracelet from her left wrist. 'This is for you, in celebration of a great performance last night. And as a public bond between us. Everyone knows it for mine; you will find it as good as a pass word.'

Or as involving, thought Beth, stammering her thanks, and putting on the bracelet.

Trust no one. The words echoed in Beth's head on the drive back from the palace. It was true. She could not. The only person she could for a moment consider telling about the Queen's revelations was Charlotte herself, but the more she thought about this the less she felt she could do so. Charlotte was amazingly better, but odd things could still throw her off balance, and then she was sick again. Besides, she was already involved in playing a part; the addition of this sinister secret to her load might well be too much. And as to the rest of their little group: impossible. Charlotte was to be kidnapped; compromised; married by a charming young gentleman. The description would fit any of their three cavaliers. No. Not three: four. She faced it. Forde could not be left out of this calculation. He, too, was charming and un-married, and though she had always thought him a rich man, fortunes had been lost as well as made in the long, grinding years of war. Only Falconi was out of it, being married, but she could not possibly turn to him in pref-erence to Forde. And John Thornton? What did she really know of him?

And behind all this was another question. How far could she trust the Queen? There had been something very disconcerting about the way Maria Carolina planned to use the local saint to distract the local popu-lace. She had been aware, since coming to Palermo, that, while conforming in public, the aristocrats took their religion lightly, but this was more than that.

Trust no one. She had failed to ask the Queen if the plan for a festival was public knowledge yet, but it must be soon, if it was to have the desired effect on the restive mob. The carriage was drawing up outside their house. What had she decided? Nothing.

She found Charlotte busy with prepara-tions for Segesta, and realised, exhibiting her bracelet, how useful it was going to prove as visible explanation of her summons to the pal-ace. No need to talk about the planned festival.

She would wait and let that come at them from another angle, though she was already beating her brains for a piece of music that would not be too totally unsuitable for such an odd occasion.

Charlotte had had a visitor while Beth was out. John Thornton had called, ostensibly to congratulate Beth on her performance, but had made no secret of his pleasure at finding Charlotte alone. As always, he addressed her formally as Miss Pennam. By tacit consent, they had still not spoken of the real facts of her case.

'But should you really be seeing me alone?' he asked now. 'Forgive me, but you perhaps do not understand how much talk there is about your unusual ménage. I have been wishing for the chance to say this to you.'

'And now you grumble because you have got it! You cannot seriously be suggesting that we hire ourselves a duenna, Beth and I? We are very well able to take care of ourselves. I really think Beth is capable of anything.'

'A remarkable woman, I entirely agree. And as for her performance last night! But that is the heart of the matter, don't you see? You and I know Miss Prior for the amazing creature she is, but in the eyes of the world, she is an actress, with all that that implies.'

'Such as —' Now her tone was challenging. 'You are beginning to talk like a mealy-mouthed Evangelical, John.' His Christian name had slipped out unawares, and she flushed, angry with herself.

'Your situation makes me feel like one.' She had led him out on to the shady terrace, and he cast a quick look about him. 'And it is all my fault! I cannot forgive myself for being the cause of your plunging into this imbroglio. And how your mother and step-father came to let you take this wild step is more than I shall ever understand! It is not just that Miss Prior is an actress; it is her past, Charlotte. I must speak of it, her relationship with Gareth Forde. How could they let you come with her?'

'They could not stop me.' She looked at him dangerously. 'And I do not want to hear about Beth's past. She is my friend, do you understand, the best friend I ever had. And it is more than that. She lives a different kind of life; a free life. I wonder if I shall ever be able to go back to Hull.'

'So do I. It keeps me awake at nights. When I remember what the old gossips did to your mother . . .'

'You have not understood me, Mr. Thornton. What worries me is whether I could bear Hull, not whether Hull would approve of me.

That's how I have changed, don't you see, thanks to Beth. I value myself now, I won't be worrying all the time about what the world would say. I think for myself.'

'And I admire you for it from the bottom of my heart. But you must be aware of the danger of your position. All kinds of dangers. There are rumours in town that you are an heiress, that that is how Forde contrived to persuade the Bentincks to receive you. And, worse than that —' He paused, searching for words. 'Men talk, you know, over a glass, over a bottle . . . There is talk about Forde . . . that he has outrun the constable . . . is here on a repairing lease . . . It's possible . . . These are bad times, Miss Pennam, and not just for bankers.'

'So what you are trying in your tactful way to tell me, Mr. Thornton, is that I must not flatter myself that you and the other gentlemen who are so civil as to call on Beth and me are motivated by anything but financial self-interest. Otherwise they would stay well clear of so contaminated a house. Well, thank you very much for your kind concern. I will think seriously about what you have told me, and how it should affect my behaviour. In the meanwhile, I have a million preparations to make for Segesta —' She moved a little forward as if to escort him indoors, and he thought again how she had grown up. His awkward, entrancing young friend was a very self-possessed young lady now, and he had done it all wrong.

'But that's the heart of it all,' he protested. 'That Segesta trip. You must see, Miss Pennam.' Formal now. 'How that must look in the eyes of the world. To be jaunting off on a party of pleasure with a group of young gentlemen —'

'Including you?'

'Well, of course, including me. Do you think I would let you go alone, Charlotte? Into such danger —'

'Danger? What do you mean?'

'Oh, there's talk about that too. There's talk about everything, here in Palermo. I never knew such a place for rumour and gossip.'

'Except perhaps Hull?'

'Oh, you are angry with me. Don't be angry with me, Charlotte?'

'Don't call me that. And don't try and prescribe my conduct to me either. I told you I had learned to think for myself, and I will.' She had got him indoors now, and rang for the servant. 'Show Mr. Thornton out, please.'

She was still simmering with rage when Beth returned from the palace.

'You've had a caller, I hear.' Beth was pulling off her gloves.

'Yes, John Thornton, full of starchy advice. I hope you don't think I should not have seen him alone, Beth. He seemed to!'

'And took the opportunity to say so.' Beth laughed. 'Having it both ways.'

'Oh, you do understand!'

'Of course I do, love, but what we are going to do about it is quite another matter. I tell you one thing: if a homeward bound ship were to come into harbour today I'd have you on it so fast —'

'Oh no you wouldn't. I wouldn't go. Besides — you need me just as much as I need you, remember.'

'More,' Beth agreed ruefully. 'I should not have brought you, love, and that is the long and the short of it. I should have known there are never second chances for women. I am doing you infinite harm, simply by my company, but what in the world can we do about it?'

'Nothing,' said Charlotte robustly. 'Nor do we need to. The people we care about don't seem to be in any sort of fuss about us, or if they are they conceal it admirably.'

'That's what worries me,' said Beth. 'What is going on under the surface. And, Charlotte, I have to tell you, I think word has got out somehow that you are an heiress.'

'Oh, yes, that's what John said. He kindly explained it's just my fortune they are all dangling after. That's all very well, Beth, except I don't believe it. What's it to the Falconis if I am rich or not, and you know how they have welcomed us into their circle. It can't just be because Lisa wants company in Segesta.'

'No, of course it can't.' Was this the moment for a warning about Segesta? She did not think so. 'And Peabody is clearly a very rich young man,' she said thoughtfully. 'Of course as an American he very likely sees things quite differently. It's disconcerting to talk the same language as someone, and yet feel you understand them so little.'

'You feel that too? It's the strangest thing, Beth, I've felt it from the moment we first met. He courts me, and listens to you. I sometimes catch him watching you with something that almost seems like dislike. But how could anyone dislike you, dear Beth?'

'Easily, love. If they thought I was a bad influence on you.'

'That's nonsense, and you know it. You've taught me to be my own woman and I shall never stop being grateful to you. You've shown me that even a woman can decide things for herself, make up her mind that she wants something, and go after it.'

'Which is not to say she will necessarily get it,' said Beth. She wished afterwards that they had managed to discuss von Achen's behaviour as well as Peabody's, but the Falconis were announced just then, come to finalise the arrangements for Segesta.

'There will just be time for the trip before this surprise festival for St. Rosalia,' Falconi told them. 'But it does mean that there must be no more delays. I am told that the King himself is coming to La Favorita for the festival. It will be a chance for you two ladies to get a glimpse of Ferdinand the Magnificent.' No mistaking the irony in his tone. 'He and the Queen are to appear together, I understand, at the entertainment she is to give down on the Marino. You will be singing for us, I trust, Miss Prior? We are all more than ever your slaves since last night's triumph. I don't think we have quite appreciated you, up to date, here in Palermo.' His eyes lit on her bracelet. 'But I see you have received the highest possible recognition. I expect the Queen will wish to present you to her husband while he is at La Favorita. You'll enjoy that; it is his Chinese Palace, you know, something like the one your Prince Regent is building for himself by the sea. You should certainly see it. But now: to our plans. We have decided, my wife and I, that the best thing will be to drive out to Monreale. There is a good road that far, built in the last century by Archbishop Testa, entirely at his own expense. It is only after Monreale that we shall need to introduce you ladies to our country mode of travel. We have made all the arrangements for the muleteers, and guards, to meet us at my friend's house in Monreale. There is no need of guards, of course, until there.'

'Is the centre of the island really so full of brigands that one must have guards?' asked Charlotte.

'I am afraid so, Miss Pennam. And the virtue of the guards is that they are hand-in-glove with the brigands. By hiring and paying the guards you automatically protect yourself from the brigands.'

'You mean,' said Beth, 'that it is really an elaborate form of blackmail.'

'I suppose you could put it like that, Miss Prior.' With a disconcerting look of quick dislike. 'What you must remember is that the peasants, here in Sicily, have been so ground down by unjust laws and iniquitous taxes that there is no way they can make a living from however rich a farmstead. What can they do but turn to banditry? We have to reform the system, Miss Prior. But, forgive me, I am boring you.'

'On the contrary,' she told him. 'You are

interesting me very much indeed. But, forgive me, I must leave Miss Pennam to entertain you. I promised to see Signor Bartolucci and discuss the programme for the Queen's entertainment.'

Bartolucci was appalled to learn that Beth proposed to be out of town for the days preceding the St. Rosalia festival. 'But, signora, how can I go on without you? This programme of sacred music you have suggested is admirable so far as it goes, but how can we manage without you there for the rehearsals? You know there is hostility to you enough in the company due to your great success — any chance will be taken to spoil your performance. And if you are not there for rehearsals —'

'I do see what you mean.' She made a business of thinking it over. 'I can promise nothing, signor. You must see that it would not do for me to make myself unpopular by withdrawing from the trip at this late date, but if a pretext were to present itself —' She left it at that, well aware that this would add something more to the volume of rumour that already surrounded them.

10

Charlotte grumbled a bit at having to drive instead of ride to Monreale, but had to admit that it made sense, granted the hot weather.

'You will be uncomfortable enough tomorrow,' Lisa Falconi told them, as they settled themselves in the open carriage, 'when we take to our *lettigas*. There is no way one can really enjoy being suspended in a sedan chair between two mules, very often with different paces. Make the most of today's comfort. Besides,' smiling, 'it is good to have you two to myself for once. I knew the gentlemen would all want to ride, so now I can ask you what the Queen really said to you the other day, dear Beth. If I may call you that?'

'Of course you may. But what do you mean? Her majesty was everything that was kind.' After some thought, Beth had decided to wear the ostentatious bracelet all the time. After all, it was probably safer on her wrist than anywhere else. She gave it a quick glance now, as if in answer to Lisa Falconi's question.

'Oh, yes, to congratulate you, of course. And, by the bye, I believe if I were you I would wear that pretty thing concealed after today. We do not want to put ideas into our escorts' heads. They are only half-tamed, you know.'

'Half guard, half brigand?' asked Charlotte, who was sitting facing the other two.

'Just so. And here we are at the Porta Nuova — so called because it was rebuilt in the last century after an explosion. The original design was by Michelangelo, I believe.'

'It's formidable.' Charlotte craned her neck to look back as they emerged on the far side of the gate. 'What are those two huge figures?'

'Saracens, I believe.' Carelessly. 'But, Beth, you have not answered my question.'

'Question?' Beth had hoped the subject would be dropped.

'My husband is politician enough to be interested in these secret audiences you have had with the Queen. He and his friends — the true friends of Sicily — are all a little anxious lest Lord William's brief visit may have done more harm than good.'

'He certainly does seem to have stirred things up,' agreed Beth. 'But dear Lisa — if I may call you that —' She thought the Countess looked surprised and not entirely pleased. 'You cannot possibly imagine that Queen Maria Carolina has been talking politics with me. I am afraid the top of her interest in me

is that she means me to sing at her entertainment for St. Rosalia.'

'A very odd business that. As if we had not
all overspent ourselves already on the July
festival. Did the Queen explain that at all?'

'Oh, yes,' said Beth. 'She thought it would
be a distraction for the public.' And was
relieved to see Forde and Falconi reining
in their horses on either side of the carriage.

'You ladies are talking so seriously,'
said Forde, 'that Falconi and I were afraid
the Countess might be forgetting to point out
the sights to you. He has been telling me that
we should have come much earlier in the year.
Then the Conca d'Oro is a paradise of colour
and scent, while now as you can see it is
burned dry by the sun.'

'Except for the orange and olive groves,'
said Falconi from the other side of the carriage. 'They give a welcome note of green to
the prospect, do they not? What did you think
of the Porta Nuova, Miss Prior?'

'I thought it very grand,' said Beth. She
wondered if he too was going to try and pump
her about what the Queen had said to her,
and was glad when Peabody sidled his horse
up on the far side of him.

'I am told that Archbishop Testa built an
ornamental fountain half way up his new
road,' he said. 'It is awkward for the ladies

to have us cluttering around them like this. Shall we make an assignation for up there? I expect you ladies will be glad of a cool drink from it by then. I know I shall.' Mopping his brow. 'I cannot tell you how wise I think you ladies are to be driving rather than riding. I expect to melt away any minute. While you ladies look cool and elegant as a —' He paused, searching for the *mot juste*.

'As a trio of cucumbers?' suggested Charlotte with a wicked look.

'Just so, Miss Pennam. But I had rather you said it than I did.' And then, to Falconi, 'It is hardly the weather for racing, Count, but I would be glad of your company, and your guidance, so far as the fountain.'

'Delighted.' But Beth did not think Falconi was. Forde had taken Peabody's hint and ridden on too, but their places were soon taken by Thornton and von Achen. 'We are really rather too well equipped with cavaliers,' she said dryly to Lisa Falconi. And then, leaning forward and adjusting her parasol, she smiled at Thornton. 'The other gentlemen have ridden ahead,' she told him. 'We decided conversation in motion was entirely too difficult and agreed that we would all meet at a fountain that the Archbishop whose name I cannot remember built halfway up the hill.'

'An admirable notion. We will look forward

to seeing you there. Are you coming?' he said across the carriage to von Achen, who had been leaning in to try and speak low to Charlotte.

Beth thought for a moment that von Achen was going to refuse, but a quick word from Charlotte settled it and the two men rode on together. A little silence fell in the carriage, all three ladies thinking, perhaps, that there was something a shade awkward about a party consisting of five gentlemen and three ladies. Satisfactory, but awkward. And not all that satisfactory, thought Beth, and wished she had decided how she was going to extricate herself and Charlotte from this expedition. She must just hope that an ideal pretext would present itself.

She was glad of the cool drink from the fountain, but not enormously impressed by the statues of children climbing up the rocks. 'Rather idealised children,' she said dryly to Peabody, who had handed her a mugful of water from the fountain. 'I prefer them real, with untidy hair and dirty clothes.'

'And maybe a dirty face, too, and a bandaged knee? I do so agree with you, Miss Prior. My children are all going to be little tearaways.'

'Have you consulted your future wife about this?'

'No. Nor about anything else, alas. I have to find the lady first.'

'I am sure there is someone, back in New Bedford, who would not agree with you.' Now why in the world had she said that?

He was laughing. 'No, ma'am. I missed the tide, you see. When I finished at Harvard, I was not ready to settle down in my father's counting house. I wanted to see the world first. My father is a reasonable man. When I asked him to let me go as supercargo on one of his clippers, he agreed with hardly a struggle. Well, it was the way he himself had started in life, he could hardly object. You see before you a veteran of two China runs, Miss Prior. I could bore you for days, if I so wished, with tales of Cape Horn and Chinese Mandarins.'

'But you do not so wish?'

'No more than you are talking all the time of sol fa and arpeggios, Miss Prior. But the thing is, a trip to the east takes time, and out of sight does tend to be out of mind. There was a young lady I had grown up with, and very charming she was too, and very much I loved her. Or so I thought. But, do you know, when I got home the first time, all laden with Chinese gifts for her, and found her married, I minded it very much less than I thought I would. But by then everyone else was paired off too. I thought about it for a bit, and was invited to make another trip to China. Well, I had enjoyed the first one. I went. But the second time I got back all my friends were starting their families. I was the odd man out indeed.'

'So you decided to continue your voyages of exploration.'

'It struck me as absurd to have been to Peking and not to Paris.'

'Paris rather than London, Mr. Peabody?'

'My dear Miss Prior, you are forgetting the threat of war between our two countries. Dearly though I would love to visit England, I do not at all wish to find myself incarcerated in your Tower of London, as an enemy alien.'

'Do you know,' shocked at herself, 'I had quite forgotten. Everything is so different here.'

'Different, yes.' Smiling at her. 'They have their own problems here. I do urge you always to remember that, Miss Prior.' And with that the conversation ended, as the little party prepared to move forward again up the steeply embanked road with its widening view of the valley, the mountains beyond, and finally the formidable bulk of William the Good's cathedral.

Peabody had left Beth with a great deal to think about. She had wondered, from time to time, whether he was not perhaps older than she had first thought him, now she was sure of it. It made it a little more puzzling that he should still be playing tourist. And how odd to find herself thinking of it in those terms. Was that perhaps just what he was doing? Was he, like John Thornton, really here on business? And, if so, what kind of business?

But Lisa Falconi was drawing her attention to the first straggling houses of the little town that had grown up along the ridge dominated by the great Norman cathedral. 'Our friend's house is close to the cathedral,' she explained. 'It is early yet. We can stop for a cool drink and then explore the cathedral and its precincts at leisure before we dine. Are you familiar with many of your English cathedrals, Miss Prior?'

'I am afraid not. St. Paul's, of course, and Westminster Abbey. And some of our provincial ones, when I have been on tour, but when one is on tour one does not have much time or strength for sightseeing.'

'I have never been in a cathedral,' said Charlotte.

'Not even —' Beth was about to say York Minster, stopped just in time and substituted 'Gloucester', and wished as she more and more often did that this masquerade was safely over.

'They say that Monreale is grander than

Gloucester,' said Lisa. 'But that the Saracen influence makes it entirely different. And here we are.' Furling her parasol. 'I am sure we will find our friends have left everything in readiness for us.'

It was a luxurious little house, but quite small, and Beth was more relieved than she quite liked when she found that she and Charlotte were to share a room.

'You won't mind?' asked Charlotte anxiously, taking off her shady hat.

'Frankly, love, I'm delighted. I don't think I snore.' She reddened, remembering a tease of Forde's. 'And I am quite sure you do not. I wonder how the gentlemen are arranged.'

'So do I.' Charlotte laughed. 'I can imagine some ruffled feathers, cannot you? I don't just see that high-nosed Forde happily sharing with Herr von Achen.'

'Or vice versa, perhaps,' suggested Beth. 'From things he has let fall, I have the feeling that von Achen is very much aware of his noble blood, however reduced his circumstances, poor fellow. I sometimes wonder if this does not in fact make life harder for him than it otherwise would be.'

'It gives him a great sense of duty,' said Charlotte repressively, and Beth felt a sharp twinge of anxiety. Just what had been going on between Charlotte and her tutor?

But it was time to join the gentlemen for the short walk to the cathedral. Lisa stayed behind, saying that she knew it well, and Beth, walking between Peabody and Falconi, was fascinated by glimpses of small town life. Ragged children, playing among scrawny hens in the gutter, came clamoring round them for alms and were briskly shooed away by Falconi. 'Oh, but please,' she protested. 'I would like to give them something.'

'Absolutely not, Miss Prior.' Falconi was firm. 'Or word will get out and the whole district will be at our heels. Believe me, just our coming will be worth a week's wages in the town.'

'But that is not the same as giving something myself,' she protested.

'I'm afraid he is right.' Peabody was beside her. 'Don't make an issue of it, Miss Prior.' He smiled down at the dark-eyed child who was holding out pleading hands to her, gave him something and spoke swiftly in unintelligible argot. 'There,' smiling at her. 'I have bribed the lot of them for you, Miss Prior. You can rest easy that they have had their Danegeld.'

'Oh, thank you. I don't suppose you have beggars in New Bedford?'

'Oh, yes,' philosophically. 'But we don't let them become our tyrants. Oh dear,' looking ahead, 'so it is true about the roof.'

'The roof?'

'I had heard that it had caught fire. Lightning, I suppose. I am afraid we are not going to get the best possible view of King William's masterpiece.'

Von Achen was saying very much the same thing to Charlotte as they reached the cathedral. 'I am surprised that the Falconis did not think fit to mention it,' he told her. 'They must have known. We will get only a restricted view, I am afraid, of the great dome, and its suffering Christ. Never mind,' bracingly. 'I am told that William's artist produced an even more moving version at Cefalu. Unfinished. The King dragged him away to work here before he had done there. This is not at all my idea of a religious building, I must say. Looking around him at the glowing mosaics. 'You should see Melk, Miss Pennam. There is true grandeur for you.'

'Interesting you should say that.' Thornton joined them where they stood just inside the great bronze doors of the cathedral. 'A friend of mine was there during the last peace, and said he found it truly vulgar. An orgy of blood-red marble.'

'Oh do let us stop talking, and just look.' Charlotte moved forward to take in the towering splendour of the smoke-darkened cathedral. Beth had moved a little further down the nave to gaze up, speechless, at the huge figure of Christ in the central dome. Tears stood in her eyes. She felt trivial, useless. I must sing better, she thought. I must do everything better.

'What's happened to Falconi?' Forde had come up behind her and she turned to him reluctantly, the moment's vision lost. 'I want to find the figure of St. Thomas à Becket in the mosaics, and he chooses this moment to abandon us.'

'I believe he is trying to arrange for us to see the treasury.' Peabody appeared from behind a pillar. 'For myself, I think I would rather stay and try and take in this magnificence.' He, too, was gazing up at the great Christ. 'It puts things into proportion somehow,' he said to Beth.

'You feel that too?'

But Forde had seized her arm. 'There's Falconi at last.'

The treasures were magnificent and Beth disliked them very much. Escaping at last into the cloisters, she was soothed by the sound of water from the fountain in one corner, and entranced by the variety of the slender columns that held up the arcade. 'I do hope I shall be able to remember all this when I get home to London,' she turned to Peabody, who was beside her again.

'We will never see anything like it again,' he said seriously. 'The whole thing . . . That Christ . . . This . . . I wish I could paint . . . To try and remember it — have a record.' He looked across the arcaded cloister to where the rest of the party were admiring the diaper work round the fountain. 'Miss Prior, you speak of home. I wish you would take your charming young friend, and go there.'

'To Palermo?' It chimed in disconcertingly with her own thoughts.

'No, Miss Prior, to London. On the first ship.' And then, looking past her, 'I believe no two of the columns are the same. A remarkable piece of workmanship, as I said.'

'Time to be going.' Forde had approached them silently across the cloister. 'Falconi says we must make an early night of it, and an early start in the morning.'

'Is there time for one more look inside the cathedral?' Beth asked, hoping for another moment alone with Peabody. And with the Christ.

But in the end, everyone came, and there was a great deal of talk about St. Thomas à Becket and the Normans' use of antique columns from the local temples for their cathedral. 'A great advantage they had over their cousins building in England,' said Falconi.

'But you will see the sad result of their depredations at Segesta tomorrow.' And an animated conversation broke out among the men over the problems of moving these vast marble pillars across country.

'And such rugged country at that.' But Beth was only pretending to listen. She could think of nothing but Peabody's warning.

'Miss Pennam.' Von Achen took Charlotte's arm to guide her past a pile of filth in the road. 'I must speak to you.'

'You are.'

'You know I mean alone. I hope you know what I want to say to you. It is intolerable to see you all the time and never to be able to speak. You see!' John Thornton had turned back to join them.

'I begin to think that everything the Falconis say about the state of things here in Sicily is true,' Thornton said. 'Did you ever see such wretched poverty, Miss Pennam? I am sure there is nothing like it on the Welsh border.'

He was teasing her again. 'No,' she told him. 'But I have heard things about the industrial north, Mr. Thornton, that I have not much liked. Of children working all hours in factories . . . crawling there from filthy hovels, falling asleep over their work, and being killed by the machines they are slaves to.'

'I am afraid you are quite right,' he said gravely. 'But I do not think the fact that we are not perfect ourselves should make us suspend judgment about others. One must continue to think, Miss Pennam.'

'Of course one must,' said von Achen. 'And anyway, these peasant children of yours, what else are they born to, but the toil of their hands? I only wish we had industry like yours in the Rhineland, my home, Mr. Thornton. What a difference it would make. There is nothing at all romantic, Miss Pennam, about starvation in a country hovel among the pigs.'

'It's not romance I am talking about,' she said crossly, 'but —' She hesitated for the word.

'Civilised living?' suggested John Thornton. 'Awareness of other people?'

'Yes. That's it!' She turned to him eagerly, grateful to be understood.

'And talking of civilised living,' he told her, 'here is Countess Falconi to welcome us to what I have no doubt will be a perfectly delicious meal, however much she apologises for it as a kind of picnic.'

He had summed up the situation admirably. They were all soon sitting down to a cold collation washed down by a chilled local wine, which Falconi explained would not even travel so far as Palermo. 'It is one of the pleasures of a trip to Monreale,' he told them. 'And it is light as a breeze; no chance of its spoiling your sleep.'

Beth did indeed surprise herself by falling instantly into sleep in the room on the terrace that she shared with Charlotte. But the wine that puts you to sleep also wakes you up. She woke, suddenly, she did not know how much later, and was aware of a disconcerting stillness in the room. No one else was breathing here.

She got up, threw a shawl around her, and moved to the lighter patch in the darkness that was the french window that opened on to the terrace. She had looked at it askance earlier on; now knew she had been right to do so.

The marble of the terrace was cool under her bare feet. Not a sound. It must be very late. The other bedrooms that also opened on to the terrace were dark and silent. The moon was rising behind the stark bulk of the cathedral. And where was Charlotte?

She moved forward, sure-footed on cool marble, to the edge of the terrace and leaned on the balustrade, peering down into darkness. Not silence. She could hear whispering down there, voices totally unrecognisable at this pitch. But one of them must be Charlotte's.

She could not remember about steps. There must be steps. She was responsible for Charlotte. She groped her way along the balustrade, feeling with feet and hands for an opening. Found it. Heard one of the whispers rise to a kind of squeak, started swiftly downward, lost her footing and fell, helpless and headlong.

11

When she came to herself, Beth was lying in bed, with Charlotte leaning anxiously over her. 'What happened?' For a moment, she could not remember.

Charlotte put a warning hand on hers. 'You fell, Beth dear. You must have been sleep-walking. I heard you get up; too slow to stop you. You fell down the terrace steps. I am so sorry!'

There was truth in that at least. Beth was remembering it all now. Did Charlotte hope she would not? Certainly, some fast thinking must have gone on, out there on the terrace. 'I've hurt my foot.' It was stiff and ached. 'How did you manage, Charlotte?'

'Mr. Peabody and Herr von Achen heard you fall. They are in the next room, you know. I think I must have screamed. Oh, Beth dear, how do you feel?'

'Not very strong.' Beth had had time to think. 'My foot hurts and my head feels strange.' It was true about the foot. 'Was I unconscious long?' Here was the chance she had hoped for, the chance to cancel the Segesta trip, and she was going to make the most of it, even if it did mean behaving like a fussy invalid.

'Just long enough for Mr. Peabody to carry you to bed,' Charlotte told her. 'He has gone now to rouse the Falconis and ask if there is a doctor in Monreale.'

And von Achen was presumably quickly taking off the day clothes that would have hinted at his assignation with Charlotte, who was herself wearing an extremely becoming negligée that could almost pass for a dress.

Beth put a hand to her brow. Or had she got it all wrong? Had the assignation been with Peabody? What was he wearing? She had to know. 'Charlotte —' But here was Lisa Falconi, full of anxious questions. The chance for private talk was gone.

There was no doctor in Monreale, but Lisa said there was a good one in Alcamo. 'He retired there from Palermo, just the other day. I am sure you would find the ride there in the *lettiga* restful, poor Beth; and then he could look after you, if you did not feel quite like going on to Segesta.'

'Nonsense.' Peabody was standing in the doorway, holding a lantern. He was fully dressed, Beth saw. 'After a fall like that, Miss Prior should not be moved until she feels very much more the thing. And when she is moved, it must be back to Palermo.'

'But all our plans —' protested Lisa.

'Could we not talk about it in the morning?' Beth made her tone plaintive, and disliked doing so. 'I am sure I will feel better after a night's sleep. But whether I shall be fit to go on . . . I am so very sorry, Countess.' She reached out to touch Charlotte's hand, busy with cold compresses. 'Charlotte?' It was at once request and command.

'Yes, of course you must get some sleep, poor Beth. Let us talk about it in the morning, Countess.' Charlotte was suddenly decisive. 'But you will be better in the morning, won't you, Beth?' she implored, as she settled her for the night.

'I don't know, love. You won't leave me?' Again it was as much command as request.

'Of course I won't.' Charlotte's hand was warm on hers. 'We'll talk in the morning.' They were both very much aware of the nearness of the other rooms on the terrace.

Sleep was all Beth's healthy body needed, and she woke feeling herself again, aside from a stiff and swollen right foot. Charlotte was still deeply asleep, and she lay for a while deciding how to make the best use of what had happened. It had been disconcerting to realise just how set Lisa Falconi was on going on with the trip. When she heard the first sounds of stirring along the terrace, she called softly to wake Charlotte.

'How do you feel?' Charlotte was across the room in an instant, bending eagerly over the bed. 'Oh, dear Beth, do say you feel better.'

'A little, but, Charlotte, I have to say it: I cannot possibly go on. Even if I felt like it, which I do not, it would not be right to do so, granted my commitment to Signor Bartolucci and the theatre. As a performer, one's duty to the stage must come first. I cannot risk making myself ill, or unable to walk. I'm sorry, love.' She saw how hard it hit Charlotte. 'Truly sorry.'

She hoped that that would be the end of the matter, but when she limped to breakfast on Charlotte's arm, and made her position clear, it was to have Lisa Falconi shift her ground. Of course she respected dear Miss Prior for remembering her commitment to the theatre. If she did not feel up to the trip, she must most certainly stay at Monreale and look after herself. The rest of them would ride on to Alcamo, send the doctor back to her, and return to pick her up after visiting Segesta. 'It is but to change our plans a little, my husband says, and it will work perfectly well. And the servants here will look after you admirably, Miss Prior. I promise you that. And of course I will watch over Charlotte as if she were my own sister.'

'You are too good. And I am ashamed to be such a weak fool, and spoil things for the rest of you. But — this sleep-walking! It frightens me. Suppose I were to do it again, and dear Charlotte not here to watch over me. I might have been killed last night. I keep thinking about that. I might have been killed. I must go back to Palermo, where my bedroom is safe.' How she hated behaving like a silly, frightened woman, but it must be done.

'Oh, very well.' Lisa Falconi was beginning to sound cross. 'If you feel like that, Miss Prior, we can perfectly well send you back to Palermo today in the carriage. My servants can be trusted to look after you as well as they would me. Then you can coddle yourself to your heart's content until it is time for you to figure at this festival of the Queen's. But you will surely not deny your young friend her once-in-a-lifetime chance of seeing the ruins at Segesta.'

Beth was aware of eyes fixed on her. The whole party was suspended, waiting to hear what she would say. She drank coffee, thought for a minute, put a hand to her brow. 'You will think me a fool of a nervous female,' she said. 'That fall last night shook me badly, but not so much as the idea does that I walk in

210

my sleep. Charlotte, dear,' she looked across the table at Charlotte, 'is it asking too much to ask you to come back with me?'

What could Charlotte say? But Beth, glancing this way and that, was deeply interested in the various expressions of the rest of her audience. They were all there, all watching, all listening, all waiting.

'Oh, Beth —' Naturally, she knew as well as Beth that the plea of fear of sleep-walking was false. But she could hardly say so. She took a deep breath, made up her mind. 'Of course I'll come back with you, dear Beth, if you want me. I am so sorry, Countess,' to Lisa, who was looking furious now.

Her point made, Beth relaxed to listen to the babble of discussion that broke out. She found it enormously interesting. Von Achen, she saw, was looking even angrier than Lisa, and saying nothing. Peabody was keeping quiet too, and this surprised her. He was usually such a very positive young man. She remembered again that he had been dressed last night. How long would it be before she managed a safe word alone with Charlotte?

Forde surprised her very much indeed, by suggesting that the party split up. 'I know you for such an intrepid traveller, Miss Prior, that I am sure you will not mind going home with Miss Pennam and the servants. The

Count and Countess have taken such kind trouble to arrange this trip, and I know the Countess longs to see Segesta quite as much as I do. We will all undertake to describe it to you, I promise. If you are absolutely sure you are not able for the trip? I am told that there is something remarkably soothing about the motion of the *lettiga*. A little like a ship at sea.'

'And you remember what that does to me, Mr. Forde!' Her tone was sharper than she had intended, and she caught a quick, quizzical glance from the silent Peabody.

'I would be delighted to escort the ladies back to Palermo.' John Thornton spoke up. 'It has been on my conscience that I ought not to be away for so long. It would be a great pleasure to feel myself of use.'

'Thank you, Mr. Thornton.' Beth smiled at him, and could not help a side glance at Forde.

But Lisa Falconi broke in at this point to make it brutally clear that she had no intention of going on without the support of another woman. Which cast an interesting light, Beth thought, on her readiness to leave her alone, either here or at Alcamo. There was clearly one law for countesses and another for actors. But what was surprising about that?

Forde had crossed the room to bend over

her. 'I know you for such a trouper, Miss Prior. Look at the disappointed faces around you. Look at poor Miss Pennam! Are you absolutely sure?' His look was a personal plea.

'Yes, Mr. Forde, absolutely sure.' And that, at last, seemed to settle the matter. Beth knew herself in disgrace with most of the party, and there was nothing to do but bear it. Charlotte looked miserable, von Achen looked like a thunder cloud, and Lisa's tone towards her had changed entirely. There was, suddenly, a great gulf between them.

'You must forgive my wife.' Falconi made a point of helping Beth back to her room. 'She has wanted to make this expedition for so long; and she is a child to disappointment, I am afraid. But she will get over it, Miss Prior, you are not to be minding.'

'Thank you.' She was relieved, and interested, to find Lisa friendly again when they all set out on the disappointed drive back to town.

Beth pleaded headache, and sat silent. By the time they reached Palermo she had decided to play the invalid for the few days the trip would have lasted; could not decide what to say to Charlotte. There must be a scolding for that secret assignation. With von Achen? With Peabody? If only she knew. But there must also be an explanation of her own behaviour. The excuse about sleep-walking would not do for Charlotte, but neither could she tell her about the Queen's warning. Arriving at last, it seemed only common sense to tell their attendant cavaliers that she wanted no visitors for a while, but it got her a reproachful look from Charlotte.

She was anxious about Charlotte. She had noticed that she had eaten no breakfast, and had a horrid feeling that she had been quietly sick the minute they got home. But her own foot was stiff; her head did ache; she felt as if she had not slept for days; it was wonderful to be back in her own room. She would rest for a moment, then have it out with Charlotte, doors and windows safely closed. But sleep overpowered her.

She woke, with a start, to gathering dusk, and rang for her maid. Miss Pennam had gone riding, the girl told her, with a look at once complicit and disapproving.

Charlotte and von Achen had left their grooms far behind and reined in their horses to look at the sea. 'It breaks my heart to have offended you,' he told her. 'You must blame my passion; your beauty; the moonlight . . .' He blamed himself, savagely, for having frightened her into betraying them. For a fatal moment, on that moonlit terrace, he had forgotten that she was not one of the easy Sicilian girls he was used to. 'Forgive me?' He put everything he had into the plea.

'Of course.' She surprised him. So it was going to be easy after all, the chance merely postponed. 'You have to forgive me too, Herr von Achen,' she went on. 'I am ashamed . . . I did not understand — did not know what I was doing. Playing at love! I'm grateful to you really . . . You made me realise . . . I am so sorry. I don't love you, you see. Don't want to marry you. I've been a fool. I am so very sorry.' She was frightened now by what she saw in his face.

But it passed in a moment. 'You make me more ashamed than ever,' he told her. 'I have frightened you indeed, dear child. We will be master and pupil again for a while, shall we not? Dear friends and companions, until you can find it in your heart to forgive me.' He had switched to German to underline his position as tutor. His brain was racing, searching for new plans, new expedients, anticipating the fury of his fellow conspirators. But they would salvage something out of this disaster, he was sure of it. It might mean waiting until the Rosalia Festival, but there was sure to be a chance then, if he could keep the wretched girl in hand. Only a week. The others would just have to wait a week.

215

Charlotte had been quiet for a moment, gazing at the sea. Now she turned to look at him very steadily, dark eyes opaque under the heavy brows. 'No, I'm sorry,' she said again. 'One can't ever go back, can one? It's been all a dream, hasn't it? A dream of love. A girl's dream of love. Unreal. You don't love me, Herr von Achen. You told me that, last night, more clearly than words could do. It's all been a charade, so far as you are concerned, and now we have stopped playing.' She held out her hand. 'Goodbye, Herr von Achen. And, thank you. You have taught me a great deal.'

For a wild moment, he actually thought of seizing her, throwing her across his saddle, carrying her off. Not impossible. Her groom was in his pay, as well as his. Something must have changed in his face; he saw fright in hers, and turned at the sound of a cheerful voice.

'There you are,' said Nathan Peabody. 'I have been looking all over for you two.' And then, 'What's the matter, Miss Pennam?'

'I'm sorry,' said Charlotte. 'I'm going to be sick.'

It was Nathan Peabody who helped her dismount, held her head, mopped her up, and finally said, 'Well, do you think that is all?' as if it were the most natural business in the world.

'I think so. I do thank you, Mr. Peabody. I am so sorry —' She looked about her.

'He's gone,' said Peabody without emphasis. 'I do not think illness is just his line. I hope you don't mind?'

It was more than a formal question, and she gave it the answer it deserved. 'Not in the least, Mr. Peabody. I am just so grateful to you. I've been all kinds of fool . . . I'm so glad you came.'

'We're all fools when we are young, Miss Pennam. It's part of growing up; being a fool, and realising it.'

'Oh, you do understand.'

'I hope so. But are you well enough to start home? I am afraid Miss Prior may be quite anxious about you by now.'

'She sent you?'

'She certainly did.'

Beth had hardly seen Peabody leave on what she horribly feared might be a vain search, when Forde appeared, ostensibly to ask how she was.

'Oh, better, thank you.' She dismissed her state of health as of no interest. 'I am only sorry to have spoiled everyone's pleasure. I am afraid you are not best pleased with me. There was more to that trip, was there not, than met the eye?' No use worrying about

Charlotte, but odd to feel such confidence in Peabody.

'There did seem to be considerable overtones to it,' Forde conceded. 'But how did you come to know that?'

'Oh, I can see through a pane of glass as well as the next man — or woman.' She was not going to tell Forde about the Queen's warning. More and more, she was aware of things he did not choose to tell her. Well: two could play at that game.

'You're right, as usual. This island is a perfect hotbed of conspiracy. We thought, Fagan and I, that we might learn something of the plotters and their plots, from what happened on that curious trip. And now all we know is that you have taken to sleep-walking, which is an odd come-out for you, my dear Beth.'

'Not really your dear Beth, am I, just now?' she challenged him. 'I'm sorry if I have upset your and Mr. Fagan's plans, but it seemed to me too good a chance to cancel that ill-fated trip. How was I to know that you had your own spy-catching hopes attached to it, since you did not choose to tell me. I thought we were to be partners in this enterprise, you and I.'

'And so we are. And as your partner I have to tell you that that tale of sleep-walking is not going to hold water for an instant, here in gossipy Palermo. That's why I came to-night, to warn you. I wouldn't like to see you hissed off the stage, dear Beth.'

Would he not? She was horrified not to be quite sure of this. 'But why should I be? It's just as good a story as any one of the Sicilian ladies would use.'

'Ah, but you are not a Sicilian lady.'

'No, I am not, am I? I am an actress with not much reputation to lose.' She was angry now, and it did her good. 'Are you trying to tell me that I am becoming a liability to you?'

'Nothing has gone as we intended, has it? I begin to think this island is bewitched. People do the strangest things. Look at Lord William, flouncing off like that; it has made things enormously difficult for poor Lady William. And I don't quite know what I am going to do when these stories about you reach her ears, my poor Beth.'

'Oh, that's the trouble, is it? I do see. How very awkward for you, Gareth.' She wondered if it might not be the last time she called him by his first name, and felt enormously sad. Perhaps he was right. Perhaps there was something strange and dangerous in the air of this island. 'I suppose I am just going to have to hope that the Queen's continued patronage, on which I believe I can count, will outweigh any disapproval of Lady William's. The Queen is Queen, after all, though you would hardly have thought so from Lord William's behaviour to her.'

'You feel so sure of her support?'

'I think I do. I certainly hope I do, because I can see no way of changing that sleep-walking story without doing infinitely more harm than good. I'm afraid I will just have to brush through it as best I may, and, one thing, I really do not expect to be hissed off the stage, here in Palermo. Not after the other night.'

'I do hope you are right. Because of course anything that affects you will also affect your engaging young friend. I take it you are hoping she and that rich young American will make a match of it, and solve all her problems for her.'

'Nothing of the kind!' If she had been angry before, she was furious now. 'I never heard such nonsense. My plans, such as I have, for Charlotte go no further than returning her to her family restored to health. She is much too young to be thinking of marriage.'

'If that is what you think, perhaps you should be keeping her on a tighter rein. Where is she now, for instance? And what assignation of hers were you really covering by that tale of sleep-walking?'

'Oh dear,' she sighed. 'Was it so obvious?'

'Well,' tolerantly, 'to me, of course. Because I really did not imagine you would be having secret meetings with anyone but me, dearest Beth. So, which was it? Peabody or von Achen?' Smiling. 'I know it was neither Thornton nor myself, because we were sharing a room.'

'I'm relieved to hear it.' Had she really loved this man, who was teasing her so unkindly? What had happened to them?

But here were Charlotte and Peabody, and that was the end of the anxiety that had been distractingly gnawing at her throughout her conversation with Forde. Welcoming them, she thought Charlotte looked wretched, and was grateful when Peabody left almost at once, and contrived to take Forde with him.

'Oh, Beth,' said Charlotte, when they were alone at last, 'I've been such a fool. And I'm going to be sick again, too!'

Beth put her firmly to bed. Only then, when she was lying flushed but more tranquil against the pillows did she take her hand, and say, 'Now, tell me all about it, love. We're all fools once or twice; it doesn't too greatly matter, if we just recognise it.'

'That's what Nathan said. Oh, Beth, he was so kind. I do thank you for sending him after me. Do you know, for a moment, there, I thought I was in danger.'

'Danger?'

'We were out of sight of anyone but our grooms, von Achen and I. I've been such an idiot. You see, what he did last night, why I cried out, woke you . . . He was so rough, Beth. Horrid.' The dark brows drew together. 'It was the strangest thing. I found myself, suddenly, remembering John Thornton. So kind. Different. I just knew, all of a sudden, that it was all untrue, what Gustav had been telling me. He doesn't love me; it was all lies, Beth, wicked lies.'

'But, dear child, if you had seen that, why in the world did you ride with him today?'

'Because I was a fool. That's what I mean. I don't altogether blame myself for letting him deceive me in the first place. He's good at it. He's had a lot of practice, I rather think.' Colouring. 'But, today, don't you see, I thought I owed it to him to explain, to tell him why it had to be all over between us. After all, I had promised to marry him, Beth.'

'I'm ashamed of myself,' said Beth. 'A fine guardian to you I have been!'

'Well, you did send Nathan to rescue me,' said Charlotte, colouring again. 'He was splendid, Beth. I was so frightened. I'd told Gustav, you see . . .'

'Told him?'

'That I knew he didn't love me, that I couldn't marry him. He looked absolutely furious, Beth, and then I saw him glance back at our grooms, and I knew what he was thinking — that they were both in his pay. I could see right through him somehow. He was actually thinking of carrying me off. Abducting me! Gothic! But, Beth, real. With three of them, what could I have done? I was so frightened, I knew I was going to be sick. And then, there was Nathan!' She smiled, remembering. 'I was sick, Beth, and he was wonderful. So calm; so friendly; so kind. And when it was all over, Gustav had just vanished, and Nathan said I wasn't to be too hard on myself, and brought me home. Isn't he wonderful, Beth?'

'I'm glad I sent him,' said Beth.

12

To Beth's relief, Charlotte joined her cheerfully for breakfast next morning, and ate a little. She had convinced herself in the night that she had been merely imagining things when she thought von Achen was going to carry her off. 'Like a heroine in a melodrama,' she said scornfully. 'But I think I'll stop my lessons, Beth. I don't much want to see him after that night at Monreale. After being such a fool!'

'I doubt he'll come.' Beth was so glad to see Charlotte herself again that she decided not to say that she was inclined to believe in the melodrama. Charlotte was better; she was going to avoid von Achen in future; why frighten her unnecessarily? 'I think we'll take things quietly for a few days,' she said. 'Until we both feel really better.'

Charlotte submitted to this decree with a fairly good grace, though she was very much on the lookout for callers, Beth thought, and grew increasingly restless when none came.

'I did say I wanted to be left alone,' Beth reminded her.

'But surely Nathan — Mr. Peabody should come and enquire about me? I want to thank him properly,' Charlotte explained.

'I expect the rules of behaviour are quite different in the United States,' Beth told her.

'I doubt he bothers much about rules, after the venturesome life he has led. He told me the most amazing stories about the China trade on our way home. I was so busy listening, I never did thank him. I feel ashamed now. Could I write him a little note, do you think?'

'No, you most certainly may not. I am afraid we have given the town quite enough to talk about already, without starting writing little notes to young men. I just hope we don't find ourselves cut when we go to the *conversazione* next week.'

'Cut? You and I? You cannot be serious, Beth?'

'I'm not sure. I did write to Lisa Falconi — to thank her and apologise all over again for spoiling her trip. There has been no answer, no enquiry about my health.'

'Oh.' Charlotte looked so thoughtful that Beth rather wished she had not spoken, but on the other hand the child must be warned. And at least the improvement in her health continued. So did her grateful talk about Nathan Peabody and Beth was growing uncomfortably certain that she had fallen straight out

225

of one adolescent passion into another. And it would not do. She was absolutely sure it would not do. Despite the youthful good looks that had misled her at first, Nathan Peabody struck her as one of the most grown-up men she had ever met. Charlotte was a darling child, but she was still a child. She would not do for him, she would not do for him at all. Anyway, Nathan Peabody had told her his marrying days were past, and she thought he was probably right.

She did rather wish he would call, but all their cavaliers seemed to have taken her prohibition seriously, and she began at last to be anxious for news of what was going on in the town.

It came, two days before the *conversazione*, in the form of a royal summons. The Queen sent a page with an invitation to the two of them to call on her at La Favorita, the King's house a few miles out of town.

'I suppose he has come there for the Santa Rosalia Festival,' Beth said. 'A royal carriage is coming for us. I wonder what one wears for an al fresco entertainment at La Favorita.'

'One's best, I should think,' said Charlotte. 'Oh, Beth, I'm so glad! I thought the Queen would never invite me too! Will it be very grand, do you think?'

'Not if King Ferdinand has any say in the

226

matter. He is more likely to welcome us in hunting clothes. I shall be enormously interested to meet him.' And then she had an anxious moment, remembering something Gareth Forde had said, back in England, about King Ferdinand the Licentious, and hoping Charlotte did not catch his eye. Charlotte was quite better, eating again, and in tremendous looks.

They were both at their most elegant in pale muslins when the royal carriage came for them. Beth was delighted to be greeted by Flora Cottone, the lady-in-waiting who had taken her to the palace the first time she was summoned.

'I hope you will find the drive interesting,' Flora Cottone told Charlotte. 'We start out through the town, and it will give you a chance to see the preparations being made for the festival.'

And to be seen in a royal carriage, thought Beth, and was grateful to the Queen. 'We are so much looking forward to that,' she said. 'It is to be something quite out of the ordinary, I believe.' They had passed into town through the Porta Felice now, and while she looked at the wooden arches that were being built over the road to hold decorations, she was very much aware of people looking at them. The tale of the royal visit would be all over town by nightfall.

'Nothing to touch the usual festivities in July,' Flora Cottone told them. 'They go on for three days and leave us all quite worn out with pleasure. But this one will certainly give you a taste. The Queen has asked me to tell you that she has arranged places for you to watch the review of the royal guard, by the way. It takes place early, before the rest of the festivities.'

'Oh dear,' said Beth. 'Then I am afraid I shall not be able to attend. I have absolutely promised Signor Bartolucci that I will come to the morning rehearsal of the concert he is to give at the end of the day down at the Marino.'

'The Queen will be sorry,' said Flora Cottone. 'I know she counted on your presence.' She turned to Charlotte as they crossed the Ottangolo Square. 'Have you been this way before? We go out by the Porta Macqueda for Colli and the King's house. We shall pass my family's house on the way. A great many of the first families built their country houses on this side of town when the King built his. Perhaps on the way back you will honour us with a visit,' turning to Beth.

'We would like to, if there is time. Is that Monte Pellegrino we are beginning to see?'

'Yes. La Favorita is on the flat just under

the mountain. You will find it quite out of the ordinary.' Was she warning them to admire the King's favourite palace?

'In the Chinese style, I believe.' Beth remembered something Peabody had said. 'I confess I was never able to take to our Prince Regent's Chinese palace at Brighthelmstone.'

'Oh, you'll like La Favorita,' said Flora Cottone, and that was a clear instruction if ever there was one.

Quite soon they were turning in between sleepy lions at gates held obsequiously open. 'The King is a great farmer,' explained Flora Cottone as the carriage bowled along a broad road between well-tended olive and orange groves. 'He was experimenting with silk farming at Naples, I believe. If only he ever gets back there, as we must all hope he will. But what's this?' Startled.

A little group of men in hunting dress, carrying shotguns, had emerged from the olive grove that masked the precipice of Monte Pellegrino to their left. 'A prize! A prize!' The tallest of them stepped into the road and gestured to the driver to stop. Beth clutched Charlotte's hand. Could von Achen be hoping to attempt a kidnap here in the royal gardens?

But, 'It's the King!' Flora Cottone whispered, as the coachman pulled in his horses.

'A great honour. He will want to show you his improvements. You won't mind?'

'Of course not.' But she did. The footman had the carriage doors open now, and the steps down. There was nothing for it but to alight, be presented and say the proper things, aware all the time of the huge hooked nose dominating a countryman's tanned face, and the dark eyes that were looking her and Charlotte over. Like a pair of cows at the market, she thought angrily, and found that the little group had somehow resolved itself into couples and that she was walking with King Ferdinand while Charlotte followed behind with the young Prince Leopold, and Flora Cottone with another man whose name she had failed to catch. Well, at least it was a relief that she had drawn the King. Prince Leopold was his mother's favourite and in his teens still; Charlotte would come to no harm with him.

The King was leaning down to her from his great height, and she caught the smell of game, and man, from his hunting clothes. 'I know that you English ladies are all great walkers,' he told her in odd but understandable French. 'So I shall show you my latest improvements while the Queen is busy about her papers.' And he surprised her by plunging into knowledgeable talk about farming, and crop rotation. 'Not much use trying to apply it here in Sicily,' he went on. 'Except like this, immediately under the landlord's eye. They are such an idle set of dogs, our Sicilian peasants, that they would rather starve than work. Your peasants in England are quite another kettle of fish, I believe, except when they take up Jacobin ideas.'

She was tempted to tell him she was a peasant herself, but was almost breathless with adjusting her stride to his long one, and found it simpler just to agree with whatever he said.

'Now I am going to show you something you will like.' He took her by the arm, and whisked her suddenly on to a smaller path that led off at right-angles through an orange plantation, and she was shocked to realise that they had left the rest of the party far behind. 'It's my latest project and I fancy you will be as pleased with it as I am. Look!' They emerged from a fringe of ilex and laurustinus into a clearing with a Chinese pagoda in the centre. Recently planted shrubs were wilting around it, and the blue and crimson paint was so new it hurt the eye. 'I know an amazon like you will not mind a trifling smell of new paint.' He led her across the clearing to the open doors of the pagoda. 'Yes,' looking in. 'All's right and tight and ready for us.' A table was set with bottle and glasses, and behind it an elegant chaise longue was heaped with cushions. But of the servants who must have made these preparations, there was no sign.

'But the others.' She hung back in the doorway. 'Miss Pennam —'

'No need to be fretting about her, my dear. My son Leopold's a mother's boy; butter wouldn't melt in his mouth. She'll be safe enough with him, if that's what you want for her. And no need to be worrying that they will surprise us, either. Nobody comes here without my invitation. So come in, my beauty, and let us drink to my new pagoda, and our happiness.'

'But, your majesty —' She watched with horror as he closed the doors behind them. 'You don't understand. I'm not —'

'Oh yes you are,' he told her. 'The Queen is not the only one with spies. I know all about you, m'dear. Turned Beau Brummell away, didn't you? And quite right too.' He was pouring wine into priceless Venetian glasses. 'Saving yourself for me? I rather think not. So who was it the other night at Monreale? You'll find things more comfortable here.' He handed her a glass. 'So, here's to us.' A large, brown hand came idly out to cup a breast, too easily reached under the light muslin.

'No!' But it had been a long time. She felt her body begin to betray her. 'Your majesty! No!' The hand continued its explorations. In a moment, she would be lost. Lost? He was bending over her now, and she got again the smell of man, and dog, and garlic. 'No!' She boxed his ears. Hard. And was terrified. She saw the thoughts chase each other through that simple mind: surprise, rage, lust. He was going to rape her. He was roaring with laughter.

'What a vixen,' he said. 'You really mean it?'

'I really mean it, sire.'

'I'm sorry,' he said. 'Have some wine.'

'Thank you.' They drank a silent toast.

Then, 'What a disappointment,' he said. 'I think we had better find the others, Miss Prior.' And that, amazingly, was that. He talked about tunny fishing as he set the same cracking pace through the plantations to a grotto in the side of the mountain, where the rest of the party were admiring what Beth privately thought a perfectly hideous triton and attendants all made of shells and bits of glass. 'I wanted to show Miss Prior my new pagoda,' said the King carelessly. 'But the smell of paint was too strong to be borne.'

The Chinese pavilion, when they got there, was quite as outrageous as Beth had expected, and all hung about with bells, which tinkled, not very musically, in the light breeze. But she felt she owed the King unstinted praise, and gave it lavishly. It was easier when they got inside. The Queen was waiting for them in an eastern suite decorated with Morland prints and was looking predictably stormy. The tale of the strong paint got Beth a sharp glance, but what the Queen saw must have satisfied her and the little party moved amicably enough to the upstairs dining room, where it was easy to admire the mechanism that brought a loaded table up from below, and thus dispensed with the need of servants. 'Not that we are talking secrets today,' said the Queen, with another of her sharp glances, and turned the conversation to the forthcoming festival.

It gave Beth the chance she had wanted to explain that she was desolated not to be able to attend the royal review.

'Oh, but you must,' said the Queen. 'Everyone will be there.'

One does not contradict royalty, but Beth promised herself that she would be the exception. She absolutely owed Bartolucci that final rehearsal. To make amends, she agreed readily enough to sing for the little party when they had disposed of a cold collation and the table had vanished to reappear with fruit and ices. 'What shall I sing for your majesties?' she asked them both.

'Oh, a love song by all means,' said the King. 'And not too sad a one either, signora.'

She was beginning to like him very much. In England, she thought, he would be a country gentleman, running his estates, loved by his tenants, visiting London once in a blue moon when he felt it his duty to vote in the House.

'I have the very thing, your majesty,' smiling at him. 'Stephen Storace wrote it for me to sing with his sister Nancy. It's a reply to a song of Mr. Gay's from *The Beggar's Opera*: "How happy could I be with either were t'other dear charmer away". Instead of a man, it is two girls, discussing their various lovers, and dismissing them with the refrain, "Change Partners in Love's Dance". Stephen worked out a version we could either of us sing alone. You will not mind if I sing it in English?'

'Of course not,' said the Queen. 'The English are our dear friends, are they not?'

It was a catchy, dance-like tune, and Beth had often sung it as an encore when an audience would not let her go. How strange to find herself singing it here in Sicily, with a royal audience. The King was delighted and demanded more, but the Queen, she saw, had vanished. 'A servant came, while you were singing,' Charlotte told her afterwards. 'I heard the name Castroni. The Queen looked angry, I thought.'

Reappearing to bid them farewell, the Queen reiterated her insistence that Beth and Charlotte attend the review that was to open the Rosalia Festival, and Beth was reduced to half-lying promises. 'You really cannot say "no" to a Queen,' she told Charlotte ruefully, safe back in the seclusion of their terrace.

'Specially not that Queen,' said Charlotte. 'She frightened me a little, Beth. She put me in mind of my grandmother; perfectly reasonable most of the time, but blind bigoted in some respects. Almost mad?' And then, 'Goodness, I wish I had realised that sooner about Grandmamma! But, Beth, seriously, that's not a woman to be trifled with.'

'I should rather think not. I wish I knew what to do for the best.' She must have advice, but from whom? She rather thought Forde was avoiding her, and was thinking of swallowing her pride and asking him to call when Nathan Peabody appeared.

'Thornton and I think it is a little cooler,' he told them. 'We are hoping to persuade you two ladies to come for a ride with us, in the fresh of the evening, since there is no performance at the theatre tonight.'

'Oh, do let us, Beth.' Charlotte was blushing.

'If your foot is better, Miss Prior, I am sure the air would do you good.' He was teasing her, she thought. He knew perfectly well she had not hurt her foot so badly as she had pretended. 'And Thornton and I long to hear what you thought of the King's Chinese palace.'

And to talk without the chance of eavesdroppers. 'Yes, my foot is remarkably better, thank you,' said Beth. 'We will be with you directly.'

She watched with interest and a touch of amusement, as Nathan Peabody let Charlotte stammer out her thanks for coming to her rescue, threw her up on to her horse, and handed her over to John Thornton.

'High-handed in the extreme,' she told him, as he helped her to mount in her turn. 'I can see you are the experienced brother of many sisters, Mr. Peabody.'

'Well, yes, I am, and an uncle of many nieces by now. It is a sobering business for a man. It certainly makes one feel one's age. But if I live to be a thousand I shall never understand the workings of the female mind. What in tarnation's name possessed you to go off alone with King Ferdinand?'

'You are well informed, Mr. Peabody.'

'The whole town knows it.'

'Then I hope the whole town will tell me

how I might have avoided walking alone with the King, granted he wished me to. You Americans may know how to say no to royalty, Mr. Peabody, but it is not something I am trained to.'

'But you came to no harm?' This was the heart of the matter.

'Will you believe me if I say so? And, more important, will the whole town?'

'That's just what they are saying; that you turned him down, and kept him sweet, and nobody understands it.'

'Frankly, Mr. Peabody, no more do I. And I think it is time that we joined the others. My reputation can hardly stand any more *tête-à-têtes*.'

'Damnation!' A hand on her bridle. 'That's not what I brought you out to say. Not what I meant at all. Miss Prior, I do beg you to be deathly careful. There's danger in the air, danger for you British. Lord William has left a powder keg behind him here; it needs only the fuse to light it. Did you ever hear of the Sicilian Vespers?'

'When they turned on the French years ago? Yes?'

'Years ago, perhaps, but they still speak of it as their finest hour. I've heard them. And "turned on" is something of an understatement. They killed the French, man, woman and child. It was a massacre, Miss Prior, a massacre that went on for weeks, until there were no more French to be found in the island. Remember that, next time someone speaks of it as a glorious moment in Sicilian history. And think what might happen to you English now if the Queen were to sell out to the French.'

'But she hates Napoleon.'

'He is married to her granddaughter. And, do you not think she hates Lord William too?'

'I know she does.' She looked back at Charlotte and John Thornton. 'You don't really think . . .'

'I am desperately afraid, Miss Prior. If there were a British ship in harbour, I would see you two on to it. I would see you on to an American one, come to that. Our countries may be on the verge of war, as I very much fear, but you would be much safer there.'

'You sound very sure.'

'I am sure. I do earnestly beg you to believe that. I am telling you this, partly to warn you, and partly in the hopes that you may have some influence with the Queen.'

'I? Absurd.'

'I'm not so sure of that. Poor woman, you have to be sorry for her. She is so very much alone. Her husband is a cipher; her daughter and her husband have taken the British side.

I wonder what would happen to them . . .
It was touch and go, you know, whether the
Duke would be arrested when the five barons
were.'

'Her own son-in-law? And daughter? And
their little boy?' But she was remembering
what Charlotte had said about the Queen.
'Charlotte thinks she is a little mad,' she told
him.

'Acute of Charlotte. A little mad and very
dangerous. I am taking it for granted that you
will pass on this warning to your friend Forde,
though I would as soon you kept my name
out of it. Perhaps if the Queen sees the British
taking extra precautions it will make her think
again.'

'If it does not precipitate the explosion.'

'I think that is the risk we have to take.
Miss Prior, I do beg you, if you get the chance,
take it. Try and turn her mind.'

Try and turn a whirlwind. But what was
the use of saying it?

13

Left to ride with John Thornton, Charlotte
was both disappointed and embarrassed. It
was the first time she had been alone with him
since the night at Monreale, and she found it
awkward enough. Here he was, behaving as if
nothing had happened, making polite remarks
about the weather and the view. She found it
maddening. She looked back; the grooms
were far behind, and anyway she was sure
they spoke no English. 'Oh, come on, John,
ask it,' she burst out. 'You must want to know
what really happened the other night.'

'Only if you want to tell me.' He, too, had
glanced quickly first forward to the other two
and then back to the grooms. 'It is none of
my business, after all. Except as an old friend
of your family.'

'Do you write to my parents?'

'Not so far. Nor did I see them before I
came away. It was all arranged in such a hurry,
in London. Have you written to them?'

'No, I haven't.' She was suddenly
conscious-stricken. 'They will be worrying,
I am afraid.'

'I am sure Miss Prior has written. I hope you realise just how much you owe her, Charlotte. And, yes, since you have mentioned that unlucky night at Monreale, there is something I want to say to you about it. Your assignations with von Achen are entirely your own affair — though a shocking mistake, in my opinion — but to use Miss Prior as cover was a disgraceful thing to do. Her reputation cannot stand it, don't you see? Forde has been keeping away, has he not? And the talk in the salons has not been pleasant. The Queen's invitation might have done something if it had not been that the King had heard the talk too. So now there is still more talk. I have to say that it was a miracle she managed to extricate herself . . . If she did.'

'Of course she did.' If Charlotte was sure of anything, she was sure of this. But he had opened her eyes to what she had done to Beth, and she did not like what she saw. 'I'm ashamed,' she went on. 'Truly ashamed. I never thought. It all happened so fast, that night at Monreale. I was desperate. And she never said a word of blame. Oh, John, what can I do to set things right?'

'Nothing, I think. Done's done. Anything you say now would only make matters worse. He thought for a moment. 'Unless of course you were to announce your engagement to von

Achen. Tell the whole story. And I should hate to see you do that.'

'I should hate to do it. That's all over. I've been a perfect idiot, but it is all over.'

'I'm glad. And do write to your mother.'

'Yes, I will. I'm ashamed about that too. I was all wrong about her, you see. My grandmother had told me a pack of wicked lies. Beth set me straight about it. But I can't tell mother what I thought: it was too horrible. So I've put off writing.'

'She will be worrying. Even if Miss Prior has written, she is bound to be worrying.' His tone was reproachful, and she knew she deserved it.

'I'll write tonight. What a mull I've made of things.' She was looking ahead to where Peabody had put a hand on Beth's bridle. 'It would serve me right —' She paused. 'Could you not tell Mr. Forde the truth, John?' she asked. 'In strictest confidence.'

'You're not thinking! How could I tell him without explaining who you are, and then all that Beth has done for you goes for nothing. I like Gareth Forde well enough, but I would not trust him with a secret. Nor do I think it would do any good. It's not the truth he cares about, but what the public thinks. His prime consideration is to keep in with the Bentincks, and you know what a starchy lady she is. If she cuts the connection, don't think he won't. He cares only for himself. If you ask me, Miss Prior is better off without him. What a woman! It would have been worth coming to Sicily, just to hear her sing Violante the other night. There were tears in my eyes at last, and I was not the only one. I hope you realise how lucky you are.'

'Oh, I do!' But she was oddly disconcerted, just the same, and glad when she saw Beth and Peabody turn to ride back towards them. And Thornton, watching her colour rise and her eyes sparkle as they approached, came to a disconcerting conclusion of his own.

But there was one thing he could do. When he and Peabody were riding home after leaving the two women, he said, as casually as he could manage, 'By the way, I made bold to ask Miss Pennam what really happened at La Favorita the other day and she absolutely supports the story of the brief visit and the strong smell of paint.'

'I am sure she does, and so must we.' It was not quite an answer, but they rode on very well satisfied with each other.

Beth was glad to be appearing at the theatre before the next *conversazione,* so that she would have a chance to get the feel of the public. In fact, her greatest anxiety was for

Charlotte. Normally, when Beth sang, Charlotte joined the Falconis in their box, but there had still been no word from Lisa. It came at the eleventh hour, in a note not to Beth but to Charlotte, confirming that they would send the carriage for her at the usual time. There was no message for Beth.

It sent her off to the theatre in a great worry, and the eager questions of her fellow actors did nothing to reassure her. 'You're the talk of the town, my dear,' Bartolucci told her. 'I just hope it works out for the best. I am sorry now that I did not follow my first instinct and have you sing Violante again tonight, to confound the lot of them.'

'I'm glad you did not.' She only had a small part, with one tremendous aria. 'I am not sure I could have carried it.'

'I think you can carry anything, signora.'

She could only wish she shared his confidence, but when she made her first entrance, it was to a wave of applause that stopped the performance.

After that, it all seemed easier, and she was happily aware of singing her best. 'Everyone is here,' Bartolucci told her, when the curtain fell at last. 'I'm told that stiff Lady Bentinck was applauding with the rest. By the way, you have not forgotten our final rehearsal for the Rosalia Festival? There is talk in town of an invitation to the royal review. But we must have that rehearsal; there is no possible way I can change the time.'

'Of course not. I promise I will be there. Don't listen to the talk of the town, Signor Bartolucci.' But she knew that what she had just said would be town talk tomorrow, or more likely, tonight, on the Marino.

Changing out of her costume, she wondered how she and Lisa Falconi would meet. It was going to be more than awkward if Lisa meant to cultivate Charlotte and cut her. So it was a relief to find Falconi himself awaiting her at the stage door. 'I am to escort you to the *conversazione*,' he told her. 'And make an apology for my wife. She is an idle, good-for-nothing girl and tells me she never answered your last note. But you are going to forgive her, are you not?'

'Of course I am, signor. I am only grateful to my good friends for standing by me so faithfully.' She was glad to have the chance to say this.

'I think we should be apologising to you, Miss Prior, for the behaviour of someone we will not name. I am only glad it all ended so well. I am sure you will understand better now why we are so eager for a constitution, some check on absolute power.' He had been leaning close, to speak low, as he guided her through the crowd to the carriage, now helped her in. 'You sing better every time I hear you.' She thought he meant it.

The *conversazione* was more crowded than usual, and she felt herself at once the focus of all eyes. It is not everyone who is said to have rejected the advances of a king. She wondered how King Ferdinand felt about it all, and comforted herself by the thought that he probably just found it comic. Surprising how much she had liked that boorish man.

No time to be thinking of that now. Falconi had her firmly by the arm and was guiding her through the crowd to where his wife was talking to Lady William. He was plumping her right into it, she thought, and was grateful. She also thought, for a breathless minute, that Lady William might turn away, but if she had considered it, she changed her mind, and they were soon carrying on a civil, uninteresting conversation about the performance.

Forde joined them almost at once and she wondered bitterly if he had been waiting to see what Lady William would do. He soon had her alone, on the pretext of finding her an ice. 'I am delighted to see you well enough to sing.' He had her in a corner by the ornate table where refreshments were served. 'I trust that means that you are receiving again.'

'Of course I am.' Surely he knew that she would have received him at any time. How far apart they had drifted and how strange not to mind it more.

'Then if I may, I will call tomorrow, and hope to find you alone.' And that was an instruction, if ever there was one.

'I shall do my poor best,' smiling at him. Had she really been intending to discuss Peabody's warning with him? She thought that she should be glad he had not called sooner. 'I think the Duchess of Orleans is wanting a word with you,' she told him now, and turned away to talk to John Thornton, whom she found most timely at her elbow.

But if she did not mean to talk about Peabody's warning with Forde, with whom could she? The answer was obvious: no one. And where did that leave her? Back at home, she said an absent-minded good night to Charlotte, and retired to bed, but not to sleep. This was the first real chance she had had to think about what Nathan Peabody had said to her, and the more she thought, the more it frightened her. Because she knew that he had been afraid himself. She knew so little about him. He was American: he was older than he looked, but, she thought, still young in his enthusiasms. He had come to Sicily by way of France and Naples. And he had been fully dressed that night at Monreale. Charlotte had not been the only one to keep an assignation there. And what he had learned had frightened him. He must have brought messages. From Napoleon? From Murat? Very likely from both. Secret messages to the Queen? He had been very much the prime mover of the whole Segesta trip, she remembered. And at his secret meeting — with Castroni, perhaps, or his representative — he had learned enough of the Queen's plans to frighten him, to make him speak of the Sicilian Vespers.

Face it. They had massacred the hated French all those years ago. This time would they be throwing in their hands with the French and massacring the English?

She suddenly realised that she even knew when it would happen, which was obviously more than Peabody did. The Queen had insisted that she and Charlotte come to the review of the royal guard. That must be when it was planned for, and the Queen's party would be protected. Presumably a simultaneous rising would deal with the British troops at Messina. Deal with. Kill. She faced it coldly. And Peabody wanted her to turn the Queen's mind!

If it could be done, it must be done soon, with time for a message to reach Messina. But how? Racking her brains, she thought of the alternatives. If she were to warn Forde, she knew well enough what would happen. He would use the information to disgrace the Queen. He might even let the attempt be made, with preparations ready to scotch it. Then the massacre would work the other way. The pretence of Sicilian independence would be ended, and the Queen would be lucky if she was only banished to Vienna.

She did not want to tell Forde. She did not trust him; that was the long and the short of it. Peabody was right. An appeal to the Queen was the only hope, but how to get to the Queen? It was one thing to be summoned to the palace, quite another to ask for an audience. Who could speak for her? Not the Falconis, they were of the British party themselves, would have no influence with the Queen. She thought of the Duchess of Orleans, but felt her a cipher, manipulated by her husband, who had also thrown in his lot with Bentinck and the British. How odd not to be able to turn to the very people who were threatened, because she could not trust them either. But she had seen enough of the lord-of-creation behaviour of British officers in Palermo to know that she could not.

Flora Cottone. It came to her as the first light began to seep through the shutters. Flora

Cottone had pointed out her family's country house on the way to La Favorita. There had not, of course, been time to call on the way back. She and Charlotte would call on them, and they would start early, so as to be out when Forde paid his threatened call. Threatened? Yes, she thought that was the word.

'The Cottones?' Charlotte was surprised but compliant. 'Yes, of course I remember about them, but, Beth, why?' She very obviously had other plans for this fresh September morning and Beth found herself wondering what they were. But there was no time for that now.

'Because I want to,' she said uncompromisingly. 'And, Charlotte dear, I want to start early, before there is a chance of callers. Please.' Charlotte was not always the most punctual of people, particularly when her heart was not in it.

'If you really want to go.' Charlotte was still meek from her scolding by John Thornton the day before, and made a sacrifice of her hopes that Peabody would call.

So they set out in good time for the drive through the town to the Porta Macqueda and the road to Colli. The preparations for the Rosalia Festival were finished now, arches overhanging the road all along the way were trimmed with artificial flowers and lights to be lit when the great day came. If we all live till then, thought Beth, and realised for the first time that the Queen must have planned this whole festival for the chance it gave her to get loyal troops into the town for the royal review. And that was not a cheering thought.

The Villa Cottone was a startling red building set well back from the road, and Charlotte was still giggling over the statues that ornamented its entrance as Beth sent in their names. 'Hush,' she said repressively, and Charlotte looked startled, and suddenly sober.

The Marchesa Cottone was sitting among a crowd of children on a terrace at the back of the villa, where a cool breeze came in from the sea. 'I am afraid my daughter is not here,' she explained, after the first greetings. 'She is in attendance on her majesty at La Favorita all this week. She will be sad to have missed you.'

'I was afraid of that,' said Beth. 'I do very badly want to see her.'

'Do you?' The Marchesa looked thoughtfully at the children. 'I am sure that can be contrived. Will tomorrow be soon enough?'

'Today would be better.'

'Very well.' She clapped her hands and gave swift orders to the servant who appeared. 'Now, you must take some refreshment after your hot drive, and tell me how you are find-ing life in Palermo.'

'Interesting,' said Beth, and got a long grave look from her hostess.

'I am sorry my husband is not here to meet you,' the Marchesa said as servants poured iced drinks for them all. 'He has gone tunny fishing with the King; I doubt they'll get much sport so late in the season, but it is a party of pleasure they all enjoy. I don't expect Rinaldo back until tomorrow night at the ear-liest.' And having provided Beth with this use-ful bit of information, she turned to condole with Charlotte over the Segesta trip. 'Though I think you would have found it dull enough when you got there,' she told her. 'A lot of columns lying about every which way. If you really want to see something magnificent, you should make the trip by water to the cathedral at Cefalu. I am told that is something quite out of the ordinary, though in a sad state of disrepair. The Sicilians are a wretched, idle set of fellows, I'm afraid. I can't tell you how we long, my husband and I, to be back at our real home in Naples. But what is the use of longing? If the King and Queen can make the best of things, here in Sicily, so must we, but it is a miserable come-down just the same. I hope one day to be able to entertain you ladies in proper style at our country house in Capodimonte, Miss Prior, and hear you at the San Carlo. The theatre here is nothing but a hovel compared to that magnificent building, but what can you expect of so barbaric a race? Oh — no need to pull faces at me, Miss Prior, you must know by this time that the Sicilian peasants one is served by speak nothing but their vile patois. They have no idea of bettering themselves. Thought for them is wasted thought.'

Beth, who had been watching the servant's face throughout this speech, was certain that her hostess was deluding herself, and did her best to turn the conversation by speaking of the Rosalia Festival, but this proved an equally unlucky subject, since the Marchesa made it clear that the cult of Santa Rosalia was merely another example of the Sicilian peasants' barbarism. 'We are sorry, my husband and I, that their majesties think it necessary to cater to the vulgar with this expensive and unnecessary festival. A touch of firm government, in the face of these republican stirrings is what is needed. Just imagine the Sicilians with a constitution! Did you ever hear of anything so ridiculous? A hanging or two would be very much more to the point than all this public outlay. Which falls, naturally, on us aristocrats. Who will pay, do you think, for the free wine Beppo here will be drinking from

254

the fountains, come the festival? See, Miss Prior,' with a sharp upward glance at the impassive servant, 'he does not even recognise his own name in French.'

Beth read the closed countenance quite otherwise, and managed a successful diversion, at last, to the Marchesa's children, wondering rather desperately how long it would take to get a reply from La Favorita, where she now knew the Queen was alone.

Conversation was just beginning to dwindle and die when Flora Cottone appeared at last, with just what Beth had hoped for, a summons from the Queen. 'Her majesty was delighted to hear that you are so close,' she said. 'She hopes she can persuade you and Miss Pennam to take a collation with her in the pagoda. She often goes there in the cool of the evening, when the King is away fishing.'

What a useful pagoda, thought Beth, accepting with alacrity. The King used it for pleasure, and the Queen used it for business. And what an odd couple they made, with seventeen children between them, too. It was hard to decide for which of them she was sorrier, but, as a woman, she thought it had to be the Queen.

Saying civil goodbyes to the Marchesa she caught a disconcertingly thoughtful glance from the servant, Beppo, and wondered just to whom he would be reporting the whole episode.

Should she mention this to Flora, who was driving with them in their carriage? She thought not. The less one said, in this dangerous island, the better.

'I am so glad you have come,' Flora told her as they started on the short drive to the pagoda in the royal grounds. 'We are all worried about the Queen; she is not well; there is something on her mind, but she will not speak of it. Poor lady, she has enough to trouble her at the best of times, but this is worse than usual.'

And no wonder, thought Beth. She remembered the previous occasion when the Queen had confided her troubles to her, and found herself very much hoping that this might happen again. It would make it so much easier to leave Peabody out of the discussion, something she was determined to do.

14

It was strange, and perhaps good, to come back so soon to King Ferdinand's pagoda. Beth had never thought to see it again, and was amused to find herself thinking quite kindly of King Ferdinand. He had only been acting on information received, after all, and had taken no for an answer like a gentleman. And it struck her for the first time, dismounting from the carriage, that she almost certainly had him to thank for saving her reputation. Had he made a funny story of her refusal? She thought he must have, and was grateful.

And now she had to deal with his formidable wife. Flora Cottone spoke briefly to one of the servants who had run out to greet them. 'Her majesty is awaiting you in the little theatre,' she told her. 'The servant will show you the way. You will find it interesting, I am sure. We used to have performances there when the royal children were young. I am to show Miss Pennam the pagoda, which you have already seen.' The lady-in-waiting was blushing.

The little theatre was formed from a natural

ledge, improved into a terrace, with a paved court beneath it for the audience, and a screen of ilex and other evergreens all round. The Queen was awaiting her, seated on a rustic bench, placed centre stage, with a stool to her right and a table with refreshments to her left. Beth, approaching from below, had time to see what an admirable setting for confidences it made. There could be no eavesdroppers here, once the servant had left.

It was the first time she had seen the Queen out of doors by daylight, and she was shocked at what the strong southern light revealed. Maria Carolina looked as if she had not slept for nights; the hand that held the silver goblet shook, and there was just a suggestion of tremor about her head. She looked as if she had been on the rack, Beth thought, and wondered if perhaps, in a way, she had.

But the Queen's greeting was composed and regal as always, and she waved the servant away when he had poured Beth a glass of chilled wine from a golden bucket. 'You wished to see me, Miss Prior?'

So it was not going to be easy. 'Your majesty, I felt I should come. It is about the royal review; you were so good as to invite Miss Pennam and me, and I thought I must explain in person why I feel I owe it to Signor Bartolucci to attend his rehearsal.'

'Oh.' The Queen thought about it, looking past her at the view of evergreens and beyond to the dusty brown of the plain. She took a long draft from the goblet. 'You must come,' she said. 'I owe you something, Miss Prior, for what happened the other day. You must come to my review.'

'Majesty, I have given my word.'

'Then you must break it.'

'I don't think I can.' She reached out gently to take the shaking goblet from the Queen's hand and set it safe on the table. 'We are two working women, you and I, your majesty. We keep to the terms of our contracts, do we not?'

'Yes, but what are they? The terms? Pour me more wine Miss Prior, and tell my why you are being so obstinate.'

'Because I think there is more to it than just a royal invitation, your majesty. This island is full of rumours, and I have heard one that frightens me.' She had to help the Queen get the refilled goblet to her lips, but the wine seemed to steady her.

'What have you heard, Miss Prior, and from whom?'

'From everyone, and no one. You know how it is. But something terrible is going to happen at that review. Unless you stop it, majesty. Which you can. You are the Queen. And nothing is ever settled by blood. It just calls for more blood. You should know that, watching the vendetta, here in Sicily. Just imagine a vendetta with the British! They'd hound you to the ends of the earth, once roused. Besides, it's not our way, not a woman's way. We work by persuasion, not violence.'

'And look where it gets us. Try using persuasion on Lord Bentinck,' said the Queen.

'I know. As well persuade the whirlwind. But just because one man won't listen to reason . . . There has to be some other way . . . Violence is no answer, majesty, believe me, it merely breeds more violence.'

'You want me to turn the other cheek? It's not what my mother did, when the world turned against her. She fought for her rights.'

'She fought fair.'

'Mostly,' said Maria Carolina. 'She was a great lady, my mother.'

'And is remembered as such. Imagine going down to history as one who betrayed an ally. What heritage would that be for your children?' Beth was afraid, for a moment, that the Queen would strike her, but what she did was worse. She seemed to crumple where she sat, and two slow tears traced a disastrous course down the painted checks.

Maria Carolina sat silent for a long moment,

ignoring the tears, gazing at the far view as if at horrors. At last: 'Promises,' she said. 'Nothing but promises. Who can I trust?'

'No one, I think,' said Beth. 'Your own instincts, majesty. You have ruled a long time, you must have learned to see through people.'

'Forty-three years,' said the Queen. 'Much longer than you have lived. How he adored me. And now he fears my tongue. But he told me about you, Miss Prior, and I'm grateful to you. Boxed his ears for him, did you? He thought it a great joke, but you're a brave woman, just the same. It might not have ended like that. I think perhaps I trust you.'

'If you trust me, majesty, remember I am English. Trust the English. I am sure you can.' Passionately, she hoped she was right.

'You think so? Despite Lord William's threats? Nelson would never have treated me so. I trusted him. But I was young then. Everything was easier. Sometimes, now, I feel an old woman, and afraid. Suppose he comes back, that Lord William, with absolute power. He hates and fears me. He might do anything. I still have friends. Now is my chance to strike, to pre-empt him.'

'And go down to history as a murderess? What kind of a friend is it suggests that? If they ask you to break your faith, how can you trust them to keep theirs? I beg of you, majesty, think again, think hard.' She had seen a servant come out from the shrubbery, obviously wanting to catch the royal eye.

'You must come to the review.' The Queen had seen the man and beckoned him forward.

'Your majesty, forgive me, I cannot.'

'You must.' The Queen turned to hear the servant's message. 'Cassetti here? I'll see him at once. Bring him to me. And show Miss Prior the way to the pagoda. No more now,' to Beth. 'But I thank you.'

One does not argue with royalty. Beth curtsied and left, wondering who Cassetti was, and what, if anything she had achieved. And how terrifying to have committed herself to staying away from the royal review.

They were very late home. The quick southern night was falling when they drew up outside their house. 'Just as well I am not singing today,' said Beth, as they got out of the carriage. 'Would you mind very much if we did not go out tonight, Charlotte?'

'Of course not,' said Charlotte, and Beth thought for the second time that day that the child was beginning to be more considerate, and was glad of it, and wondered why.

Everyone had called while they were out.

'The Signor Forde waited a long time,' the servant told Beth. 'He did not seem best pleased.'

'Did he leave a message?'

'Only to say he would see you tonight at the Marino.'

Which confirmed Beth in her decision to stay at home. John Thornton and Nathan Peabody had also called, the servant told her, and so had the Herr von Achen. There were notes from them all, Peabody's for Beth, the other two for Charlotte.

'Too many men,' said Beth, laughing. 'Peabody wants to ride in the morning. I hope John Thornton does too.'

'Yes. But, Beth are you certain you don't feel like going to the Marino tonight? The air would do us good, I am sure. It's been a long day.'

'And a dull one for you, I am afraid,' said Beth, suddenly contrite, since she had always found kind Flora Cottone rather heavy going herself. But she really did not want to jump to Forde's bidding, and there was so much to think about, to decide. 'I'm truly sorry, Charlotte dear, but I am on stage again tomorrow. I really must have an early night after this long day, and I am sure you would be the better for it too.'

'I'm not a bit tired,' said Charlotte rebelliously. 'Could I write a note to Lisa and go with them?'

'I'd much rather you did not. Should she explain her doubts about the Falconis? No, how could she? 'Please, Charlotte,' she said instead.

'Oh, very well, I suppose I must find myself an improving book, and go to bed early, like a good girl.'

'Just what I feel like.' Once again, she was pleased at Charlotte's ready compliance.

Charlotte had quite other plans. Having yawned her way to her room with a volume of *Clarissa* under her arm, she pitched it on to the bed and sat down at her dressing table to reread von Achen's note. He must see her; at once. 'Miss Prior is in danger; deadly danger. I dare not write of it, I must speak to you tonight, alone; you will know what to do. Please, let me make this amends for frightening you the other night.' He was hers, for ever, Gustav von Achen. And then: 'Tell no one; it might increase the danger. Bring this note with you to our rendezvous on the Marino.'

Tell no one. She ought to tell Beth. But if she did, Beth would not let her go. That was the easy way out, the coward's way, and she was not going to take it. Besides, Beth was always keeping things from her. Here was her chance to act for herself. And she thought she owed it to von Achen to give him this chance to redeem himself, just because of the monstrous things she had imagined about him. A final chance to put a civilised end to the affair, and forget all about it.

He wanted her to meet him at a spot they had used before, a secluded corner of the Marino close to the royal gardens, where the lights in the gardens cast a darker shadow outside. As the carriage drove, it was some distance from the house, but masked and cloaked she could slip down there through the alleys in a few minutes.

Beth had played into her hands by sending the servants to bed too. She had wanted the house to look closed for the night, so that if Forde should come he would go away again. Charlotte wrapped herself in her cloak, picked up a loo mask, and crept down the marble stairs, feeling the well-known way in the dark. Marble does not creak. Nobody stirred. Shooting the bolts on the heavy door, she realised she would have to leave it on the latch. Well, all the better; von Achen would see her home and she would be able to slip in unobserved.

It was quiet in their little street, but she could hear music from the royal gardens. No distance away, she told herself, suddenly daunted by the largeness of the night. She had been used to going out, when there was as much moon as tonight, back at Windover, to look at the stars and dream of a different life. Now she was in that life, and she was suddenly very much afraid. Go back? Go on? Cowards go back. Someone with a lantern was approaching from the direction of the Porta Felice; she dived quickly into the alley that led down to the Marino, then paused, frightened again because it was so much darker there. She stumbled, reached out and found a wall, and felt her way down uneven steps, pausing at the bottom to put on the mask, glad that she would have von Achen's company on the way back.

Now she could hear the familiar sounds of the Marino against the background of music. Low voices, laughter, the jingle of harness. Absurd to be so afraid; the place was full of her friends.

But they must not see her. She wrapped the cloak more tightly round her and made her careful way among the carriages to the place of assignation. She had no idea how long it had taken her to come down that dark alley, but of course von Achen would be waiting.

Yes; a darker figure moved in the darkness, a cautious voice whispered, 'Miss Pennam?'

'Yes. Thank God you are here. Tell me —'
But a hand closed roughly over her mouth.

'If you speak, if you struggle, you are a dead woman.' Not von Achen's voice. 'Come quietly and you will not be harmed. That's a knife at your back. It's sharp; it won't take a moment: you're dead, and we are gone. But we want you alive. Nod if you understand.'

She nodded. What else could she do. And felt a gag slipped into her mouth. Horrible. Disgusting.

How many of them were there? Too many. Each of her arms was firmly held now, one by a woman, which seemed more horrible than anything. The prick of the knife under her left shoulder was insistent. They were moving slowly through the crowd, the man and woman who had her by the arms talking lightly across her in the Sicilian patois she could not understand.

She must watch for her chance. When they reached their carriage, there must be a moment when the knife was withdrawn, when she could wrench away, run for her life, attract attention somehow, even through the gag. They must be passing the Bentinck carriage now. She heard Lady William's voice, and Forde; and felt the knife sharper against her ribs. It had cut through her cloak, she realised, and shivered.

'Quiet,' said the man on her left. 'Don't try anything.' A different voice; none of them von Achen's, thank God, but the note had been in his handwriting, she was sure of that. Had he been captured too, forced to write it? What a fool, what an idiot she had been to come out without telling Beth.

And thinking this, she missed the moment when the knife was withdrawn and her arms pulled behind her and tied, before she was thrown into a carriage like a bale of hay.

A big old-fashioned family coach, she thought, lying helpless among rushes, and smelling feet. She must keep her head, try not to faint, try and work out which way they were going. But it was impossible, down there in the heavy darkness. Better just to concentrate on keeping her head, on not fainting, on not losing any chance.

But there were no chances. She was aware for a while of the lights and noises of the town centre and thought they must have passed through the Ottangolo, but could not tell which way they turned there. It got quieter, darker; no one spoke. She did not even know how many people there were in the carriage. It was all horrible beyond imagining.

And at home, no one would know she was missing until morning. They were outside the town now, she thought, but still on hard road;

they might be on their way to Monreale, to the Colli or to Bagaria. So far as she was concerned, it hardly mattered which, but she still felt it was desperately important to know. Or was it just that it was important to keep her head, to keep thinking?

After some time, the movement of the carriage changed, as if it had turned off the road on to a not very well cared for drive. And not before time. She was getting extremely stiff in the uncomfortable position into which she had been so carelessly tossed. Her captors said they wanted her alive, but beyond that they cared little enough about her. It was not a cheering thought.

The carriage stopped. Rough hands pulled her to her feet. 'No use struggling,' said the voice. 'We are among friends here. Do what you're told; you won't get hurt.'

She was so stiff that she almost fell down the carriage steps, but the hands held her upright, pulled her forward up a shelving flight of steps. The large bulk of a house loomed ahead, a few lights showing. Someone's country house.

They were expected. A door had swung open, there were torches, and something dark fell over her head, blinding her. But she had seen a wide hall; balustraded stairs leading upwards, someone's rather neglected country house. Going obediently where her captors led her she made herself concentrate on the brief vision, itemising every detail, to be sure she would know it again.

If she survived. What could these ungentle men possibly want of her? It was the first thing she asked, when she was pushed into a room and the gag removed. 'What do you want of me?'

'Money of course. What else?' It was the same voice, speaking the same fluent but accented French. Would she know it again? Hard to tell, but the more he talked, the more likely it was. So, keep him talking.

'Money? But I have none. It's all a terrible mistake.' Or was it a terrible discovery? Had the secret of her identity been blown? As Miss Comyn of Comyn's she was afraid she would be worth a great deal of money.

'Not worth much in yourself, maybe,' said the voice. 'But they'll pay for your life, those British tyrants, pay handsomely before we're done with you. If they are slow, it is only to send them an ear or two. But they'll pay, no need to worry, they'll pay if you write what we tell you. And you'll go back unscathed, if you do as you are told. Do you understand me?'

'You make yourself very clear.'

'Good. So, sit here.' She was pushed on to

a chair, nearly missed it and fell to the floor, but recovered herself, furious at her own helplessness, her hands still tied behind her.

'We will have to remove the blindfold for you to write.' The voice came from behind her, a heavy hand fell on her shoulder. 'I do earnestly recommend that you do not try to see us. If you do so, it will be the worse for you. We will be compelled to kill you.'

'How do I know you won't anyway?' She tried for a coolness she was very far from feeling.

'Not if we can help it, I promise you that. It spoils the trade for the others, don't you see, if we start killing off the victims. No one will pay up if there is no hope. So, try not to see us, Miss Pennam.' Someone untied her hands, the blindfold was pulled away, and she saw that she was sitting at a writing desk, with ink and paper ready.

'Write what I tell you and you will be left alone.' He was standing behind her left shoulder and she was aware of one or two other people in the room, also behind her. She was facing a curtainless window, in a room without furnishing so far as she could see except for a cot bed and a bucket. It must have been an elegant room once, with frescoes and moulded cornices, but now the torchlight revealed only cobwebs and dilapidation.

'Write,' said the implacable voice. 'Dear Beth — you call her Beth, I presume?'

'Yes.' An educated man, she thought, and wrote: 'Dear Beth —'

'I have been kidnapped,' went on the voice. 'They promise not to hurt me if I behave, and you pay them five thousand ounces.'

'Five thousand ounces!' So far, Charlotte had been obediently writing as he dictated. 'But that's impossible! An ounce is a day's wages.'

'Here in Sicily, it is,' said the voice. 'In England, it would be nothing. Write, Miss Pennam: Five thousand ounces, to be ready tonight, when you will receive instructions as to delivery.'

'Tonight?' asked Charlotte, appalled.

'She will have the note first thing in the morning. With her powerful friends, she will be able to collect that sum in a day. You surely do not wish to stay with us any longer than is strictly necessary, Miss Pennam. You might be so unfortunate as to see one of us.' No mistaking the threat in his voice. Charlotte went on writing. What else could she do? She was translating ounces into sterling in her head as she wrote, and thought that in fact Comyn's would, eventually, be able to pay the upwards of two thousand five hundred pounds this represented easily enough. But whether Beth would be able to raise it so swiftly was another question. It was a huge sum in Sicilian terms, and she did not know whether to be flattered or appalled. Mainly, she was just frightened. And she longed to be alone, for all kinds of undignified reasons. She finished and put down the pen.

'Go on,' he told her: 'They say, any delay, and they will send you one of my ears, with the earring still in place. Now: one sentence of your own to convince Miss Prior that you have written this yourself. Careful now: no tricks.'

She sat for a moment, helpless, desperate. Her chance, but how to take it? Then she picked up the pen and wrote.

'What do the initials signify?' he asked.

'It's an old joke between us. She'll know it's me. You said that was what you wanted.' She made her tone plaintive; easy enough to do so. Would it satisfy him?

It seemed to. 'And the note?' he asked. 'You brought it?'

She had longed for another look at it, to be sure if it was von Achen's hand, now saw it snatched from her. 'Good,' said the voice. 'Sleep well, Miss Pennam.'

15

'Gone?' Beth had been roused by a frightened maid. 'What do you mean?'

'The front door was unlatched, signora, and her bed has not been slept in.'

'Dear God!' Beth was remembering how easily Charlotte had yielded about staying at home the night before. She must have planned to go out to some secret assignation. Something in one of the notes she had received. Dressing rapidly, Beth tried to marshal her thoughts. Three callers; three notes. Two for Charlotte, one for her, from Peabody, asking her to ride. 'Too many men,' she had joked. She remembered it savagely now. Charlotte had confirmed that Thornton wanted her to ride too. She had said nothing about von Achen's note. Bitterly, now, Beth remembered the Queen's warning about the plot to kidnap Charlotte, compromise her. Had she really deluded herself that she had scotched it for good by putting a stop to the Segesta trip? There simply had not been time to think about it. But at least she should have warned Charlotte, taken precautions. Idiotic. Fatal.

And there was worse; she saw it now. Von Achen. She had not quite decided whether she really believed he had intended to carry Charlotte off; now she saw that it might all make appalling sense. And she had let Charlotte convince herself that she had been imagining things. I'll never forgive myself, she thought.

She was dressed and trying to swallow some coffee and decide what to do first when the note arrived. One of the servants had found it on the doorstep, the maid told her. No, they had seen no one.

Bold capitals for the address. A covering note in the same disguised hand: 'We do urge you to do as Miss Pennam asks.' No signature, no other clue, just Charlotte's note, with its chilling postscript: 'I think they mean it when they speak of my ears. I am so sorry, Beth, forgive me? C. P.'

Charlotte never signed like that. So, what was she saying? Presumably that she thought she had not been recognised as Charlotte Comyn. Beth could only hope she was right.

Now she knew what she must do. It was still very early; she would be sure to find Gareth Forde at home. She would go there rather than lose time asking him to come to her. At least, she thought, there was no injunction about secrecy in the note. Why should there be? She remembered meeting Castroni, whom

Flora Cottone had described as Chief of Police, and Forde as the Queen's spymaster. Not much chance of help from him; he might even be involved, she thought. Anything could happen, here in Sicily. No: the only hope for Charlotte was to collect the money fast. And for that she must have Forde's help. For the first time, she found herself wishing Lord William was not away.

The carriage was at the door when she remembered that Peabody and Thornton would be calling, and sat down to dash off a breathless note, asking them to await her return. She was bound to need their help too.

She had never been to Forde's first-floor apartments on the Toledo and found them surprisingly luxurious. But then Gareth Forde had always liked his comforts, she thought, giving her name to the surprised servant and telling him it was most urgent.

Something faintly supercilious about the way the man received her? He knew her, of course. Everyone in Palermo knew her. But he showed her civilly enough into what was obviously Forde's study, a snug little room with a desk littered with papers and a view of the decorations ready in the Toledo. It was a frightening reminder that it was now only two days until the festival, and the royal review; and all the danger that implied. At all costs, she must have Charlotte safe by then.

She was still standing by the window, looking unseeingly down at the crowded street, when Forde joined her, resplendent in a velvet smoking jacket.

'I am more than honoured.' He kissed her hand. 'But very much surprised. Is this a wise move, dear Beth?'

'No.' She wasted no time. 'Charlotte has been kidnapped, Gareth. They want a ransom of five thousand ounces, by tonight. I need your help.'

'Oh dear.' It seemed miserably inadequate to her as a reaction. 'And Bentinck away. You must see, dear Beth, that in his absence I am powerless. It will mean getting in touch with Maitland, at Messina. You will have to ask the kidnappers for time.'

'There is no time.'

'Oh, come now, there has to be time. There is an accepted formula, I believe, for kidnappings, here in Sicily. They will expect you to negotiate, to haggle if you like. It's the way they do business here.'

'It's not the way I do. Not with Charlotte's life at stake. She speaks of her ears, Gareth, you know what that means.'

'Fool of a girl,' he said. 'How did it happen? By one of her mad starts, I have no doubt, and now she counts on you to get her out of it. And you have rushed from your house, like the heroine of one of your dramas, without so much as a bite of breakfast, I have no doubt. We will remedy that at least, and put our heads together, without dramatics, to think what to do for the best. And I shall tell you how much I have missed you, Beth, how glad I am to have you back.'

'Back?' She could not believe her ears. 'What do you mean?'

'Well, of course,' he said. 'You came to me, didn't you? Publicly. You might as well stay now; your name is gone anyway.'

He was actually trying to pull her into his arms. 'No!' Her hand itched to strike him as she had King Ferdinand, but something in her knew that this would be fatal, unforgivable. Only kings could laugh at rejection. 'No, Gareth,' she said instead. 'You have understood nothing. I am sorry I came to you. Goodbye.'

He was so surprised that he let her go. She turned in the doorway. 'If you think of anything helpful,' she said. 'Perhaps you would come to me? I mean to have the money by tonight.'

She found Peabody and Thornton waiting for her, as she had known she would. Or had she? After all, she had known Forde would help her. What in the world did she know?

'Thank God you are back.' Peabody greeted her without ceremony. 'What's this about Miss Pennam being missing?'

'Kidnapped.' She wasted no words. 'I've had the demand. Five thousand ounces by to-night. Or one of her ears tomorrow.'

'In her own hand?' asked Peabody.

'Yes. No question of that.'

'You've been to Forde, of course. What does he say?'

'That he can do nothing without consulting Maitland at Messina. That we must ask for time, negotiate.' She minded horribly having to tell them this.

'So much for that,' said Peabody. 'How much can you raise in a day, Thornton?'

'Hard to tell.' John Thornton was chalk white, but there was a dangerous gleam in his blue eyes. 'We'd best get started. There is no demand for secrecy?' to Beth.

'No. I suppose they know it's impossible.'

'Yes.'

She had to trust these two men. 'There's more.'

'More?'

'I'm so ashamed; so angry with myself. The Queen warned me, you see, that there was a kidnapping plot in the wind; told me not to go to Segesta. I didn't tell Charlotte; didn't want to frighten her. And there's more still:

the Queen said the release would be so handled that Charlotte was compromised, forced into marriage —'

'Von Achen?' Peabody spoke savagely. 'I notice he's not here. We'll see about that. We'd best get going, Thornton. Try not to worry too much, Miss Prior.'

'Nor to blame yourself,' said Thornton.

'I'll get my jewels valued.' She looked down at the Queen's bracelet. 'And tell Bartolucci I can't appear tonight. And wait.'

'Hardest of all,' said Peabody. 'But, think while you wait, Miss Prior. Of course we are going to do our utmost to collect the ransom, Thornton and I, and pay it, but the other approach would be better still: to find her. The Queen warned you, you say. Might she know more?'

'She said she must not be involved. She had it from her spies, you see. They thought something else was going to happen on that trip.' She caught Peabody's speculative eye and blushed for the first time in years. Maddening. But he had turned to look thoughtfully at John Thornton.

There was a little silence, then: 'Something was,' Peabody said. 'Miss Pennam's life and reputation are at stake.' He went to the door, opened it, found no one, closed it again. 'They are all busy exclaiming in the kitchen,' he went on. 'I promoted that Segesta trip because I had someone I wanted to meet. Secretly. At least, I thought I promoted it, but when I look back, I do wonder a little if my cousins did not steer me into it. They were very keen.'

'I have been thinking that,' said Beth. 'It's all been just a little odd. A little off. Lisa started to cut me, after the scandal the other day. I don't think I would even have blamed her. But her husband made her change her tune. I think they are using us. I wish I understood why.'

'So do I,' said Peabody. 'They are of the English party, after all. On your side, you could say. But there's no time for this talk. We must get started, Thornton. We'll keep you posted, Miss Prior. And why don't you try to find out if the Falconis have any old disused country houses anywhere near town. Tactfully, for goodness sake!'

Left alone in the absolute dark, Charlotte felt her way to the bucket, then fell on to the hard bed and, amazingly, slept. Waking to dawn light, hunger and absolute silence, she hurried to the cobwebbed window and peered out at a deserted stable yard. She had heard the bolt shot, last night, on the outside of the door; now she saw why they had left her ungagged and with hands untied. The window might not be barred, but it would not open, and there was no way down from it anyway. And even if there were, she would only find herself in the empty stable yard with its solidly closed wooden gate. Nothing for it but to wait, and pray, and trust Beth. And castigate herself, over and over, for the idiotic impulse that had driven her out into the dangerous night. She had no money, no jewels, nothing to bribe a servant with, even if there were a servant to bribe.

But nobody came near her all day. There was no sign of life in the yard below, nor in the house around her. Nothing in the room but the cot and the bucket, and she was grateful for both as the long hours passed. Her captors must simply have abandoned her here while they went back to Palermo to await the ransom. What did they care if she was hungry?

Which she was. Visions of all the meals she had ever refused to eat tormented her. If I get out of this, she thought, I'll be different. Better not to think about food. Instead, she made herself apply her mind to what had happened to her. It seemed important to try and work out who was behind it. They had taken the note away from her. What did that mean? Reading it hastily she had been sure it was von Achen's hand. Well, of course it was from him. The servant had said he had left it. Or had she? Horribly, she found she could not be sure. It made her recognise that so far she had been too frightened to think straight, and that would not do.

She sat upright on the hard cot and thought about von Achen. Of course the note had been from him. Looked at coldly, as she was doing now, it all made horrible sense. He was not just a fortune hunter, he was a criminal. She made herself think back to that scene at Monreale. What had his plans been for her that night? What would have happened if the careless roughness of his embrace had not startled her? If Beth had not come? Obviously she would have been kidnapped then. And then, fool that she was, she had gone riding with him, and been saved by Nathan Peabody. And even after all that she had let herself be taken in by his lying words about Beth.

And here she was. She would not be such a fool again. She might not get the chance. She wished she was not so hungry. It was beginning to make it hard to think. She lay down for a while on the cot and even slept a little, restlessly, and dreamed she was at Windover eating the first strawberries and cream and waked to find herself crying, and was angry. The light was beginning to fade, and the hot little room to cool off. She felt dirty, and dishevelled and hungrier than ever.

What would Beth have been doing all day? She would have had the note first thing; what would she have done then? Gone to Forde of course. He would help them. Would he? She wished she could be sure of this, for Beth's sake as much as for her own. John Thornton's scolding about what she had done to Beth weighed heavy on her. John Thornton. Beth would go to him and he would put up the money. She was completely sure of this. It was only to wait.

It was full dusk when she heard a sound in the stable yard below and hurried to the window. Nothing to be seen. And then she heard the sound again; someone must be trying to break open the gate. It gave suddenly with the rasp of breaking wood and a cloaked figure half fell into the yard.

Rescue! Gustav von Achen. He was looking about him as if he had never been here before. How had he come here now? He moved to the middle of the yard, looked up, cupped his hands round his mouth, called, quietly: 'Miss Pennam, are you there? Can you hear me?'

Rescue? Or a pretence at rescue? But a chance to be taken. She banged on the window, and he looked up, saw her. 'Thank God! Don't be afraid. I'll find my way to you.' He disappeared from sight and she heard a banging as if he were forcing a door. All too easy? Why was he alone? But the very fact that he was improved her chances.

It seemed a very long time before she heard his footsteps in the echoing hall outside, and his voice calling softly, 'Miss Pennam, where are you?'

'Here!' She had decided what she must do. When he opened the door at last, she fell into his arms. 'Oh, thank God, you are come. I have been so frightened!'

'And no wonder, my poor darling. Your pretty little ears! But come, quick. We must get you out of here before they come back. Forde wouldn't help; Miss Prior is at her wits' end, turned to Peabody, of all people. You and I know how deep he is in the plot.'

Did they? She did not ask it. Let him hurry her down the long corridor to a back stair. It was all unfurnished, dilapidated. She leaned confidingly against him. 'How did you find me?' she asked admiringly.

'I knew who to suspect. Those Falconis! Jumped up lot of Sicilian snobs. Why do you think they were so keen on that Segesta trip? They had something planned for it, I am sure, only your prudery, my little love, put paid to it. We shall do better in future, shall we not? Understand each other better.'

'Oh, yes!' She put all the heart she could

into it, and the arm that was hurrying her along tightened round her.

'My precious one. My little love.'

How could she ever have believed him? 'I've been so frightened.' It was the thing she knew she could say with complete conviction.

'My poor child, of course you have. And right to be.' They were in the stable yard now and he hurried her across it, and out through the broken gate. It was getting darker by the minute now, and she had no chance to see how convincing a job he had made of it. Much better that he did not see her looking.

'You've been so clever!' She made herself look at him with adoration, and wondered when her chance would come. His accomplices must be in Palermo now, making the arrangements to collect the ransom. He would hold her somewhere until they had it, then take her back, in triumph, 'rescued' to Palermo.

Rescued, and without reputation. What were his plans for her tonight? She did not like to think about them, but must. Or rather, she must get away. 'I'm so hungry.' It was easy to put a quiver into her voice. 'They gave me nothing, all day. How soon will we get to Palermo?'

'My poor child, I am afraid I dare not try to take you there tonight. Suppose we met the kidnappers on their way back. We would not know them, but they would know us. Fatal. One man against a gang of brigands. No, love, we must hide for tonight, hope to get in touch with one of the search parties tomorrow. They are bound to be out after you by then.'

'Hide? But how? Where?' She pulled back a little to look at him. 'Where are you taking me?'

'To find my horse, love.' Laughing a little. 'I did not dare bring it too near for fear of being overheard. I know you for an intrepid rider, and it's not far to safety.'

'Safety? Oh, Gustav —' She had never used his first name before, thought this was the moment for it. 'And food?'

'Yes, indeed, my poor child. Food and sleep are what you need. Ah, here we are.' He let go her arm to untie his horse, and she wondered whether to run for it there and then, thought she must wait for a better chance, and let him settle her on the saddle, awkwardly enough in her muslin skirts. Now the temptation to try and make a dash for it was greater, but still she thought it must be resisted. Higher up now, she could see no light, no sign of human habitation, and her seat on the strange horse was too awkward for any kind of control. She had to be grateful for von Achen's firm arm, steadying her.

'Where are we going?' she asked. 'Where are we?'

'You don't even know that! No wonder you are so frightened, my poor little love. But you are safe with me now. I am taking you by back ways to a convent I know of, where the daughters of the aristocracy are educated. They will give us asylum there, my own, and then, in the morning, I will send to Miss Prior to fetch you home.'

'But she will have paid the ransom by then.' She thought this a reasonable objection to make.

'Of course she will, but you didn't seriously think those ruffians would have let you go, did you? Oh, if you'd been Sicilian they might have, because of the code of honour they set so much store by, but as an alien Englishwoman you'd not have had a chance. There's too easy a route for captives down to the south coast of the island, for sale to the Algerine pirates. A beauty like you would fetch a good price too.' He was enjoying frightening her, she thought, and was frightened and made a point of showing it.

'Thank God you found me! How long will it take to get to the convent?' And what would they find when they got there?

'Not long now, my brave girl. Which will you have first, a bath or your supper?'

'Oh, a bath I think!' It would give her more time, and besides, she was beginning to be aware that her dishevelled state was making him feel dangerously her superior. But perhaps this was a good thing. She wanted him confident, sure of her, but very much disliked the way the arm that steadied her was beginning to stray. It roused her, and that made her angry, and she started telling him all over again, rather shrilly, how clever he had been to find her.

She thought she was actually beginning to bore him a little when she saw lights ahead.

'Is that the convent?' she asked eagerly. 'A big building, with lights.'

'It must be. Nearer than I thought, what a blessing. Not long now, my own.' He tied the reins to a hitching post and lifted her down, his arms too tight around her. 'You are exhausted, and no wonder.' He kept one arm firm round her waist while he beat a resounding tattoo on the big door. No chance of escape now, but surely there must be help for her inside?

The door swung open on to a blaze of light and raucous sound. A marble hall, brilliantly illuminated by chandeliers that cast sharp shadows on frescoed walls. The sound of revelry from rooms beyond, and a smell of tallow, and wine, and man. Not a convent. Every

sense told her what this place was. 'But —'
She stopped, pulled back, looked at him, questioning.

'I must have missed the way.' He hardly pretended to conviction. I am so sorry! How could I be such a fool! But at least it is warmth and safety for you, my little love. No one need ever know. It will be our secret yours and mine, for always, where we spent our first night.' He turned to speak rapidly to a servant in the patois she had not thought he knew.

She was taking in what he had said. 'Our first night.' He was sure of her indeed; by tomorrow he meant to be surer still.

'My bath?' She put a hand on his arm and looked at him with big eyes. 'I feel so dirty and disgusting.'

'Yes, of course.' Now he laughed. 'You will find the facilities here much better than they would have been at the convent where I meant to take you. Perhaps it is all for the best after all.' He snapped his fingers, very much at home. It frightened her more than anything that he was not even pretending never to have been here before. He was beginning, she thought, as he meant to go on.

She had planned to appeal for help to the servant who took charge of her, but saw the way she ogled von Achen and changed her mind. Her heart sank when the girl took her arm and led her across the tiled hall to a stair going down to a lower floor. What chance of escape from a basement? She was silent, making herself lean confidingly on the girl's arm; easy enough to pretend exhaustion; it was real.

Like the hall above, the stairs were brilliantly painted with human figures. She caught glimpses of what they were doing, and was shocked.

It was not a bath; it was a pool, fed by a bubbling spring of warm water, but at least it was empty. She very much disliked having the girl undress her, and tried in vain to make her go away.

'No, no, the milord told me not to leave you.' She laughed. 'No need to be shy with me, save your blushes for him.'

16

Beth could hardly bear to sit inactive while Thornton and Peabody collected the ransom. She was racking her brains as to how to find out if the Falconis had a country house, when the servant announced Mr. Fagan, and she remembered that she and Charlotte had promised him a final sitting for their joint portrait today.

'I am so glad to see you.' She greeted him warmly. 'But you cannot have met Mr. Peabody or Mr. Thornton, or you would not be here.' She explained quickly what had happened to Charlotte, cut short his sympathetic speeches, and went to the heart of the matter. 'I am sure they will need your help in raising the necessary funds, Mr. Fagan, but before you go, tell me something. You know Palermo so well. Where do you think the kidnappers would be holding her?'

'Not here in town,' he said at once. In this heat, every house stands so open to the breeze that it would be difficult to keep someone captive without it being obvious to the neighbours. So — somewhere not too far out of town.'

'That's what I thought. I have been wondering about country houses. Ones standing empty . . .' She let it trail, hopefully.

'Plenty of those,' he told her. 'With times so hard, and taxes so high, it is not everyone can afford to keep up a proper style both in town and in the country. Some people, like your friends the Cottones, have decided to live entirely in the country, while others — the Falconis, for instance, and the families of the exiled barons — have closed their country houses to live entirely in town.

'I didn't know the Falconis had a country house.' She made it casual.

'Oh, yes, out towards Bagaria, less popular now the King has settled for La Favorita, in the Colli direction. They have quite closed the house, I think, and prefer to visit friends when they feel the need of country air.'

'Very sensible.' Beth dismissed it. 'But, Mr. Fagan, I am sure Mr. Peabody and Mr. Thornton will be needing your help.'

'A fortunate thing both their credit is so good,' he told her, picking up his hat. 'This is a time when we miss Lord William sorely.'

'Do you know, I had been thinking that too.' She wondered whether she dared ask for more information about the Falconis' country house, but decided against it. He had probably given her enough for them to go on. At least she knew it existed. He had given her something else to think about too. He had obviously been surprised that the demand was for so comparatively small a sum. It worried her very much.

It was almost the first thing she said when the two men arrived, weighed down with money bags, later that afternoon. 'It's not enough, is it?' she said. 'It sounds ungracious to say so, when you have so splendidly managed to raise it, but they haven't asked enough.'

'No,' said Peabody. 'That's just what we had decided, John and I. It's the reaction we got from everyone we talked to: that it was an absurdly small sum.'

'Yes, so there is more to it, as the Queen warned me,' she said. 'They meant us to be able to raise it in a day. And von Achen is going to "rescue", and compromise her, tonight.'

'We are very much afraid so,' said Peabody. Both men seemed to her to have aged in the course of the day. 'Fagan told us you and he had talked a little about country houses.'

'Yes. The Falconis have one in the Bagaria direction. But, even if we are right in what we suspect, she won't be there by now, will she?'

'I'm very much afraid not. Von Achen is

bound to have moved her. But where would he take her?'

'Not back to Palermo until morning.' Peabody seemed to be acting as spokesman. 'If there were an inn he would take her there, spend the night with her, bring her back to you in the morning, with his gallant proposal of marriage.'

'But there are no inns.' Beth paused as a servant appeared to announce the signor Forde.

'I came to see if I could be of any help,' he told her. 'Have you had the instructions yet?'

'No, but we have the money ready, thanks to these two gentlemen.' With a very cool look. 'We think it possible that she may be out Bagaria way. Can you think of any sort of public place there where she might be being held?'

'Well, of course,' he said. 'But I devoutly hope not.'

'What do you mean?'

'The House of Persephone. You must have heard of it —' to Peabody. 'It's — how to describe it? — a very expensive club built on the site of a Roman bath. There's a natural spring, warm water there, they always made the most of those.'

'Of course,' said Peabody. 'I had heard of

it, but not where it precisely was, since it did not much interest me. Let us not mince words, Forde. Why say club when you mean brothel?'

'Oh, my God,' said Beth, and the maid appeared with a note. Once again, it had been found on the doorstep, and once again Beth wondered if the kidnappers had an accomplice in her household. No time to be thinking of that now. The note was in the same anonymous capitals as before, and its instructions were simple and precise. The money was to be left in a disused chapel off the Bagaria road. The goods would be returned in the morning.

'They are very sure of themselves,' said Peabody.

'Yes, it's terrifying. What are we going to do?' Beth looked from one of the three men to the other, but all were silent for a few minutes.

At last Peabody spoke. 'Do we think she is probably being held in this House of Persephone?'

'It does make horrible sense,' said Beth.

'I think so too. Obliging of them to have made the drop in this direction. Convenient for them, of course, but more so for us. We leave the money as directed, don't we, then put on dominoes and masks, and go on as a party of pleasure to this place of Persephone. You have the entrée I take it, Forde.'

'Yes.' Avoiding Beth's eye.

'Good. Once inside, we separate, find her.' He made it seem simple. 'You can describe the customs of the place to us as we ride there, Forde. I imagine we can count on finding enough men we know, when we get there.'

'Certainly, but will this not precipitate just the kind of scene and scandal we wish to avoid?'

'Not if I go too,' Beth surprised them. 'Then it becomes a rather foolish prank that has gone agley. No use to try to work out the story until we see what we find, but everyone knows Charlotte for a termagant child. It will be easy enough. Some kind of innocent dare.'

'Just like her,' John Thornton spoke for the first time. 'But, Miss Prior, we can't let you do it.'

'I doubt you can stop me,' she told him. 'And I shall be in men's clothes, of course. It's ages since I played a modern young man. I hope my breeches still fit. How soon do we start?'

Charlotte turned a deaf ear to the servant's hints that it was time to emerge from the pool and get dressed. 'It is making me feel so much better,' she explained, turning luxuriously in the warm, fizzy water.

'But milord will be waiting.'

'Let him wait.' How much did the girl

know? Worth trying anyway. 'I believe I've
changed my mind about milord. Is there a
back way out? I'll make it very much worth
your while.'

'Oh, no, signora.' Frightened. 'They'd kill
me. And it is all for your best interests, really.'
Charlotte wondered what story she had been
told, and whether to try and spin out the time
by asking, but at this moment a door opened
and a man's voice called something in the
maddeningly incomprehensible patois.

'A group of men are coming to use the pool,
signora,' said the girl. 'Come, quick, if you
don't want them to see you. I have clothes
for you through here.' She wrapped a huge
towel round Charlotte as she emerged from
the water, and led her into a small room where
fresh clothes lay ready.

All planned. All ready for her. Terrifying.
And the muslin gown was deplorably scanty,
its slip as transparent as the dress itself. 'I'm
cold,' Charlotte protested. 'A shawl, please.'
At all costs she must keep up the pretence
of being in command.

'You'll be warm enough soon.' The girl
winked, but produced an ephemeral gauze
scarf, which Charlotte was glad to drape round
her shoulders and across the front of the low-
cut gown. 'You look every inch the bride.'
The girl was patting Charlotte's damp curls

into place. 'I hope milord knows how lucky he is.' She evidently thought she was assisting at an elopement, and Charlotte wondered whether to try to undeceive her, but a man-servant was tapping on an outer door, the moment had passed.

She felt a lamb to the slaughter as she followed the man upstairs. It was a different stair, and her half-formed plan of screaming and making a scene when they reached the main lobby had to be abandoned. Von Achen was awaiting her in a private dining room, the table set with a lavish feast, and she could not help a moment of pure pleasure at the sight of food. She was going to make a fight for it, of course, but she would do it much better with a square meal inside her.

She clutched the scarf more closely round her and made herself greet von Achen gushingly. 'All my favourite food.' Oh, how clever you are, and how hungry I am! Do you know, I have had nothing to eat for more than twenty-four hours? Do I dare have a glass of wine?'

'Of course you do.' He was pouring it for her. 'Here's to us, my beauty.' And then, to the hovering servant. 'You may go. We will wait on ourselves.'

She had managed to wolf four little savoury pastries by now, while looking nervously round the room. Nothing but the marble-topped tables, loaded with food, two elaborately carved chairs, and an eastern-looking divan, heaped with cushions. This meal had better take a long time, she told herself, and ate another pastry, more slowly.

'Here's to us,' he said again, impatiently, and she touched her glass to his and sipped. Would it be drugged, or would he want her conscious at the seduction scene — or call it rape — that he was planning? She was not going to risk it. Putting the Venetian glass goblet down, she contrived to miss the table so that it shattered on the marble floor. 'Oh, forgive me! I am clumsy with hunger. And so thirsty.' She reached out, took his glass from his hand, and drank.

For a moment, he looked furious, the real man revealed, and not a pleasant one, then he smiled at her, took and filled another glass for himself. So there had been a drug in hers. What did that tell her? That he wanted her complaisant, of course, but she let herself hope that it also meant there were people among the merry-makers outside who might take her part if she could only appeal to them. He must have bribed the servants, but not the guests, in this house of ill repute. She wished now that she had contrived to change her glass for his, rather than breaking it. Too late for that.

'Food for my starving girl.' He was carving one of the scrawny Sicilian capons, and she made a note of the sharp knife. 'And let me refill your glass.'

'Oh, yes, please. It is doing me the world of good.' She made herself smile adoringly at him, and noted that he was using the same bottle as he had for himself. Having failed with his drug, he was simply hoping to get her drunk. Well, two could play at that. Or might he be more dangerous drunk? It was a chance she must take. When he turned away for a moment to fetch a dish of savoury rice from the side table she poured swiftly from her glass into his. Not enough for him to notice, she hoped. 'This is so good.' It was true; she had eaten half her helping of garlic-rich chicken already, realised her mistake and asked eagerly for more, to eat more slowly. While he was carving it, she managed to get rid of the rest of her wine into a soup tureen. 'Tell me how you found me.' She leaned confidingly towards him. 'I had quite given up hope.'

'As well you might.' He emptied his glass, and refilled them both. 'That penny-pinching Forde refused to help raise the ransom; said he was powerless in Bentinck's absence. He wasn't going to chance his arm for a nobody like you, my poor girl. That's when I decided to play a lone hand, look for you. I've not wasted my time here in Sicily. I've been learning something about the island and its ways. And what I have learned terrified me for you. How were we to know that they would not take the ransom and then send you south for sale to the Algerine pirates? While Peabody and Thornton were running round the town, begging on your behalf. I made some enquiries of my own. They led me to the house where you were being held. I was prepared for a fight, lucky to find you alone there.'

'Clever to find me! Whose house was it?'

But he was on his feet, carving more capon and pretended not to hear the question, and she did not dare repeat it. 'Anyway, you found me,' she said. 'That's the main thing. I'll never forget it, not so long as I live.' And that was true enough.

'My own.' He reached for her hand, planted a moist kiss on the palm, and began to pull her towards him.

'You've not finished your capon.' Holding back. 'You must be just as hungry as I am, after all your labours on my behalf. And thirsty too.' She held out her own glass, which she had once again contrived to empty into the chilled soup. How surprised the cook would be, she thought.

'Greedy child!' But the distraction had worked. He let go her hand to refill their

302

glasses, and returned to his eating. His manners were slipping, she noticed. He was using his fingers where most people would have preferred a fork. It did not endear him to her, but it frightened her. It was a foretaste of how he would treat her if he succeeded in forcing her into marriage. She drank a little wine and came to a cold conclusion. Whatever happened tonight if no help came; if she could not fight him off; if he raped her — she would still refuse to marry him. She promised herself this, and turned to him, smiling, and asked for more rice.

'How long will it take?' Beth asked. There had been nothing in the instructions about who or how many should leave the ransom, so the four of them were riding through the town, two by two, the heavy bags shared out among the men. She was with Forde, and sorry for it.

'Hard to tell,' he told her. 'An hour, perhaps longer. It may take a while to find the chapel they speak of, but the moon will be up by then.'

'Suppose it clouds over?'

'Unlikely,' he said. 'But it would mean it took longer.' And that was not much comfort. 'Mad of you to come.' He had said this before, would probably say it again. 'The rags of your reputation gone, my poor Beth. We will have to think hard what is best for you, when this is all over. Back to England at once, I think, the pair of you. I doubt Lady William will feel able to receive either of you, after tonight.'

'I do wonder if you are right, Gareth. For myself, I think better of Lady William than that.'

'But she has her husband's position to consider,' he told her, and obviously felt that ended it.

In the lead, Peabody and Thornton were discussing, all over again, what they would do when they reached the House of Persephone. What Forde had told them about the set-up there while Beth was putting on her breeches had not been encouraging. There was an entry lobby, leading into a series of public rooms, but the private rooms were set apart. He had shuffled a little about this, unable or unwilling to tell them whether sounds in the public rooms were audible in the private ones, and vice versa.

'I still think we should not have let Miss Prior come.' Thornton had said this before.

'How would you have set about stopping her?' asked Peabody.

'But whatever happens tonight, and, please

God, we will save Miss Pennam, Miss Prior's reputation is gone beyond recall. First the King, then this.'

'And you think she should have thought that more important than coming to the rescue of her friend? What very odd views you British have both of friendship and of women. You blame Miss Prior for coming; I don't think I would have forgiven her if she had not.'

'Forde agrees with me.'

'Of course; he is English too. And while we are about it, shall we stop calling our young friend Miss Pennam? I admire the way you have stuck to it, but it seems a bit absurd now, between you and me.'

'Oh.' Very much taken aback. 'You know?'

'I rather think all of Palermo knows by now. Penniless girls don't get kidnapped, Thornton.'

'No. I should have thought. What a wretched business it all is. Even if we get there in time, and fudge up a story among us, they are both in deep trouble.'

'I am afraid so, and young Charlotte is less well equipped to endure it than Beth Prior. That's a woman who would stand against the world, and enjoy it. Your Charlotte is something else again. What do you bet me she is sick when we rescue her?'

'Not my Charlotte, alas.'

'Well, the sooner you make her so, the better.'

'What? But, I thought —'

'Nonsense,' said Peabody. 'Beth Prior is worth twenty of her. And as for that schoolgirl's passion the child has been showing for me, you can count on me to disabuse her, brutally if it must be, the first chance I get.'

'If we only get the chance.' And they rode on in silence until it was time to look out for the turning to the disused chapel.

It was exactly as described, its door hanging drunkenly on its hinges, and an empty chest for the ransom money just inside. They had agreed among themselves that the gang were bound to be waiting within earshot, and stacked the money bags in the chest in absolute silence. What they had not been able to decide in advance was whether it would be safe to ride straight on to the House of Persephone after making the drop. Now, riding back towards the main road, they discussed this in low voices. Forde wanted to ride part way back to town, and take another track to the house, but Beth would not agree. 'No,' she said. 'The gang will have no further interest in Charlotte now. What they care about is the money. They will be too busy helping themselves, and, if we are lucky, quarrelling about it, to notice which way we go. And why should they? Besides, they will be loaded now, we are not. I am sure we should not waste a moment.' They were at the main road now, such as it was. 'I vote we go on,' she said.

'And so do I,' said Peabody.

'And I,' said Thornton.

'Oh very well,' said Forde grudgingly. 'But on your heads be it.'

Was it by her contrivance or his that Beth found herself riding with Peabody now? She was not sure, but was very sure they must hurry. 'Can we not go faster?' she asked him, horribly aware of time ebbing away for Charlotte.

'I think we must all arrive together,' he told her. 'We need Forde, remember, to get us in. But, yes.' He turned to speak quietly over his shoulder to the other two. 'What's keeping you?'

'Forde lost his stirrup.' Thornton spoke through clenched teeth. 'We're with you now.'

'And must sound like a merry party,' Peabody reminded them. 'It can't be far now, thank God.'

'And no sign of pursuit,' said Beth.

'No. So, a catch, do you think?' And he surprised her by leading off in a powerful bass. She followed his lead and they were all at it in full cry when they saw the lights of a large house ahead.

Von Achen leaned towards Charlotte, smiling that false smile. 'Feeling better now?' he asked.

'Oh, much, and longing for an ice, Gustav. The food is so good here, I am sure they must make wonderful ones. And a little more wine, perhaps? Or do you think I have had enough?' She looked at him with large eyes, every inch the little woman.

Had she put it on too thick? No. He swallowed it all, congratulated himself on his easy conquest, and sent for the waiter to order ices, and a dessert wine.

It was sweet to stickiness and she disliked it very much, but forced a little down because he was drinking it with such obvious pleasure. She was sorry to see the waiter remove her useful soup tureen, and afraid for a moment that he would say something about its contents, but he gave her a speculative glance instead, and she risked a wink at him while von Achen was refilling their glasses. A wink, and a prayer. Would he recognise it for the appeal it was? No way of knowing.

'That will be all.' Von Achen dismissed him. 'Don't disturb us again.' And to Charlotte, handing her her favourite orange ice. 'You see how well I know your tastes, my little love.' His words were slurring a little. 'But, come, time to be comfortable together. I'll be your servant; I'll be your slave.' He pulled her to her feet; put an owner's arm round her waist to guide her to the divan. 'We will be married tomorrow,' he told her. 'No need to be worrying your little head about that. But tonight is ours!' He pushed her down on to the divan, pulled away the gauze scarf, and bent to kiss her breast.

His breath smelled of wine, and his hair of pomatum. She opened her mouth to scream, to protest, and was horribly sick all over him.

17

When they arrived, still singing, grooms came running to take their horses, and the doors of the House of Persephone swung wide in welcome. While Forde spoke to the porter, Beth was aware of something going on; an angry voice raised; a servant running by with a bucket and cloths.

She remembered her first meeting with Charlotte. 'Someone is ill?' She grabbed the man's arm. 'I'm a doctor.' It was her man's voice. 'Show me the way.'

'A doctor?' It was the waiter Charlotte had winked at. 'Well, she surely needs help. This way, sir.'

Forde was still talking to the man at the door, but the other two followed her down a long frescoed corridor.

'Here!' The servant flung open a door on a tableau that Beth would never forget. Von Achen, with his back to her, was standing in his shirtsleeves, swearing unintelligibly in German, as a servant girl tried to mop him down with an inadequate piece of gauze. Behind him, Charlotte was sitting on the edge of a gaudy divan bed, her dress awry, her head in her hands, shaking with hysterical laughter.

Beth heard Peabody say, 'Pity I did not name the stake,' and wondered what he meant. But he had his domino off already and was wrapping Charlotte in it. She needed cleaning up too, Beth saw, and admired the matter-of-fact way he ignored this.

'Best get her home, don't you think, doctor?' Peabody took no notice of von Achen who stood there demoralised, goggling at them, still swearing, but on a lower note. 'We don't bother with him, do we?' Peabody went on, low to Beth. 'We're in time, thank God.'

'Yes.' She was aware of a little crowd beginning to gather in the doorway, and stepped forward to slap Charlotte briskly in the face.

'That will do.' She kept her voice deep. 'Time to go home, child. Miss Prior sent me for you, and a rare scolding is waiting for you, I can tell you, for this prank of yours. And as for you —' turning to von Achen. 'Think shame to yourself for encouraging the child in such a shameless caper. You should be old enough to have some sense, even if she is not.' She saw Forde push his way through the crowd in the doorway. 'Will you take care of the gentleman, sir, and may we borrow your horse to take the young lady home to her friends?'

And that was that. Ten minutes later, the four of them were riding back to Palermo. There had been an anxious moment when Beth wondered whether Charlotte was fit to ride, but Peabody dealt with that. 'You can do it.' He hoisted her skirts and lifted her bodily on to the saddle. 'I'll be close by. Just hang on.'

They did not talk much on the long ride home. All of them were tired, Charlotte exhausted, and each of them felt that anything they said now might be a mistake. Only at last, when they reached home, and Peabody lifted Charlotte down, she looked round at the three of them. 'I do thank you all,' she said. 'I am so grateful, and so ashamed, but, truly, I am not such a fool as you think me. It was not for love that I went out to meet Gustav von Achen.'

'But, Charlotte,' said Beth, 'then why in the world?'

'Time to get the child to bed, I think,' Peabody intervened brusquely. 'Your neighbours are all agog, I am sure, and Miss Prior will be anxious.'

Thus reminded of her disguise, Beth hurried Charlotte into the house, and into bed. 'Time to talk in the morning. What you need now is sleep.'

'Oh, Beth,' Charlotte leaned up from the

pillows to put her arms round her, 'I thought I was done for.'

'I was a little anxious myself,' said Beth.

'Well, thank God for that,' said Peabody as he and Thornton remounted for the short ride home. 'I never thought we would brush through so well. I'm sorry if you thought I stole your thunder, back there, Thornton, but believe me, it will be for the best in the long run. I don't think this is a night young Charlotte is going to enjoy remembering. She did smell, you know, poor child, and she is bound to remember that, and mind. I told you she'd be sick.'

'And what a mercy that was. Otherwise, I think we would have been too late.'

'Yes, so do I,' said Peabody soberly. 'But, just the same, not a habit to encourage her in. I do think, Thornton, it is time you took the gloves off, told her why you came, married her, and took her home.'

'You think it so easy? Oh, if only she would. And poor Miss Prior could come too. Do you think there is any hope that news of tonight's doings won't get out?'

'Do you?'

'No.' They had come to the parting of their ways and both rode home with a great deal to think about.

313

★ ★ ★

Beth woke late and was glad to remember that there was no performance today as everyone would be busy with last-minute preparations for the Rosalia Festival. And that was another threat to be faced. There had been no time to think about it yesterday, but now she found herself wishing passionately that she had seized a chance to tell Peabody about what she feared were the Queen's plans. But on the way out, their thoughts had been all for Charlotte, and on the way back he had been looking after her. He would come today, she was sure, and ask for Charlotte's hand in marriage. She ought to be glad about this. He would be the making of Charlotte. The way he had handled her last night had made that obvious, and the way she had looked at him made her answer equally so. No wonder John Thornton had been so quiet on the ride home. She felt immensely sorry for him.

And for herself. What a curious thing. Depression was no habit of hers, but today there was no fighting it. Charlotte would marry Peabody and vanish into those far distant United States of America. And what will I do? She faced it over her breakfast coffee, refusing food. She had given orders that Charlotte was not to be disturbed, and was grateful for this interval before she started comforting her. I need a little comforting myself, she thought, and then: that's not like me.

No comfort from Forde. If there had been any chance of that, she had put paid to it by leaving him so ruthlessly behind to deal with von Achen. But it had seemed the right thing to do at the time. Besides, she did not want to be comforted by Forde. He was over. That whole episode in her life was over. I am grown up now, she thought, at last, and I am not sure that I like it.

And what in the world was she going to do with her grown-up self? It was a pity she had spent all her savings on this trip. And that brought her uncomfortably back to Forde. He and Mark Weatherby between them, had paid the initial expenses of the trip, but the further funds Forde had promised her had never been forthcoming. It had been awkward to raise the question, still more so to raise it and find it somehow shuffled aside. She had been meaning to try again after the Festival was over, but now felt less than hopeful. He was not going easily to forgive her for leaving him behind at the House of Persephone.

The result was that she had not even enough money to pay her passage home, and the chances of saving it out of her pay were nil. But at least she had not had to sell the Queen's bracelet, thanks to Peabody and Thornton.

And that brought her back to the Queen, and her own suspicion of a massacre planned for tomorrow's festival. Well, to be killed would solve everything, she thought, and was ashamed of herself.

A timid knock on the door introduced a chastened Charlotte. 'Beth, I am so sorry. I should have told you!'

'Of course you should,' cheerfully. 'Tell me, love, why in the world didn't you?'

'He said: "Tell no one." And you were worn out, remember. But it wasn't just that. He said you were in danger, you see; that he dared not write about it, must tell me himself. I knew if I told you, you wouldn't let me go. How could I be such a coward? But it wasn't even only that. I'm ashamed now, it seems so trivial, but I was tired of being left out of things, left to talk to the old Cottones while you hobnobbed with the Queen. This was my turn for the action! And, besides, he still wrote like a lover; I thought it a chance to make him see it was all over. Oh, Beth, I have been all kinds of a fool, haven't I?'

'Not a bit more than I have,' said Beth ruefully. 'And there is no excuse for me. I had actually been warned that there was a plot against you. One of the times I went hobnobbing with the Queen that's what it was about. I should never have let you convince yourself that you had only imagined von Achen meant to carry you off that time. I'm disgusted with myself now, but I truly thought it for the best.'

'Sparing the sick child anything that might upset her,' said Charlotte. 'No need now, Beth. I'm not a child, and I'm not going to be ill any more either.'

'No, you're not, are you?' said Beth. 'So that's a great thing gained. Now we must hope that the gossips don't make too much of a meal of yesterday's doings.'

'Drat the gossips!' And then, conscience-stricken, remembering John Thornton's scolding, 'Oh, Beth, will it have made things worse for you? Is that why Gareth Forde looked so Friday-faced?'

'Never mind Gareth Forde,' said Beth, surprising them both. 'I don't.'

'Then no more do I. Oh, Beth, wasn't Nathan wonderful? Lochinvar, and Sir Charles Grandison, and Galahad all rolled into one. Why are you laughing?'

'I was thinking how surprised he would be to hear you — if he has ever heard of any of the gentlemen.'

'Of course he has. I think he knows everything that matters. Will he come today, Beth? I must thank him.'

'You must thank all three of them.' Beth felt her tone a little quelling and regretted it. 'Yes, I am sure they will all come today, and we had best be getting ready for them.' She pushed back her breakfast tray, ready to get up.

'Beth.' Charlotte turned in the doorway. 'One thing?'

'Yes?' What now?

'If Mr. Peabody comes . . . May I see him alone? Will you help me? I'm so ashamed of the state I was in last night. It's going to be difficult . . . I want to thank him properly.'

To throw yourself into his arms, thought Beth. But best get it over with. 'Very well. I'll contrive to play the absentee chaperone. But he expected you to be sick,' she went on. 'I rather think he had a bet on it with Thornton.'

'A bet?' She did not much like it.

'Let's not play it for more of a drama than it was, love. The first thing he said, when we broke in and found you, was, "Pity I did not name the stake." I asked Thornton about it on the ride back and he told me Peabody had bet him you'd be sick. And thank God you were. I think it just made the difference.'

'Yes,' soberly, 'so do I. I didn't think I could fend him off much longer. One thing I had decided, Beth. Whatever had happened, I wouldn't have married Gustav von Achen.'

'Good for you,' said Beth. 'And now we must get dressed, love, ready for our visitors.'

Charlotte was torn between wanting to be ready, in case Peabody arrived first, and wanting to look her very best. She gave her maid a great deal of trouble before she was done, but was satisfied at last with the vision confronting her in the glass. This was a very far cry from last night's dishevelled victim.

She was downstairs, watering the plants on the terrace, when she heard the first visitor arrive and recognised Peabody's voice with a little leap of the heart. But she had known he would come first. She longed to run to meet him, but they would be more private on the terrace, so she made herself await him there, and was bending gracefully over a late-flowering shrub when he appeared.

'Mr. Peabody!' She held out both hands to him. 'How can I thank you?'

Had she hoped he would pull her to him in a masterful embrace? Instead, he took them both, and held her a little away from him, looking her over with a smile. 'Well, I must say, you look very much more the thing this morning, Miss Pennam. I'm delighted to see you so visibly none the worse for your escapade. I hope the same is true of Miss Prior.'

'Escapade?' She could not believe her ears. 'But —'

He went on as if she had not interrupted. 'Had you ever thought that the only disadvantage of this delightful terrace of yours is that you can have no idea whether your neighbours may not be standing just above or below you, listening to every word you say? Not exactly the place to play a scene of high drama, I have always thought. But then, I have never much liked scenes of drama. We Americans are plain people, Miss Pennam, who like our bread without too much butter, our dishes not too highly seasoned. That is one of the reasons why I am so devoted to your remarkable friend. She can play a tragic scene on the stage, and bring tears to your eyes, but off it, she is more likely to make you laugh than cry.'

'You speak of Miss Prior? Now? To me?'

'Well of course I do.' Looking down at her smitten face, he was sorry for her, but it had to be done. 'Will she be down soon?' he asked. 'I am afraid there are bound to be other callers any moment, and I do badly want a moment alone with her, to be sure that she is none the worse for last night's adventure.'

'Beth?' She looked up at him with large, tragic eyes, understanding at last. 'You did it all for Beth?'

'I'd do anything for her,' he said. 'And now

you know my secret, Miss Pennam, if a mere American can have anything so romantic. And I beg of you to keep it just that, a secret, until I get a chance to tell her myself.'

'Of course I will.' She stiffened her jaw, and he was proud of her. 'But I am afraid you are not going to get a chance now. I can hear someone else arriving.'

'Dammit, so can I. I am your very humble servant, Miss Pennam.' And he raised her hand to his lips and kissed it.

Thornton found them in this elegant pose, and felt a moment of pure rage until he saw the expression on Charlotte's face. And then he was angry with Peabody for hurting her so, for being able to hurt her so.

Beth joined them while they were still saying the proper first things to each other, and Forde appeared soon after that. By tacit agreement, they were all speaking of last night's adventure as just that, a mad prank by a couple of irresponsible young people, from which they had been extricated by their elders.

'But I am afraid your part in it is known all over town,' Forde told Beth. 'I came early, as I thought,' with a glance for the two who had preceded him, 'to warn you of that. No use, I think, to pretend that you did not gallantly accompany us in travesty.'

'Then I most certainly will not try to do

so,' said Beth. 'And I do thank you for the timely warning, Mr. Forde. I knew I could rely on you for all the gossip. What else is being said in town?'

'Gustav von Achen has gone to Messina,' he told her. 'And I hear that the Queen has sent for Carlo Falconi.'

'Oh.' There was a brief, telling exchange of glances. 'Is she back in town then?' Speaking to Forde, Beth wondered more and more what could have gone wrong between Charlotte and Peabody. The poor child looked on the verge of tears, but was fighting them gallantly.

'Yes, she came back from La Favorita last night, ready for the Rosalia Festival tomorrow. No one seems sure whether the King is going to come to it, but I suppose he may make one of his last-minute decisions to do so. One good thing, the celebrations will take the gossips' minds off last night's doings.' With a not very kind look for Charlotte.

'They certainly will.' Beth wondered if she should tell them of her fears for tomorrow. Would they think her mad? She thought she must risk it, but she must get them indoors first. Like Peabody, she had gradually become aware that the terrace was much less private than she had first thought.

But before she could suggest they move in,

a servant appeared with an urgent summons to the palace. 'The Signora Cottone is outside in the carriage, waiting.'

'Forgive me, I must leave you,' she told the three men. 'Would you like to come too, Charlotte, for the ride?'

'I don't believe so, thank you just the same. I find myself a little tired today, somehow. I believe I will just sit in the shade with a book.' There was a sad little dignity about Charlotte as she said this that both worried and impressed Beth. What in the world could Peabody have done to the child?

It was the gentlemen's cue to leave, which they did in a body as Beth hurried to collect a shady hat and join Flora Cottone in the royal carriage.

'How is her majesty?' she asked at once.

'Not at all well. We are all anxious about her. There is even more than usual on her mind. Well, of course, the last few days have not been easy. Their majesties are not often together these days.'

'Does the King mean to come to the celebrations tomorrow?'

'Nobody knows. He calls it a lot of nonsense, you know, and I think he and her majesty have argued about it more than a little. He thinks it an extravagance; she says it will be a great boost for public morale. They are both right, of course.'

'Of course.' Beth had become very fond of this plain, sad lady, whose whole life had been swallowed up by royalty. 'What do you think, signora?'

'Me? Oh, I try not to.'

The Queen had aged visibly since Beth last saw her. The shake in her hands was more pronounced as they clasped the inevitable goblet, a vein throbbed in her scrawny neck. But she was regally jewelled, as if for an audience, the tiara only slightly askew in the white hair.

'Miss Prior, I am glad to see you.' She had dismissed the servants. 'And glad to hear you managed to rescue your young friend last night. She is none the worse, I hope?'

So much for secrecy. 'No, I think she will come out of it well enough, once the first shock is over, and I do thank your majesty for your concern.'

'My responsibility,' said the Queen. 'I have had Falconi here this morning. He confessed of course; he's a nothing that man. The idea of some years in one of my prisons had him talking fast enough. Castroni knew most of it already. That's what I pay him for. You'll have the ransom money back by tonight, Miss Prior. Falconi promised that, in exchange for exile to an island for him and that wife of his. As for the German, I don't think he matters much, do you? He was their tool, though he did not know it. Castroni will keep an eye on him.'

'But the Falconis?' Beth had to ask it. 'Why, your majesty?'

The Queen drank deep from the goblet. 'You're not a fool,' she said. 'You surely see why, Miss Prior.' And then, when Beth sat silent, puzzling it out. 'I can see you may not much like to recognise it, but you know as well as I do that those Falconis are hand in glove with Lord Bentinck, with the party that wants to send the King and me packing, or maybe turn us into puppets, turn our country into another Ireland, a British possession. The Falconis were extorting money from the British, Miss Prior, to finance a sell-out of Sicily to the British. Not very pretty, do you think?'

'No.' Beth had been frightened before, now she was terrified. She was beginning to feel the Queen had reason to be plotting to dispose of the British, here on her island. Dispose of? Massacre? 'But, your majesty —'

'So you must come to the review tomorrow.' The Queen said it as if it followed logically from what had gone before, and Beth was very much afraid that it did.

'I cannot, majesty.' Was she mad to say it?

But what else could she do? They had become, in a curious way, almost friends, the Hapsburg Queen and the woman who lived by her wits. Where Maria Carolina might imagine massacre in the abstract, might she not blench at the planned death of a friend?

'You must,' the Queen said again. 'It is an order, Miss Prior.'

'One I cannot obey, your majesty.' There were red spots on the Queen's cheekbones now, and her head shook a little, so that the jewelled tiara flashed in the light. I must get away, Beth thought, before she realises that I know what she is planning. She had visions of being held a helpless prisoner overnight, unable to warn of the impending disaster. Why in the world had she not done so sooner? Fool. Idiot. But if the Queen were to hold her, she thought that in itself might be a kind of warning.

She watched the angry thoughts chase each other across the Queen's face, a frightening study now in scarlet and blanched white. She had put down the empty goblet and her hands were writhing together in her lap. More and more Beth feared a seizure of some kind and was wondering whether to call for help when a servant appeared, looking frightened, to announce an urgent messenger from Messina.

'From Messina?' Had the Queen forgotten

all about Beth? 'Send him in.'

'Majesty!' The man was covered in the journey's dust, and looked exhausted. 'Cassetti has been arrested.'

'Cassetti? Dear God!' Maria Carolina's hand clutched feebly at her necklace as if it were suddenly too tight. 'Cassetti!' she said again, and Beth caught her as she fell.

18

While Beth was at the palace, Charlotte sat in the shade and pretended to read her book, and no one came to see her. Well, who had she expected? They had all been — and gone, with Beth. Peabody had said his say, and left her to digest it as best she might. It had not been pleasant. Looking back, she thought she had made a fool of herself at every step of her short life. Being abducted and nearly raped concentrates the mind wonderfully, she found. But not to pleasant effect.

Peabody loved Beth. She had deluded herself about him, and he knew it, had as good as told her so. Worse still, he had bet John Thornton that she would be sick in a crisis, and she had. They were doubtless laughing about it still.

I want to go home, she thought. I'm tired of being hot, and dressed up, and polite. The autumn winds would be beginning to blow at Windover. At Hull, plans would be making for the winter assemblies. Suddenly, passionately, she longed for the safe structures of her childhood. If only she could stop play-acting, be Charlotte Comyn again, a young woman with a future, a place in society.

It had all seemed such a game at first. Now the game had turned sour. Forde and von Achen had wanted her for her money, Nathan Peabody did not want her at all. Horrible to have exposed herself to him as a lovesick girl, to be warned off. Lovesick? Idiotic. He had treated her always like a friendly uncle. He had patronized her, now she came to think about it. Besides, she had not the slightest wish to go and live in New Bedford, Massachusetts, of all barbarous places.

Windover was where she wanted to be. But what would it be like going back there? Planning this mad trip, she and Beth had assumed she would simply return as from a visit to her family in the west country. Now, the very idea seemed ridiculous. It would never work; the world was too small for that. And there had been something basically false, she saw now, about her life here, because of the pretence that she was Charlotte Pennam. Having always to remember, to play the part, had cut her off from real life somehow. No wonder she had been such a fool in so many ways. When I go home, she told herself, there will be no more pretending. I shall go home and tell the whole story.

And be cut dead in Hull? She remembered

something John Thornton had said to her, that unlucky day when he proposed, back at Windover. He had tried to warn her of something precarious about her mother's position in Hull society. Not her fault, but there it was. And, if about her mother's, then, of course, also about her own. She had been born, in curious circumstances, in London. He had urged this as a reason for marrying him. That would make all right, he had implied. He had not even known of those lies her grandmother had told about her mother, but they had added a horrible conviction to his argument. Who else had old Mrs. Comyn told that her supposed granddaughter was a bastard?

It had all worked together to push her into this mad escapade — which had made everything infinitely worse. She faced that now. And not just for her. She had done Beth untold harm. She made herself remember and face what had happened the night before: Forde's furious look as Beth demanded his horse for her. She had always known, deep down, that Beth had come on this strange venture in the hope that it would lead to marriage with Gareth Forde. That was why she had been so particularly outraged when he had proposed marriage to her. And now all hopes in that direction must be at an end. Poor, brave Beth.

How gallantly she had pretended not to mind about Forde.

Charlotte dropped *Clarissa* and moved across the terrace to look unseeingly at the far view of sea and sky, and one ship far out. I shall go home, she decided. I shall face them all. I shall behave like a rich woman who can afford to be eccentric. And I will take Beth with me. Look after her. We will neither of us be forced into a marriage we do not want, just for appearances' sake. I must say all this to her. Quickly, before she does anything desperate. And then we will go home.

Her mother would help them. She knew that now. Playing so hard at being Charlotte Pennam she had thrust the question of her mother to the bottom of her mind. Now she brought it up, and, guiltily, faced it. Believing her grandmother's lies, she had let a great gulf widen between her and Kathryn, then blamed her mother for it. My fault, she thought; all my fault. When Beth had told her the true story, she could not bring herself to confess her groundless suspicion of murder in a letter. How could she? But it had meant an inevitable element of untruth in the letter she had finally written home after being reproached for her neglect by John Thornton.

He was always scolding her, that man. His expression, last night, had been as bad as a scolding. And he had stood back and let Nathan Peabody look after her. Making his position clear? If he had ever truly wanted to marry her, which she had always doubted, that was all over now. Even the idea of uniting their two banks would not make up for what he must think her inexcusable behaviour.

Small town thinking, she told herself; I will have none of it. But she had been admitting her homesickness for Hull. It suddenly struck her that her mother, too, must have felt like this. She had run away from Hull, but in the end she had gone back there, had worked through the *Hull Review* to change things there, make them better. How childish to have resented being neglected for the paper. Of course it was more important than she was.

And what would it do to her mother, who had faced down one scandal in her life, to have her daughter come home trailing another one? And bringing scandalous Beth with her?

She tried, and failed, to imagine Beth settling down to life in Hull, where she had once been a servant. She had been romancing again, on a new tack, and was angry with herself once more. It was almost a relief when Beth came home with her dramatic tale of the Queen's seizure. No time to think or talk of anything else today. And tomorrow was the Rosalia Festival and she was belatedly becoming aware that Beth was, most unusually, anxious about her part in it. She felt more and more, guiltily, that she had not thought enough about Beth's career, had not realised its importance to her, had been selfish as usual. No wonder John Thornton scolded her. But at least he and Nathan Peabody had promised to escort her to the royal review in the morning. She was upstairs searching her wardrobe for a particularly becoming dress for the occasion when Fagan called.

Beth had been searching her heart as to whether she could safely assume that Cassetti's arrest and the Queen's illness must have put an end to all threat of a new Sicilian Vespers. She was sure it was safe to assume this. Was she sure? Of course she was. She wished she were. She also wished she knew whether the Queen had ordered the Falconis' arrest and the return of the ransom money before her seizure.

Altogether she was delighted to see Fagan, who had questions of his own. 'Do you think her majesty will recover?' He plunged right into it. 'You must see as clearly as I do how gravely the situation here would be changed if she were no longer in command of affairs.'

'Not necessarily for the worse.' Beth was glad of a chance to say this. 'I have been more and more aware of how anxious she was about British plans for Sicily.' And rightly so, she thought, but did not say.

'You think that?' Thoughtfully. 'It is true Lord William did not give a very friendly impression. It's that brusque manner of his —'

'Not what royalty is used to,' Beth agreed. 'Mr. Fagan —'

'Yes?'

'Think me an idiot, think me an anxious fool, but should some extra precautions perhaps be taken for the review and festival tomorrow? You know what the Palermitans are like, what a volatile lot they are . . . I had wondered if there might not be some explosion of popular feeling.'

'Had you indeed?' With another sharp look. 'Well, Miss Prior, so had I. You have heard, I have no doubt, of the arrest of the man Cassetti at Messina. In fact, this was a result of some extra precautions we have been taking. Things are screwed down tight there, I can tell you, and there is a detachment of British troops on the way here, ostensibly to take part in the review tomorrow. A gesture of courtesy, we are calling it. This place is a powder keg, Miss Prior, and I shall be more glad than I can say when Lord William returns.'

'Will you?' she asked, and got a very

thoughtful look indeed.

'That reminds me.' He changed the subject. 'I have a message for you and Miss Pennam from Lady William. You may not have heard of the surprise arrest of the Falconis. They are off to an island for their sins, whatever they may be. Mind you, if her majesty continues unconscious . . . But the case is, they will most certainly not be present at the review tomorrow, or the festival. Lady William has suggested that Miss Pennam might care to join her party.'

'Oh, that is *good* of Lady William!' exclaimed Beth. And then, 'Mr. Fagan, she does know?'

'About Miss Pennam's troubles? Indeed she does.'

'Then I am more grateful than I can say.'

With Charlotte's plans for the morning settled, she had time to worry about her own. Bartolucci had been vague when she asked him exactly what he planned, explaining that it was all to be settled in the morning of the day itself, when the float on which Saint Rosalia's image was paraded through the town was fetched out of store on to the Marino. She could not much like the idea of being paraded through town. Suppose there really was an anti-British claque. She would be exposed to anything they chose to throw at her.

She must not let herself think of that. But she would be very glad when tomorrow was over.

She found Charlotte in her room surveying most of her wardrobe, spread out on her bed, and gave her Lady William's message.

'The Falconis arrested!' This was amazing news to Charlotte. 'But Beth, why in the world? Is the Queen mad?'

'Well, I do sometimes wonder,' Beth admitted. 'But for goodness' sake, Charlotte, never say I said so. But she's not in the least mad when it comes to the Falconis. I had thought to spare you the knowledge, but, Charlotte I am afraid they were behind your kidnapping. There's been so little time to talk, but that is how we found you. They had had you taken to their own disused country house. Once we worked that out we got to thinking about the House of Persephone which was close by. There weren't that many places where von Achen could have held you overnight. Charlotte dear, I can't tell you how I regret that I didn't tell you of the Queen's warning, but I truly thought you had enough on your hands playing one part, without having yet another pretence thrust upon you.'

'Oh, Beth.' Charlotte dropped the pale muslin she was holding and raised desolate eyes to her friend. 'It's all been a terrible mistake, hasn't it?'

'Oh, I don't know about that.' Beth smiled at her lovingly. 'You have to admit it's been interesting. And now, I think early bed, don't you? It's going to be a long day tomorrow. But I can't tell you how glad I am about Lady William. At least I shan't be worrying about you.'

'Oh, Beth, I'm so angry with myself. I've been thinking about it all day.'

'Don't mind it, love. We all have things we wish undone. Nothing for it but to forgive oneself, tie a knot, and go on.'

'I'll try.' With a watery smile. 'Beth, I do wish you luck for tomorrow. Will I see you between the rehearsal and the parade?'

'I'm afraid not,' Beth told her. 'Bartolucci wants us all to stay together after the rehearsal, and I don't blame him. There are going to be such crowds in town tomorrow that it would be easy just to find oneself unable to get back to the float. That's why I am so particularly grateful to Lady William. You will stay close to her, won't you, Charlotte?'

'I most certainly will. No more mad starts, I promise. But you look worn out, Beth. Was it very dreadful with the poor Queen.'

'It was quite sad, poor lady.'

'Will she recover, do you think?'

'It's hard to tell what to wish for her.'

And on that sombre note they parted for the night.

It was a heavy night, with a threat of September storm in the air, and Charlotte slept badly, dreaming of Windover, and a faceless man who turned away from her on the cliff. She woke early and unrefreshed and hurried downstairs to see Beth off and wish her luck.

'There are going to be British troops as well as the Neapolitan Guard at the review,' Beth told her, as if casually. 'It should be a splendid spectacle.'

'One review is very much like another, if you ask me,' said Charlotte. 'It's the procession I am looking forward to. I was reading about it in Brydone yesterday; he makes it sound a splendid occasion: everyone so happy, with their beloved saint in their midst.'

'I do hope it turns out like that. But there's the carriage, love, I must go. I'll send it straight back for you. Enjoy yourself.'

It was on the tip of Charlotte's tongue to say she hardly hoped to do so, escorted by two men who cared nothing for her, but why spoil Beth's day? She smiled instead, and wished her luck, and felt a little pleased with herself for a change.

As she had expected, her two escorts arrived

punctually and together just as the carriage drew up again outside the house. She wondered what they had been betting on this time.

'That's good,' said Thornton, after the first formal greetings. 'Lady William particularly asked that we arrive prompt to the minute. She expects a good deal of confusion at the palace, which is not the usual scene for royal reviews. But of course it can hardly take place on the Marino, with all the preparations being made there for the procession.'

'You have seen Lady William today?' Charlotte asked, as he handed her into the carriage.

'No, yesterday. I hope Miss Prior went off in good heart for her rehearsal. Does she know any more of what her part will be?'

'No. Signor Bartolucci said he could not plan anything until they had the float to work on.'

'A long day for her,' said Peabody. 'And a long one yesterday, by all reports. We longed to call, Thornton and I, when we heard the rumours of that dramatic scene at the palace, but decided she needed her rest more than our solicitude.'

'Considerate of you.' Naturally neither of them had given a thought to her own long, lonely day. Was she being sorry for herself again? Something in Peabody's quizzical glance disturbed her. 'I'm worried a little about Beth,' she told him. 'I think she's worried herself. About being up there on the float. But Brydone says it's a happy occasion.'

'Yes,' said John Thornton. 'I've read that too, but that is the real festival. No one seems quite to understand the reason for this one.'

'Specially now the Queen is ill,' said Peabody. 'What did Miss Prior say about that, Miss Pennam?'

'She said —' She put a hand to her mouth. 'She said I was not to say.'

'Then you most certainly must not,' Peabody told her, and changed the subject.

They found Lady William and her party already established on a balcony overlooking the parade ground, and her hostess's cool, civil reception gave Charlotte an uncomfortable foretaste of what her life was going to be like from now on, here in Palermo. She knew she ought to be grateful for being received at all, but found this rather more than she could manage. Relegated to the farthest corner of the balcony, she found John Thornton beside her. 'The last review I attended was on the Garrison Side at Hull,' he told her. 'Do you know, Miss Pennam, for all our exotic surroundings and grand company, I find myself very much wishing I was there now.'

'Oh, so do I,' she said, and then remembered the masquerade, and blushed crimson.

'They are beginning,' he said. 'Remember to block your ears when they fire the salutes. We are a little nearer the guns than I quite like. It seems a makeshift enough business altogether, if you ask me.'

'You speak like an expert.'

'Well, of course. We are proud of our volunteer bands, where I come from, Miss Pennam.'

'John —' Suddenly, she was sick of the whole pretence. Had she been going to say, 'Take me home'? She thought so. But at that moment the salute was fired. As the sudden noise deafened her, his iron hand was on her shoulder, pressing her down to the tiled floor of the balcony; she felt his weight on top of her, heavy, formidable. Debris rained around them; people were screaming; people were cursing.

'All over now.' He was lifting her to her feet, matter-of-fact as usual. 'One of the guns must have burst. I thought they looked well past their prime.'

'But you're hurt!' Blood was streaming down his face from a cut on his temple.

'A scratch, no more.' He put his handkerchief to it. 'Ah, here come our troops. Crisis over, I think.'

19

Beth gasped when she saw Saint Rosalia's triumphal chariot. It was as high as a house, and, surely, nearly as wide as the streets it was to be pulled along by its team of fifty-six enormous mules. She could see now why it went straight down the Great Street from the Porta Felice to the Porta Nuova. There was no way in the world it could possibly turn a corner.

'But suppose it sticks in the street?' she asked Bartolucci anxiously as he held out a hand to help her on to the stage built high at the front of the float.

'We will suppose no such thing, if you please.' But she felt that he was anxious too.

The musicians of the small orchestra were already in their places at the front of the little stage. She had to climb up to the apex of the small amphitheatre and take her own place directly below the silver-gilt statue of Saint Rosalia that topped the unwieldy machine.

She felt enormously exposed as she turned to look down at Bartolucci. She was on a level now with the upper floors of the houses that faced on to the Marino, with only the slightest of handrails to steady her.

Bartolucci was outlining the order of the procession. They would make only three stops, he told them, one inside the Porta Felice, the next in the Ottangolo, and the last inside the Porta Nuova. And they would give the same simple programme of sacred songs at each stop.

'This is a solemn occasion,' he reminded them. 'Those of you who are strangers to Sicily will be so good as to remember that our Saint Rosalia is to us what Saint Januarius is to the Neapolitans. Or Saint George to the British,' looking up at Beth, perched above him at the top of the amphitheatre.

'I suppose so.' She felt her answer inadequate, and also felt that, just because she was foreign, she could not protest about the exposed insecurity of her own position. After all, other singers must have managed. Signora Bartolucci would have sung here in July.

Everyone was restless, there was unease in the air, and Beth from her high perch could see unwonted clouds gathering inland over Monte Pellegrino. What happened if it rained? Unlikely in July, when the festival usually took place, it began to seem a real possibility today.

The rehearsal went quite as badly as she

343

had expected, and Bartolucci was still haranguing them about their poor performance when he was silenced in mid-sentence by the sound of an explosion echoing down from the direction of the palace.

'What's that?' he exclaimed, and they were all silent, straining to listen. Then: 'The royal salute, that's all.' He raised his baton. 'We will take the last chorus again, if you please, with your hearts in it this time.'

The rehearsal was over at last, and Beth had climbed gratefully down from her high place to join the rest of the performers, when a breathless messenger arrived to tell of the explosion at the palace. No one had been seriously hurt, he said. The review had been cancelled, but the rest of the festival was to continue as planned.

'Who was hurt, do you know?' Beth managed to catch the messenger.

'Several soldiers who were near the gun that burst,' he told her. 'And I believe one of the Englishmen, but only slightly.'

That is what he would say, she thought, but failed to elicit any more information, since one foreigner looked very much like another to him. It added a last straw of anxiety to this wretched day. She gave the man an immense tip and begged him to try and find out more, but though he made lavish promises she

344

thought she had wasted her money. He would go off and spend it, and watch the procession.

Time dragged. They could not start until a message came to let Bartolucci know that the royal party had reached the Viceroy's Palace on the Ottangolo. The man she had bribed did not return and she told herself she had known he would not, and was disappointed just the same. But surely if something serious had happened to Peabody or Thornton, someone would have let her know. And of course there were plenty of other Englishmen. Why was she so sure that it was Peabody, that he was badly hurt and concealing it? Bleeding inwardly perhaps?

The message came from the Ottangolo at last. 'Places, please,' called Bartolucci, and Beth climbed to her high vantage point for the last time. At least, she thought, she would be able to see whether all their party were safely present on Lady William's balcony.

The band of trumpeters and kettle-drummers who led the procession struck up a rousing march and moved forward under the Porta Felice. Now the gold-and-silver-clad postillions cracked their whips over the mules, and the cumbrous carriage lurched forward on its huge wheels. Beth clutched the rail below her and hoped that someone had inspected those wheels. The huge machine was heavy enough in itself, but now it was further burdened by the orchestra and singers. She instinctively ducked her head as they passed under the Porta Felice, and looked ahead up the Great Street to the buildings of the Ottangolo, half a mile away.

The huge carriage creaked to a halt. Time for the first performance. The crowd in the street and on the balconies were waving handkerchiefs, scarves, coloured streamers of all kinds. A shower of bonbons and coloured paper fell among the singers and Beth thought how easy it would be to throw something else, and nearly missed her cue.

It all went a little better this time, but when her own solo part was done, and she was free to look about her, she began to be aware that the audience was not at all what she had expected from Brydone's description. This was a token enthusiasm which had hardly outlasted the first chorus. Her own solo had been listened to respectfully enough, but now people were turning away from the singers to talk earnestly to each other. Had there been more to that explosion than had been reported? Or had Maria Carolina miscalculated the effect of this extra festival on the volatile Palermitan public? Or was there, perhaps, drastic news of the Queen herself?

Thinking of this, Beth was caught unawares

when the huge machine lurched forward. Clutching the handrail to steady herself, she felt it begin to give under her hand. Leaning back, balancing herself with a desperate effort of will, she explored the terrifying possibilities. Wear and tear? Or had it been tampered with? And, if so, to what end? A dramatic fall in the course of the procession; the lead singer killed, or seriously injured . . . It would be at once the worst of omens for the superstitious crowd, and a pleasure to Bartolucci's wife, whose place as diva she had taken. She had been grateful to Signora Bartolucci for taking her demotion so calmly. Was this perhaps her answer?

Coldly facing facts, she thought she would be able to balance well enough so long as the carriage moved steadily forward, and stopping should be all right. It was when the float moved forward again after the performance at the Ottangolo that the danger lay. Of course, that was where a disaster would be planned. What could she do to avert it? She tried in vain to catch Bartolucci's eye, signal to him that something was wrong, but he was happily bowing this way and that to his friends on balconies as they passed. And the orchestra and chorus, well below, had their backs to her. She felt immensely alone as the huge vehicle was pulled slowly forward towards the

Ottangolo and the next crisis.

She did not dare look sideways at the balconies, for fear of losing her balance, but Lady William's house faced across the Ottangolo to where the Great Street entered it. Her friends would be on the balcony there. Might she be able to catch their attention, give some kind of signal for help? But this, too, would mean stopping the procession. And that might so easily precipitate just the kind of anti-British riot they feared. Not much comfort to think of British troops on duty up at the palace if trouble were to break out at the Ottangolo. The streets were so packed with people that there was no chance of help arriving in time.

Looking ahead, she could see that the first musicians had reached the Ottangolo. A wave of cheering greeted them, almost drowning the strident sound of their instruments. It was too noisy to think. The carriage lurched a little as the first of the mules entered the square. She made herself fix her eyes steadily, straight ahead. Soon she would be able to see Lady William's balcony, but what good would that be?

The light was changing. How strange. The gold and silver of the postillions' gala dress no longer gleamed in the sun. She could see heads on balconies across the square turning upwards to scan the sky anxiously. And now she could see Lady William's balcony, ahead and just to the left, with its gaily dressed group of people, all looking upwards. Lady William, Forde, Fagan, Charlotte rather in a corner, with John Thornton beside her. His head was bandaged. But where was Peabody?

Killed, she thought. And nobody told me. So nothing matters. The carriage moved into the square and she hardly noticed, looking straight ahead at desolation.

It had stopped, and she was still upright. Bartolucci raised his baton for the first chorus. There was a crash and a searing flash as lightning streaked down the statue of Saint Rosalia and so down behind her. Shocked by the scorch of its passage, she leaned forward, instinctively clasped the handrail, and felt it give totally under her hand.

Charlotte admired the cool authority with which Lady William collected up her little party after the explosion, saw to it that John Thornton's head was bandaged, and marshalled them to the carriages that would take them to the Ottangolo. 'That's a great lady,' she told John Thornton.

'You would do it just as well, if need were.' He smiled at her, and her heart lurched in her breast. Absurd. Ridiculous. What was she imagining now? She felt colour flood her face. He had knocked her down, fallen on her, squeezed her ribs and crushed her dress. And everything had changed between them. But had it? Did he feel it too? How could she tell?

'Does it really not hurt?' She made herself ask it casually, as he stood back to let her go first on to Lady William's balcony.

'Not the least in the world. I've a hard head.' He took her arm to steer her into the furthest corner of the balcony, and again she felt an electric shock run through her.

What is happening to me? She must not let it show. 'I think there is a storm coming,' she looked up at the darkening sky. 'The air feels strange.'

'Just the air? Charlotte —' But a servant approached them, handing out little parcels of streamers to be thrown at the procession. 'Lady William thinks of everything,' he said.

'Yes, but I don't like it.' Peabody had come up on the other side of Charlotte. 'Such a chance to throw something else. This doesn't strike me as at all the happy crowd Brydone describes.'

'Well, it's not the real occasion,' said Thornton. 'But, surely, with the Queen ill . . .'

'Is there any news of her?' asked Charlotte.

'Just the same, I believe. I wish they had

cancelled this frolic.'

'The King said his wife would wish it to go ahead.'

'If we could only see down the Great Street.' Peabody sounded anxious. 'I'm told the float is immensely high, and the lead singer stands at the very top.'

'We'll see soon enough,' Thornton told him. 'The music is getting nearer.'

'If you call it music,' said Charlotte. 'I hope poor Beth isn't supposed to sing against that. Look, here they come!' There was a ripple in the crowd, where the Great Street entered the square, and then the first drummers entered, the crowd falling back before them, so that people were squeezed close against the buildings. 'Goodness, I am glad we are up here,' she said.

'Yes,' Thornton agreed. 'They all look cheerful enough so far, but what a muddle.' They could see little scuffles breaking out all round the square as people who had been in the front row got pushed back into the crowd. 'Just so long as nothing goes wrong — Oh, here it comes!'

The musicians had managed to form into ragged ranks across the square, leaving an aisle so that the pairs of huge mules could go straight across. And at last the huge float came into view at the corner.

'Oh my goodness,' exclaimed Charlotte. 'Look at poor Beth!' And then, 'The sun's gone in.'

'Yes,' said Thornton. 'If it rains, we won't move until everyone else has gone. Better get wet than get crushed, don't you think, Peabody?'

'He's gone,' said Charlotte. 'Something's wrong with Beth, I think.' The float was still moving slowly forward towards the centre of the square, and all the time it was getting darker. The din of drums and trumpets was suddenly stilled, there was a little hush across the clamorous crowd, and into the silence came the tearing crash of thunder, with its simultaneous lightning flash. For an instant, the float was lividly lit, and she saw Beth's figure sway, dark against the light, clutch the rail below her, fall.

'It gave way.' Thornton had his arm round her, holding her tight, as panic struck the crowded balcony. 'I think someone caught her.' It was dark now, and out of the darkness came rain in torrents. 'Don't move, Charlotte,' he said. 'Not yet. I've got you.' They were both straining their eyes to see what was happening on the float.

'John, it's on fire!'

'Made of wood,' he said. 'And the statue metal. Madness. If I could only see . . . Charlotte, I'm almost sure someone caught her as she fell.'

There were screams now from the float as well as from the square, where people were fighting to get away from the flames that licked around the base of the huge carriage.

'Thank God for the rain,' said John Thornton. 'I think we should start down now. It looks as if the worst was over here.' The last spectators were vanishing through the big door into the house. 'Keep close.' His arm made it impossible to do anything else, and she was glad of it. They were both soaked to the skin, and rivulets of water were running from her hair.

'I hope there is a back way out,' said John Thornton.

'But, Beth,' protested Charlotte. 'We must find out what has happened to her.'

'Peabody will be with her.' He said it with absolute certainty. 'Don't mind too much, Charlotte.'

'Mind? Why should I mind?' But they were in the crowded salon now, and she was not sure if he heard her as he tried to make a reasonably civil way for them through the vociferous groups of people. Those who had managed to keep dry wanted to stay, those who had been drenched wanted to get home at all speed.

'This way.' John Thornton had spoken quickly to a servant, now pushed her through an inconspicuous service door concealed in a corner behind a Chinese screen.

It led to a different world: a dark, filthy corridor, then a steep little stair. 'Careful.' He let go of her to lead the way. 'It's slippery.'

With grease, she thought, and it stank. It led straight into a vast kitchen where drenched servants were too busy running about and swearing to notice them. A back door gave on a courtyard full of stinking rubbish, and so into an alley. It was still pouring with rain, but they were beyond caring.

'Are you cold?' he asked.

'No. Yes — a little. It doesn't matter. Where are we going, John?'

'I'm taking you home,' he told her. 'You're drenched. Peabody will bring Beth, I'm sure of it. Don't worry. It does no good.' He had her arm, hurrying her along a narrow lane into which soaking people were crowding as they escaped from the chaos of the Ottangolo. He took a right turn to get further from the crowd, then a left. 'Can you go faster? I want to get across the main road before it gets too crowded.'

'It's my skirts.' They were soaked and clinging round her, shortening her stride.

'Hitch them up.' He hardly slackened speed

to let her do so, urging her ruthlessly to a near trot.

She saw his point when they reached the main road to the east and saw it already filling up with fugitives from the Ottangolo. Very soon it would be impassable.

'Could you understand what they were saying?' she asked as they plunged into another alley on the seaward side of the street.

'I rather think the fire is out.' They were away from the worst of the crowd now and he shortened his stride to hers. 'What a blessing I know you for a good walker, Charlotte. We haven't a hope of finding a carriage.'

'Of course not. Besides, it's warmer walking. If only we knew what had happened to Beth.'

'No use worrying,' he said again. 'Right, here.' He was guiding her expertly through the maze of alleys. 'Lucky thing I have amused myself walking about this town. And I think the rain is beginning to slacken. Are you very cold, my poor Lotte?'

'No, just drowning.' Tears started to her eyes at his use of the childhood name.

'Oh, my poor child.' He saw, and misunderstood. 'You must not mind it so much. He's years too old for you, and, if you ask me, something of a bully.'

'I know,' she told him. 'Beth will deal with him admirably. What in the world makes you think I care about Nathan Peabody, John?'

'But you did,' he said.

'I thought I did.' She admitted it ruefully. 'He set me right. Bully's not just the word — bossy, perhaps? He told me I couldn't hold a candle to Beth, and of course he was right. But then I don't want to. I'm very happy as I am. As me: Charlotte Pennam Comyn. When this is all over, and we know Beth is all right, will you take me home, John?'

'Of course I will.' He stopped, dropped her arm, pulled her round to face him. 'Charlotte, do you mean . . . Can you really mean?'

'Well, of course I do. How can I put it more plainly.' She smiled an invitation.

'Charlotte!'

Swept into his arms, lost in his embrace, she pulled away at last. 'You taste of salt,' she said. 'Is it rain or tears?'

'Both, I think. I've loved you so long, Charlotte. I think I had given up hope.'

'I didn't know. You were so matter of fact, that day at Windover. I thought it was just our families, our banks . . . Oh, what a waste of time.'

'Don't think that, Charlotte. Never think that. We love each other better now.'

'Yes,' thoughtfully. 'Yes, that's quite true.

Well, one thing, I'm grown-up now. I wasn't before. Oh, there is so much I want to tell you, John.'

'And I you, but not, perhaps, here in a stinking Sicilian alley. Time to go home, love, and find out about Beth and Peabody.'

'Do you think she will like living in New Bedford, Massachusetts?'

'I wish I knew. But I'm sure they'll manage.'

20

Beth's fall had been broken by the group of sopranos just below her, but she was winded for a moment, aware only of screaming and confusion all around. Rain was catapulting down now, there was another growl of thunder, she pulled herself together and began to apologise to the women she had fallen on. None of them seemed to be seriously hurt, which was a miracle, she thought. But they were all close to hysteria, and no wonder; there was a hiss and crackle as fire from the dry timber of the under-carriage met the downward plunge of the rain. There was only one way out, at the front of the float, and the members of the orchestra were crowding towards it, trying to protect their instruments from the rain, fighting each other to go first.

'We'd best wait a few minutes,' Beth urged the panic-stricken women around her, but they were beyond reason, and pushed past her towards the savage crowd at the exit.

'No, Beth, this way.' Peabody's voice, she would know it anywhere. She looked about her, saw his head, topping the side of the cart.

'Can you reach me?' he asked. 'Trust me?'

'Of course.' She pushed one of the high stools the singers had used over to the side of the cart, climbed on to it and faced him. Not high enough. She reached down to tear savagely at the skirts of her drenched muslin, and, liberated, got a toehold on the uneven side of the float, lifted herself bodily to the edge, and perched there, high above the crowd.

'Do just as I tell you.' His hand was warm on hers. 'It's a climb down, I'm afraid, but there's a kind of workman's ladder. I'll go first. Do just as I say.'

'Believe me, I will.'

The rain sluiced down; she could hear screams and the crackle of flame further back along the carriage side; she put hand and foot meticulously where he told her, thinking of nothing else, and found herself at last on the flagstones of the square. The crowd had fallen back from around the burning carriage, leaving a little space where they faced each other.

She was going to thank him, but, 'No time,' he said. 'Quick, this way.'

And again she obeyed him instinctively, letting him put a firm arm round her, steer her through the crowd. 'Head on my shoulder,' he told her. 'I don't want you recognised. Be a clinging woman for once.'

They were in the thick of the panicky crowd now and she was glad enough to obey. Besides, she was in no state to be recognised. She had a horrid feeling that her torn skirt was now split to the waist, revealing more bare leg than she cared to think about. What an absurd thing to be thinking. She was alive, and so was Nathan.

She kept her head meekly down on his shoulder, but could feel that the crowd was a little thinner, the paving had changed under her feet, they must be in one of the alleys that led off the square.

'Where are we going?' she asked.

'Head down,' he told her. 'To my rooms, they are nearest. I want you off the streets. God knows what will happen if the crowd's mood takes a superstitious turn.'

' "Dastardly British," you mean. "An affront to Saint Rosalia?" I'm keeping my head down, but I can still talk.'

'You'd thought of that too?'

'Yes. When I found the handrail had been tampered with. I was trying to stand alone, but that lightning flash —'

'Tampered with? That's what was wrong! I could see something was, by the look of you.'

'I'm glad you did. I never did like crowds, and they were in a fine panic on that float.'

'If that had been the worst of it,' he said. 'I had visions of you being sacrificed to Saint Rosalia.'

'Sacrificed?'

'The Neapolitan crowd tore an innocent messenger to pieces a while ago. Here we are. At my back door. Quick, now, in with you!' He whisked her through a gate, across a yard, and into a kitchen that smelled of garlic and red wine. A fat woman, stirring something on a brazier turned and exclaimed at sight of them.

'Quiet, Maria.' Nathan spoke in surprisingly good French. 'The crowd is in an ugly mood. I have brought the signora here for safety. No one must know.' He turned to Beth. 'Maria speaks French but no English.' Was it a warning?

'Then no one will.' She beamed at them both, gap-toothed. 'You can trust old Maria. And would the signora perhaps like to borrow a dress?' She was looking with frank amusement at Beth's legs. 'It will go twice round you, I'm afraid.'

'Never mind,' said Beth. 'I'd be more than grateful, Maria.'

'I'll fetch it directly. The other servants are out, signor, watching the procession as you so kindly permitted. No need to fret about anything. Give the signora a glass of wine,

361

she looks as if she needs it.'

'I certainly do.' Beth found she was shivering and moved forward to the warmth of the brazier while he opened a dark bottle. 'Can we trust old Maria?' she asked when the woman had gone.

'For the moment, absolutely. In the long run, not at all.' He filled a goblet with red wine and handed it to her. 'You are well and truly compromised, my dear friend.'

'You sound very pleased with yourself.'

'I am. Bring your glass, come up to my rooms. Maria will not disturb us there.'

'Not even in the interests of my modesty?' She had stopped even trying to hold the soaking muslin together.

'No indeed. She knows better. Besides, think how she is enjoying herself, wicked old thing. But if it bothers you —' He had led her out into a wide front hall, reached down a cloak from its peg — 'Here. But remember that I have seen your splendid legs often enough, in travesty, on stage.'

'Yes,' she said, 'but that is different.' Wrapping herself in the cloak, she was grateful for its warmth.

'I know. This way.' He ushered her up a marble stairway and into a long first-floor apartment. 'Keep away from the windows,' he instructed.

'You think there may be some shreds of my reputation left?'

'I don't give a damn for your reputation, Beth. It's your life I care about.'

'I thought you were dead,' she told him. 'When the news came of the explosion.'

'Then you have some idea of how I have been feeling. Beth —' He held out his hands to her.

'Yes.' She put hers in his, let the borrowed cloak fall to the floor, felt her body answer his. How long? She had no idea. In the end: 'I'm sorry about my past,' she said.

'Don't be. Without it, you would be different. I like you the way you are. Like you! Love you. Beth —'

'Yes?'

'Would you very much mind a Catholic ceremony, just to be going on with? It's the only kind I seem to be able to lay my hands on, here in Palermo.'

'Catholic? What do you mean, ceremony?'

'I am asking you to marry me, dear fool. What did you think I meant?'

'Not that. Oh, Nathan, not that.' She was crying now, but did not mind.

'I can see you know nothing about us New Englanders,' he told her. 'It's marriage or nothing, dear Beth, and nothing till marriage either. Mind you,' he tilted her chin to look down at her lovingly, 'whether you will be able to bear life in New Bedford is something else again. I am not absolutely sure that I can. I thought, if you agreed, we might give it a try, making my old mamma very happy by doing so, then what do you think of Louisiana, my life? Do you know about Louisiana?'

'Of course I do.' The warm shock of his proposal of marriage was running through her veins. 'You Yankees bought it from Napoleon.'

'And now we are wondering what to do with it. I have been offered a kind of a job there. I think we might like it, you and I. And there will be a theatre there, if I know the French.'

'Which is more than you can say for New Bedford?'

'I'm afraid so,' ruefully. 'Will you be a fish out of water for me, dearest Beth?'

'I'll be anything for you,' she said.

'Even a mother?'

'Oh, Nathan!' Now he had struck her to the heart. 'I don't know . . . I've never . . . I shouldn't . . .'

'Nonsense. It is going to be quite different with me. And here I think is Maria to make you respectable.'

'Dear Nathan, it is you who are going to make me respectable.'

'As if I could! As if I wanted to!'

Maria had brought her own wedding dress. 'It's the only thing I have that's white, and might fit the signora,' she explained. 'I was young and slender then. I saved it for my daughter, but all I have is sons, heaven help me. You must keep it, signora; may it be lucky for you.' Her bright eyes went from one to the other. 'I think it is, already.'

'It is indeed,' said Nathan. 'Take the signora to my room, Maria, and help her dress.' There was a knocking at the door below. 'I'll get that. Don't come down till I tell you, Beth.'

He opened the big door cautiously, just a crack. 'Oh, it's you,' with relief. 'Come in, quick, Forde. What's happening out there?'

'Mayhem.' Shaking the rain out of his coat. 'The crowd's out for blood. English blood. You're an American, safe enough, but frankly I want to get out of here. There's a ship just docked. Peabody, we've not always seen eye to eye, but as one man to another . . .' He paused, searching for words, and Peabody watched him quizzically. 'I'm done for, rolled up,' Forde went on in a rush. 'I thought I'd remake my fortune coming here to Sicily, but it's not worked out like that. I'm desperate. Peabody, will you lend me the passage money?'

'What's the ship?'

'An English merchantman with supplies for the troops. She is going on to Messina, then to Malta. She leaves in the morning, if the wind holds. Peabody, I beg of you!'

'She didn't bring Lord William back?'

'No, only letters. Peabody, please — The crowd's ugly out there. God knows what's going to happen.'

'And the ladies?' Peabody went on with his relentless questions. 'What about Miss Prior and Miss Pennam?'

'They will be safe enough. They are royally protected, after all.'

'Is there news of the Queen?'

'None that I have heard of, but everyone knows about the King's fancy for Beth Prior. One way or another, she is sure of protection.'

'What a shabby fellow you are, Forde.' Peabody went to his desk. 'But I'm grateful for the news you have brought. How much do you need?' And then, 'But one thing first. I need a note taken to Miss Prior and Miss Pennam, something I cannot trust to a servant. Do that for me, Forde, come back here, and you shall have the money.' And then, aware of the other man's reluctance, 'No need to see them, just make sure one of them gets the note, bring me back an answer, and the money is yours.' He was writing quickly, reached for taper and wax, sealed the note and handed it Forde. 'There. Don't stand around thanking me, you've not got the money yet.'

Opening the door as little as possible to let Forde out, he saw crowds still milling about in the Great Street. The rain had stopped as suddenly as it had started and people who had expected a day of merrymaking were reluctant to go home. Presently the fountains were supposed to start running wine, in honour of the saint, and what would happen, either if they did or if they did not, was anybody's guess.

He went half way up to the next floor. 'Beth, are you ready?'

'Yes, who was that?' She came down to him, splendid in heavy white silk that had turned ivory with age. 'Did you know Maria's father kept silkworms?'

'My darling, you are blushing!'

'Yes, isn't it strange? I thought I had outgrown that years ago. What are you doing to me, Nathan?'

'What are we doing to each other?' Smiling. 'How happy I am. And that was Forde, my love, with good news. There's an English ship in harbour, bound for Messina and Malta, and you and I, and Charlotte and Thornton are all going to be on her when she leaves.'

'And Forde?' she asked. 'What an interesting party we shall make.'

'Yes. He came to borrow the fare, not to enquire after you as I thought. I've sent him with a note to Charlotte, asking her and Thornton to join us here. What's the matter?'

'Will you be safe on a British ship? Suppose our countries are at war?'

'Safer there than here, I think. And I'll suppose no such thing. If need be, we will go ashore at Malta, you and I. An old married couple, we will be by then. Better a British ship's captain than a Sicilian priest, don't you think? You won't mind doing it so in hugger-mugger?'

'Mind?' Her smile said the rest. 'And, look, I'm dressed for it already.'

'So you are. There's an omen for you! Now, stay close, love, to receive Charlotte and Thornton, while I find Fagan and arrange our passages.'

'Be careful!'

'Believe me, I will. Strange how happiness makes one cautious. I value myself now.'

'And so you should. But I think you always did, Nathan. It's one of the things I have liked about you.'

'Liked?'

She smiled. 'Loved, Nathan.'

'Oh, thank God she's safe.' Charlotte's hands had trembled as she broke the seal of

Peabody's note. 'At Peabody's. You were right, John. He wants us to go there, on foot, with just what we can carry. There's a ship come in; we are going to board her tonight, under cover of the promenade on the Marino. The crowd's still ugly, he says.'

'It certainly is.' Forde had delivered the note in person, was watching her and Thornton with interest. 'I'd waste no time, if I were you; there's a kind of afternoon hush at the moment, but it won't last. I promised Peabody I'd take him your answer. Would you write him a line, Miss Pennam, to say you are coming?'

'Write? Can't you just tell him?'

'If you wouldn't mind —' Embarrassed. 'And, quickly, Miss Pennam, if you please. I mean to be on board too, and I have all my arrangements to make.'

'Yes, of course.' She was still puzzled. 'It's good of you to have come, Mr. Forde, when you must have so much to do.'

'Just write the note, Charlotte,' said Thornton, who had been watching Forde. 'We are going to be busy too.'

'Yes.' She retired to her writing desk.

Forde followed her with his eyes, then turned to Thornton. 'Well,' he said. 'Am I to congratulate you, Thornton?'

'If you like,' said Thornton.

369

* ★ *

The air was cooling and the light beginning
to fade when Charlotte and John Thornton
were ready to leave, so that it was possible
to put on cloaks, as if for the promenade on
the Marino. The crowd was still surging
about, rather aimlessly now, a prey to rumour
and counter-rumour.

'I suppose they are waiting for the fountains
to start spouting wine,' said Charlotte.

'Then we had better walk faster,' said
Thornton.

'You keep saying that,' with a loving, teasing glance. 'Are you going to bully me, John
Thornton?'

'As if I would dare.'

They found Beth alone. 'Nathan went to
find Fagan and arrange our passages,' she explained. 'I wish he'd come back. It's been
ages.'

'Nathan?' asked Charlotte. And then, 'Beth,
what in the world are you wearing?'

'Maria's wedding dress.' She smiled at
them. 'And mine, I hope.'

'Oh, Beth.' Charlotte went into her arms.
'I am so happy for you! And you are to be
glad for us.'

'I thought so!' Kissing her warmly. 'What
a happy ship's company we are going to be!'

'If they will take us,' said John Thornton.

'And if we can get to the docks.' He had been looking out of the window. 'The crowd is getting noisier. I wish Peabody would come back.'

'He will,' said Beth.

But it was dark, and even she was growing anxious when Peabody returned at last. 'It took some arranging,' he told them. 'But arranged it is, and the sooner we leave the better.'

'Splendid,' said John Thornton. 'But first, Peabody, I am to congratulate you, with all my heart, and you are to rejoice with Charlotte and me.'

There was a great deal of indiscriminate kissing, and then Peabody dragooned them ruthlessly downstairs and out to the carriage that stood ready. 'We are all crowding in to one,' he told them. 'For peace of mind. My man is looking to the baggage, such as it is.'

'Who cares about things?' said Beth.

Their carriage pulled out into the stream that was headed towards the Porta Felice and the Marino. 'How strange to think it is the last time,' said Beth.

'Don't even think it,' Peabody told her. 'It might show. We are a party of pleasure, nothing else.'

'I am your obedient stone,' she told him, and got a loving laugh from Charlotte.

'Oh, Beth.' She found and squeezed her hand. 'How happy we are.'

'Don't be happy yet,' said Peabody. 'I'm superstitious.'

'Not you,' said Beth.

But they were all quiet as the carriage passed through the Porta Felice and turned towards the docks instead of the Marino. This was the moment of danger. This was the crisis.

Nothing happened. Nobody noticed. Back on the Marino, the fountains had begun to run red with wine, and the crowd was entirely taken up with that.

A small boat was waiting at the quayside. 'Mr. Peabody and party?' asked the man in charge. 'In with you. No time to lose. We sail tonight.'

'Tonight!' exclaimed Peabody. 'I thought it was not till the morning.'

'Cap'n says tonight. I reckon cap'n has his reasons. The lady had a hard enough time making him stay for you.'

'Lady?' asked Beth, but her voice was drowned by Peabody's. 'I hope Forde makes it,' he said.

The water of the bay was phosphorescent, gleaming under the men's oars. Soon the moon would rise. Back at the Marino, a first firework went up.

'The fountains must be running wine,'

said John Thornton.

The ship loomed huge above them. A bosun's chair came down.

'What ship is she?' asked Beth, getting in.

'The *Wilberforce*, ma'am, from Hull,' said the seaman who was helping her.

Beth heard Charlotte's gasp as she was winched into the air. Landing on the well-scrubbed deck, she was not even surprised to find Kathryn Comyn, anxiously awaiting her.

'Kathryn!' They went into each other's arms, but she knew, as she always had, what her friend was thinking. 'It's all right. She's coming. She'll be next.'

'Thank God. Beth, was I right to come?'

'It's the best thing you ever did, love.'

She stood back to watch as Charlotte was dumped on the deck, looked about her, saw her mother. 'Mother!' They were in each other's arms.

'Well, there's a happy ending.' Nathan Peabody had swarmed up the ship's side and crossed the deck to put his arm around Beth. 'Let's leave them to greet Thornton, love, and go find the captain. I mean to be a happily married man before we reach Messina.'

Postscript

Queen Maria Carolina did recover from her seizure in September, 1811, and Bentinck did return that winter with the full powers he wanted. But even the arrest of Cassetti did not provide him with hard evidence on which to act against the Queen. They carried on an acrimonious battle of wits and wills until 1813, when he first exiled her to southern Sicily, then banished her to Vienna. Since war still raged in the Mediterranean, it took her almost a year to get there, by way of Zante, Istanbul and Odessa. Greeted as a heroine by the Polish princes of the Ukraine, she reached Vienna at last in February 1814 to a cool reception from her nephew, the Emperor, who was busy with the end of the long war against Napoleon. Rusticated to a palace near Schönbrunn, she made friends with her granddaughter Marie Louise, and urged her to join Napoleon on Elba when he was sent there that spring. Ferdinand, planning to go back in triumph to Naples, sent for her to come home, but she had another, fatal stroke in September.

Whereupon her husband married his mistress and finally returned to the throne of Naples after Waterloo, having, naturally, learned nothing and forgotten nothing.

The employees of THORNDIKE PRESS hope you have enjoyed this Large Print book. All our Large Print books are designed for easy reading — and they're made to last.

Other Thorndike Large Print books are available at your library, through selected bookstores, or directly from us. Suggestions for books you would like to see in Large Print are always welcome.

For more information about current and upcoming titles, please call or mail your name and address to:

THORNDIKE PRESS
PO Box 159
Thorndike, Maine 04986
800/223-6121
207/948-2962